WASHINGTON

THOMAS J.
GEBHARDT III

WASHINGTON

The following novel is a work of fiction. All characters depicted as well as names, places and events mentioned are created from the author's imagination for story purposes. Any resemblance to persons living or dead, or to places or events past or present, is entirely coincidental.

This 1st edition has been catalogued with the Library of Congress.

Library of Congress Control Number: 2022902706

ISBN:
979-8-9857160-0-9 E-Book
979-8-9857160-1-6 Paperback

Publisher Ghoti
Honolulu, Hawaii, United States of America

Cover design by Damonza
Logo design by M. Takajiro Tobita

www.tjgiii.com

Dedicated to Scott Oshiro

Scotty
Scotto

Race in peace, old friend

PART ONE
NUMBER ONE WITH A BULLET

1

Jan 19th
11:09am

THE FIRST SHOTS fired tore a hole through their universe, through the little bubble they had been living in. The crowd surged in a panic as gunshots echoed throughout the hall. Each student pushed and shoved and clawed with urgency, but to him, they were moving in slow motion. He could see feet pounding, but heard no footsteps. He could see mouths moving, but heard no voices. The sounds were clear then became muffled, and grew mute as he shut his eyes and bit down on his teeth, clenching his jaws tight. What sounded like fireworks or maybe a car backfire, he knew was something else. Something less mundane, something more sinister.

He clutched a hand to his chest. His feet dragged across the concrete floor backwards until the small of his back tapped into a sturdy pillar, bringing the hand over his mouth. From the ledge of the second floor, across the courtyard and cul-de-sac, he could see the flagpole: its flag tattered, torn, riddled with holes. He slid down the pillar until he was on the floor, raising both hands now to cover his face. Around him, the masses scattered like roaches with the lights on. A herd of bodies squeezed into the narrow stairwell down to the first floor. The mob clogged between the rails on either side, onto each step, on the landing between the two flights of stairs all the way to the top. They were trapped.

2

9th Grade

THOUGHTS CHURNED AND turned over with his forehead against the glass, and through it, the world in a blur. There was a small shopping center. There was a public storage facility, a community park with a big baseball diamond and a playground. Larger, smaller, then larger buildings whizzed past. It was empty out in the morning hour. Like he was the last person that existed. Next to him on the chair was a backpack and composition book. In his hand, he held a letter half-sticking out of an envelope, along with a form which bore an official letterhead. His eyes narrowed as the top of a flagpole bobbed in and out of view from behind the tree line, in between telephone poles, the bus midway through a wide turn.

I wonder if it'll be any different . . .

To a certain extent, high school really is just high school, no matter where or which one. A place filled with people, a campus filled with students. This particular place had chalkboards and analog clocks and shelves with textbooks and rows of desks. This particular group of people had acne and hormones and angst. Still, it could be considered a delicate little ecosystem. There was balance. There were norms. He pondered these as he pulled the cord, slung the backpack over one shoulder, and stood in the stairwell by the door. In the round mirror, he glanced at his own reflection.

Disembarking, he folded the papers and stashed them in his pocket, tucked the composition book in the crook of his armpit, and waited for the bus to pass. He jaywalked across, hopped onto the curb, and faced the campus. Over the walkway in front that spanned from east to west was the name of the school in big white letters, all capital, sans serif. Beyond that was a long grass field with driveways on either side leading to a courtyard and cul-de-sac. A large bronze statue in the middle of an oval median was framed from this angle by a wide set of stairs leading to what he presumed was the administration building.

The grass had been freshly cut, and the chlorophyll scent filled his nostrils as he took in one deep breath. Walking beneath the branches that loomed, he gazed up at the sun in intermittent haloes of lens flares. *First day of school, I guess.* Which was odd, because it was already the middle of the second quarter. And, it was already second period, and everybody was in the middle of class.

There were motivational posters on the wall, a bulletin board with a calendar, and notices posted up with thumbtacks. He saw a flyer advertising an upcoming pep rally and spirit assembly. Fidgeting with his fingers, he leaned on the counter and kicked at the base.

A clock hung above the bench by the door. He turned, watched the second hand slide past the long hand, resting his composition book flat. On the cover was a mechanical pencil that he unclipped and tapped as if it were a little snare drum, then flipped it open and cycled through the pages. Unfinished sketches, random doodles. Staring down, he nibbled on the eraser end of his pencil then closed the book and put it away. At first, he placed the pencil behind his ear, but decided to put it away as well.

After filling out the proper paperwork, having his picture taken and talking to the counselor, he made his way down the west wing towards C-building. He glanced down at the generic map of the school, the layout of which reminded him of a circuit board. The big grassy field out front, two buildings on either side of the long driveways running parallel, then four buildings on either side of the administration building seemed to make up the bulk of the upper campus, which was all he could resign himself to memorizing for now.

According to his schedule, he had Chemistry II for second period in room C-104. He straightened the map, his schedule and welcome packet, and tucked them beneath his arm as he stepped towards the doorway of the classroom. Before he entered, he stopped, faced down to his feet, and breathed out through pursed lips. He peeped his head in. The teacher turned from behind the podium. Each kid stared up from their desks. He could almost hear their thoughts . . .

Ugh. Who is this *weirdo.*

What the hell is he doing here?

What's his *deal?*

Who transfers mid-semester?

The teacher flipped through the forms, showing the least bit of interest. "Evan, huh."

Gazing down at the floor, he made his way to his new spot as instructed. Third column from the windows, fourth row back. He was supposed to share textbooks with his neighbor but none seemed too fond of the idea. The kid in front lowered his head, leaned further forward. The one to the left grimaced then shifted the other way, the one to the right shook her head and rolled her eyes. He slumped in his chair and watched the top of the teacher's head as he read aloud. That was when he felt a tapping on his shoulder.

At first, he ignored it but it happened again. He turned back, sure it was some punk trying to mess with him. To his surprise, it was just a girl. After some hesitation, he gestured with a wave and began to scoot his desk closer, as did she. He sat like that—turned around, his back to the chalkboard—for the remainder of the period. Both leaned in, tilted their heads to see the textbook turned sideways between them. She turned the page to keep up, crinkling the paper, pointed, following each word in the sentence with the lecture.

The vowels and syllables droned on and on, the paragraphs and figures blurred, and he found himself more interested in her finger than anything else . . .

She had very pretty fingernails that were painted a clearish pink, almost metallic but not. She also had a thin bracelet around her wrist, some dinky black lace with a couple letters and symbols on it, and another bracelet with some kind of wooden beads. He noticed the pages in her book, filled with underline and highlighter and notes, the corners folded in. Then he glanced up at her, watched her eyes move as she read along. She seemed engrossed in it, like in a trance. It confused him. And then the bell rang.

The weekly schedule at school was periods one-three-five on Mondays and Thursdays, and periods two-four-six on Tuesdays and Fridays. It was all periods on Wednesdays, which were a shorter day. So the next time Evan was in Chem II was the very next day, but not for too long. This time, as he made his way down the aisle, instead of gazing down at the floor, he glanced at some of the faces while taking his seat. Evan could hear some of the thoughts again, but not as hostile it seemed.

Written on the chalkboard was a list of assignments that were due, none of which he was aware. He arched his neck back with a sigh. As he did this, the teacher took his place at the podium, opened up the textbook and instructed everyone to hand their chapter questions to the front. His mouth hanging open, his eyes screwed upward towards the ceiling, to the sound of bags unzipping, binders unclipping and papers shuffling.

"Mister." His right hand was half-up in the air, elbow still on the desk. "I just got here. Did I still need to do the homework?"

"Uh. Well, how 'bout you can turn it in late." The teacher collected small stacks from the front of each column of desks. "You can come at recess or after school, since you don't have the book."

Evan sighed, slouched in his seat. "And how much is this assignment worth?"

"Five points."

"Okay, then I just won't do it."

He could feel heads whipping over to see, others just glancing with their eyes. There was static electricity in the air.

"E-excuse me?"

"For a measly five points, I'd have to come in on my own time, go through all this hassle. Now, don't get me wrong, but this school doesn't use a plus-minus system. So a B's a B, right, no matter what." He leaned forward, rested his cheek in his palm. "I might as well say screw it and try to make the next thing. After all, anything above eighty-one percent would be a waste of my time and energy. No offense."

The teacher blinked, not upset, but like surprised. He

jutted out his lower lip, threw up a hand and nodded as if to say, hmm, you got a point.

"All right, class. Let's go and finish the reading."

Evan turned backwards again, leaned with his head tilted, as she turned the textbook sideways and scooted in closer. They listened, read along. Again, he noticed her hands . . . until he stopped himself and focused on the page. After that little display, he felt just a little compelled to at least try and pay attention.

Keeping his gaze on the reading, he reached back into his bag, fumbled to grab a piece of folder paper and something to write with, jotted, then realized he made a mistake. Evan reached again, grabbed an eraser to undo it, and before he knew, he accidentally smeared a blurred black and white swirl on the page that resembled a tornado.

"Shit . . ."

"Cool."

He glanced at the instrument on his desk, picked it up. Instead of his usual mechanical pencil, he held up a ballpoint pen. She stared at the mark on his paper with curiosity and intrigue, while he turned to her with a furled brow and a hint of a smirk. She lifted an eyebrow then faced back down to the textbook, smiled, as he sighed and shook his head.

3

Jan 19th
11:11am

In front of him, the stairwell overflowed. Students trying to run down were blocked in and huddled, students trying to go to the third floor slowed as the crowd built up. Bodies weaved in and out of pillars, some bumping into the other. One of them knocked a bulletin board that fell to the floor in a scatter of thumbtacks, construction paper and cardboard. Evan faced the toppled board diagonally leaned against the base of the wall, as feet stamped and as legs brushed past. His eyes blinked, his head tilted, then he rose to his feet.

A student ran into him, then another, but his eyes remained locked on the board on the floor, stepping towards it. His hands shaking, his feet dragging, he felt a cold sweat take over and linger. Crinkled flyers skidded with the stomp of heavy footsteps. Decorative pieces of paper wafted down like feathers and dandelions. Then he knelt down, stared at the banner with letters fallen off . . .

SHI T
C OOL

With that, Evan gazed back up, was snapped back to current reality from the muffled noise and slow motion. Every sound and movement washed over him and flooded his senses until he uncontrollably flinched. The yelling, screaming, pushing. The running, the flailing of arms.

Bang. The crowd ducked down all at once. *Holy fuck. Holy fuckin' shit.* He glanced around, saw students with tears in their eyes, mouths hanging open, hands over their faces, arms clinging to one another. Now, he felt the gravitas, the surreal situation unfolding. Now, the shock slipped away and the fear began to settle in.

Bang. Bang. The crowd ducked down again and frantically swayed. This time the sound even louder, even closer, with an echo that floated through the stairwell. He could feel the concrete vibrating. He could feel his chest pulsing.

4

9th Grade

THE NEXT TIME he had Chem II was at the end of the week. Textbook turned sideways, they both leaned in and tilted their heads, and Evan followed her pretty finger as she turned the page then found their place. She adjusted in her chair, and as she did, a puff of her perfume drifted in the space between them. It was a pleasant scent he couldn't quite define. After breathing it in, he found himself glancing over at her, just out of curiosity. Again, she was so engrossed in the reading, her eyes scanning the words and registering the information. It was almost like she enjoyed it, which was a concept unfamiliar to him.

"Okay, so that's bonds and reactions. The end of the chapter, thank God." The teacher stepped from behind the podium, began to walk past each desk. "We're going to break into groups now, for your project and assignment." He lifted a hand, pointed. "How 'bout . . . you two, you two. You two." He went on, working his way around towards the middle, towards the third column, fourth row. Staring, lingering, he pointed, this time to him and her. "And then how 'bout . . . you two." He continued. "And you two, you two. Then you three." He returned to the podium. "Come grab a handout. Free time for the remainder of the period, get started please."

Without asking or double checking, Evan stood and went to get the worksheet then brought it back. She had gathered up the textbook, some notes, her Hello Kitty pencil case and waited for him. They made their way to the lab area in the back of the class. There were about eight black counters, four on each side, with a sink, clamp and emergency eyewash station at each one. He took out his mechanical pencil (made sure it was this time) and began writing.

Class: Chemistry II

Period: 2

Date: 10/16

Name:

He turned to her, raised an eyebrow, then gestured with the pencil in his hand.

"Judith." She folded her arms, leaned her chin on them, watched as he wrote. "What does that even say?"

"Evan . . . My name."

"You write so tiny, and messy. It's like chicken-scratch." She brought her face up close, squinted. "Oh my God."

He shook his head, sighed, kind of annoyed.

"Like, seriously. How can you even read that???"

"Okay, okay. I get it. I'll try to write nicer, and bigger. All right?"

She faced down, half-smiled.

"Well, I hope you're good at chem, 'cause I'm not." Evan laid the pencil down, shrugged. "Really. I suck at this."

"Then how'd you get placed in Advanced Chemistry?"

"No idea. I asked for Marine Biology, actually. So I guess I'm screwed. And I already got like negative five points, too, apparently."

"We better get to work, then. Some of us are aiming for more than just a B."

⁂

As the clock winded down, Evan slouched in his chair with his cheek in his palm. On the desk, his composition book lay open in which he scribbled and sketched away. It was far more important than the overhead projector with its various triangles and variables. He tilted his head as he shaded in, erased, curved just so, then darkened. This time, an intentional swirl of a black and white tornado. Dark clouds flashed down jagged veins of lightning, and a twisting cone hurled debris and fluttered diagonal raindrops.

With the sound of the dull bell, each student stood and headed towards the door. Evan put the mechanical pencil behind his ear, stuffed the book under his arm and followed the crowd. He glanced down from the corner of D-building where he had his last class. From the second floor, buildings B through G were connected by a walkway that connected to the admin building in the middle. The admin building had three floors, top two the library.

He lingered a moment, leaning on the rail watching kids walk down the lower campus, past the portables, around to the auditorium, gathering like rain in their respective cliques. The brainiacs. The athletes. The basket cases. Wannabe prom kings and prom queens. And, of course, the outcasts. The delicate little ecosystem.

Turning away, Evan tugged on one strap of his backpack and made his way to the west wing of the admin building,

From the open walkway, he could see up to the roof but instead stared at his feet as he walked, random kids passing by on either side. In front of the library were two parallel rows of sturdy pillars.

The automatic doors slid open with a whoosh of cool air. As he entered, passing through the turnstile and sensor, it was like a different place compared to the rest of school. Past the front counter were study rooms to one side, open tables and shelves beyond that. By the far wall was a little cubicle area with divided sections, then stairs in the middle. Before he walked up, he stopped and gazed in a glass display case with ancient artifacts and maps.

Evan admired the space, staring through the glass panel as he ascended each step. His hand slid along the wooden rail above the panel. The carpeted floor was clean, with an interesting pattern that was soothing. He liked it quiet.

More shelves, longer, and at a slant. Private cubicles at the end of each one. There was another display case at the top of the stairs but he walked past it. From above, he could see the entire first floor and its layout. Pretty cool from that angle. He might've found a new hiding spot, he thought to himself.

Okay, chemistry, chemistry . . . Sigh.

Dragging his fingers across the canvas-cardboard spines lined in a row, he darted his eyes up, down and across the labels one by one. He picked one and leafed through its contents, putting it back then taking another. Some of them were musty and old, most wordy and bland, until he found a thinner one with lots of pictures that he checked out.

From the front of the library, he could see down to the courtyard, the flag waving, the droves of students walking past the oval median and statue along the long driveways off campus. He went down the stairwell, a hand on one of the rails, onto each step, onto the landing between, all the way to the bottom.

Ahead, to one side, a small crowd gathered that shouted and pointed, waved in the air. Bag over one shoulder, books under one arm, Evan stepped towards them as he exited the building. He peered in between backs and necks and heads, curious. Three kids in the middle lashed and shoved while the group outside heckled and cheered. One kid bounced back and forth like a ping-pong ball, in between the other two taking turns winding back and punching. The group lifted his limp body and threw him right back in the middle.

It was such injustice. Why weren't they helping him? No way this kid deserved this. No way the crowd thought this was right. Then again, the ecosystem . . .

Evan continued to circle around to see the poor kid's face. He was scrawny and pale, his voice scratchy with each wail. He struggled to break free as they grabbed him, taunted him, called him a wuss. The crowd oohed with the forceful jab, jab, and deep cross that toppled him forward onto the grass.

The victor glared, shot a look at his friend, winked and then smiled. The two stepped in again, one last time, both kicking down and stomping. One of them spit as they walked away, a confident and proud bounce in their strut.

As the crowd dispersed, Evan lingered there a second and watched the poor kid on the ground. His eyes were closed, arms hugging at his sides as he lay, breathing heavy breaths, in a slight moan.

Evan wanted to help him up, but knew better not to. He turned, started back to the front of the school. Above him, the sun shined through the branches in the trees. He glanced over at M-building where he had one of his classes, then across the grassy field on the other side at N-building. Past it, he saw there was a small shopping center. As he made his way down the long driveway, he peeked behind to the school—at the flagpole, at the admin building and library, at where presumably the poor kid lay on the ground—thought about the long day, thought about the long week, thought about the tornado.

Not sure what compelled him to go and check it out, Evan crossed the street towards the small shopping center. It wasn't much. There was a grocery store, a DVD rental place, an arcade, some restaurants and fast food. Off to the side, around the bend in the parking lot, he spotted a comic book shop hidden. Jam Comics, it was called. His hands up on the glass as if holding binoculars, he peered inside. A long table out front was lined with kids playing some tabletop game he didn't recognize. Behind them, a glass counter displayed trading cards and collectible figures. The walls were littered with posters up. Some scrolls hung down from the ceiling.

Swinging through the double doors, he glanced at the table as one of them rattled then rolled statistical die. In the glass counter, he could see special cards wrapped in plastic: mythical creatures, magical weapons and armor. One was a jester's cap, another a single black lotus.

He continued forward to the comics section. *This place is frickin' huge.* There were weekly and monthly highlights of different serials showcased, and boxes upon boxes on scattered tables. Graphic novels lined big tall shelves. On the side of one shelf was a cardboard cutout of a masked, caped vigilante and of course their grinning archnemesis. There was manga on some of the shelves. In fact, the scrolls hanging were of anime characters but it took him a second to notice.

That was when he felt a tapping shove on his right shoulder. Probably some punk trying to mess with him, for real this time. As he turned, Evan balled a fist. To his surprise, it was his friend. Someone he had been hoping to run into since he stepped onto campus, but just now had come across. Here he was, with an innocent smile and a poof of wavy hair. Best friends separated by summer vacation and different schools brought back together. They clapped hands together in a handshake then wrapped around for a bro hug.

"The hell you doing here?"

Evan laughed, returned the shove. "I was going for that dramatic entrance. I just transferred."

"What??? I thought you were at Roosevelt!"

He laughed again, stared his friend up and down in his baggy clothes. There was a chain hanging from his wallet, a long canvas belt dangling down. A goofy look crept across his friend's face.

"Crap, dude. Well, welcome to Wash."

Most of their group had gone on to Washington after intermediate school while he alone went to Roosevelt. He was a little further away from the rest, enough to be across the line of a separate district. Evan tried it out for a while, but decided to apply to get a geographic exception then waited for everything to process.

"Thanks. It ain't so bad."

"Aw, wish you came a little earlier. The guys were just here. What took you?"

"I had to go to the library. Homework, you know?"

"Lame. Well, lemme show you around real quick. I'm about to head home, I gotta help my mom today."

"Ah, okay. Cool."

They continued around to the back of the shop, an arm around one another's shoulder. His friend tapped him and pointed, showing in detail areas Evan grazed over from a distance. The stacks. The shelves, the bins. An entire area with variant covers and limited edition. Then, they swung out the double doors in front again to the outside world.

"Your house's this way, right?" Evan asked as he hopped off the curb, ready to jaywalk.

"Well, la-di-freaking-dah. I only lived there since I was a little shit."

"And you're *still* a little shit."

They both laughed.

"I know you live the other way, so—"

"Nah, I'll walk with you."

"You sure? It's pretty far for you."

"Of course, man."

Behind the school, opposite direction of the shopping center was a canal with a running path. If you headed towards the mountain side, there was a park with a baseball diamond and a playground. They turned the other way, the ocean side, right along the flowing water.

The clouds glided in the sky, and the leaves in the trees swayed in the breeze. The water appeared just a bit choppy. Evan stopped, picked up a rock that he threw in the water. His friend did the same. Evan searched for a smooth, flat rock that he could try to skip across the surface. He found one and gave it a nice hurl—skip, skip skip. His friend tried the same, knelt down and flung it hard—skip skip, skip skip, skip. They exchanged a glance. Evan shook his head, shoved at him sideways, and they returned to walking.

"So . . . What happened? Why'd you come here?"

Evan didn't say anything right away, instead faced down, his hands deep in his pockets. "I don't know. It wasn't working out there."

His friend was quiet, just nodded. "I'm glad you're here, though. It always kinda felt like there was something, well, missing."

"Missing?"

"Yeah, like in our group. Wasn't quite right. And now things seem . . . I can't find the word . . ."

"I think I get it." Evan turned. "Like, when you put a quarter in the machine, the capsule comes out, and it's the toy you wanted."

"Haha, exactly."

"I'm glad I'm here too."

"Uh, after school, we like to go to Jam Comics or maybe Game Works. You saw it, right? The arcade up top?"

"Yeah, but I didn't check it out."

"If not those, we'll prolly go to someone's house."

"Cool. I'll swing by."

They slowed as they approached the entrance of the apartment building, in front of the security door and the elevators. Staring at each other, both smirking, they clapped their hands together and hugged.

"Why didn't you come look for us in the cafe?"

"First week, ya know? A lot to take in."

"Sure, man. Uh-huh. I know you. You were probably in some corner, dazing off and overthinking, right?"

Evan shook his head. "Haha, shut up.

"Anyway. That was fun, dude. It's good to see you."

"Yeah, man. It was good to see you, too, Der." That was what he called him. Short for Derek.

Facing down to his feet, Evan paced the outside edge of the courtyard. He could've went to the cafeteria, could've found Derek and found the others, could've played and joked and laughed along like everyone else. But here he was at recess, all alone. He wasn't ready to assimilate into this universe yet, this little bubble. It was a new week for him, yet nothing had changed.

He walked to the rock wall around the base of the flagpole, from which he could see the statue, could see the set of stairs leading to the admin building. Around him, he observed it all. Cool kids talked about cool things. There were the delinquents. Preppy ones hung banners and bulletin boards, those that did their homework and paid attention in class. He wasn't sure where he fit in here, if at all. Perhaps none of the above. Perhaps somewhere in between.

In his hand, the book he borrowed taunted him. He skimmed through the pages several times but it had been a horrendous experience. It made zero sense. Formulas and equations and diagrams that didn't mean a thing. Might as well have been in another language.

Screw it already, man. Who cares.

After school, he found himself in that exact same place. In the courtyard, alone, sitting on the rock wall. There wasn't much to look forward to on Mondays, anyway, but that Monday had been especially abysmal. Tuesdays were the better day, it seemed. On Tuesdays, he had chemistry, then art which was all the way in M-building, and geometry. Evan pondered the last day in art class, which was kind of cool. They had discussed blind contour drawing, and played around with depth and with vanishing point. What makes a drawing or painting work, and how the eyes worked when you were gazing at it.

As his thoughts wandered, the rest of the world continued on. Some punk raked leaves while a security guard watched with arms folded. Another clapped erasers by the bushes nearby. There was a guy in a letter jacket walking next to a girl in a tight cheerleader outfit. The cool kids were in a circle, with their nice hair and their nice clothes and their nice shoes. Freaks stood over by the bus stop, wearing all black, one of them in a long trench coat.

Maybe coming here was a mistake . . .

Once more, Evan glanced around the courtyard, took it all in. The different groups of kids. The flagpole waving. The statue, the stairs. The admin building, and the library. The roof. He peered over at C-building, at the walkway connecting to the other buildings. All these structures. All this chaos. And there he was, in the middle of it, stagnant, lost.

He stood and kicked at the grass, then started walking. Not stopping by the shopping center for the hell of it. Not taking the long way back along the canal. Just straight home.

Taking out a pencil and some folder paper, Judith laid the textbook down. Around them, students did the same, were scattered across the lab area in pairs. Evan watched as each of them seemed so perfectly natural in this setting, so confident in their ability to tackle the task at hand. This festered in him as he unzipped his backpack, pulled out his composition book and notebook, his mechanical pencil.

". . . You okay?"

"Oh, uh." Evan noticed her staring at him. "Yeah, I'm fine. I-I'm good."

Judith's eyes narrowed as her head inclined as if to say, hey, c'mon, what's wrong. He balled his hands into fists that he knocked on the countertop, leaning over by the sink. His eyes were closed as he took a deep breath.

She stepped closer, put one hand on the sink. Their eyes then met and locked. Her lips stretched into a smile.

"Did someone die? 'Cause you look way too concerned."

He shook his head, couldn't help but force a little smirk in return.

"No, seriously. That's not the kind of face—"

Evan cut her off, almost blurting it out. "I just don't get all this. What is this?"

Confused, her face grimaced.

"Letters and tiny numbers and lines and dots. And then there's like minus signs and plus signs, and then arrows. What the crap."

She covered her mouth, trying not to laugh.

He watched, kind of annoyed, but felt some relief at least. His forced smirk grew into a natural one.

"Listen, don't worry. This class is a joke. It's supposed to be college level but the teacher doesn't care. He's lazy."

Evan didn't quite understand, but nodded along regardless.

"This project is just busy work to fill in the gap before the test, give us time to study."

Judith placed a stack of elegantly written notes that stood out like a beacon next to his chicken-scratch on the worksheet.

"Well, what exactly is it you don't get?"

"Like . . . all of it."

"Okay. Chemistry, the study of change—"

"Well, come on, I get that much. It's just I'm at least a quarter and a half behind and I'm not even supposed to be in this class."

She watched his face as his eyes fixated on the floor.

"I mean, I will say, it is kind of interesting."

"It is?"

"Yeah. Like, it's the 'study of change' as you said. Chemical reactions and things, chemical bonds. Atoms and molecules and the sharing of electrons. Different elements."

Evan motioned with his hands as he said this. She stepped forward, reaching past, grabbed his composition book. He wish she grabbed the notebook instead. As she opened it and began to scribble, he noticed her fingernail again.

"Okay, what the hell is that!?"

$$CH_4 + O_2 \rightarrow CO_2 + H_2O$$

"This is methane, this is oxygen." She wrote a little C and then a little H, H, H, H, and circled them. "There's one carbon and four hydrogens. Right?" Then she wrote an O, O, and put a circle around that. "Then there's two oxygens."

"Uh. Suure."

"And, here, this is carbon dioxide and this is water." She wrote a little C and a little O, O, and circled. "One carbon and two oxygens." Then she wrote a H, H, an O, and circled again. "And two hydrogens, one oxygen."

He tilted his head, starting to furl his brow.

"Methane mixed with oxygen, and then burning, makes carbon dioxide and water." She pointed to each part of the equation. "Now, if you count these all up, there's not the same amount of hydrogens and oxygens. It needs to be the same."

Evan nodded, with a squint.

"When things 'change,' nothing is ever lost."

He watched her scribble more, then scribble again.

$$CH_4 + O_2 + O_2 \rightarrow CO_2 + H_2O + H_2O$$

$$CH_4 + 2O_2 \rightarrow CO_2 + 2H_2O$$

"Okay, whoa, whoa, you lost me there."

They both laughed aloud. He shifted away, shaking his head. She covered her mouth with the back of her hand.

"And now I have a headache. Great."

"I guess that'll do for now." She flipped the page over. "My bad, I just took this."

"Nah, that's—"

"Hey. Wait a sec. Can you draw?"

"No, uh . . ." He took the composition book, closed it, put it back in his bag. "I can't . . . I don't."

"Yeah you do. And it looked pretty good." She smiled a big smile, nodding. "I got an idea."

He stared at her, half-turned away.

"If I take care of the notes and information and things, you can actually *make* the project. You draw, cut, paste, all that. I'm not good at that kinda stuff."

He folded his arms, rubbed his chin.

"What do you think?"

"I mean, how can you not be good at that kind of stuff?"

"Just trust me. I don't have a good eye, I'm not very creative."

"I mean . . . I guess. Are you sure?"

"Totally. You kidding? This is such a relief."

"All right, then. Cool. Awesome." Evan smiled, gazed across at her. "Thanks, Jude."

Not sure why, but that was the way it came out. Like that, he noticed the minute it slipped from his tongue and his lips. As it floated in that space between them, where a slight puff of her perfume wafted. The way the sun peered into the class just then made her cheeks the slightest touch of red. They returned to the textbook turned sideways between them, with their heads tilted in. Her elegant notes next to his chicken-scratch. His mechanical pencil. Her fingernail. The tornado.

5

Jan 19th
11:12am

ECHOED GUNFIRE SOUNDED all around, and he couldn't trace the source. It appeared to be coming from the first floor towards the bottom of the stairwell, but it might have been the floor above or even the roof. Evan couldn't be sure, had no clue, darted his head around, peeked down the hall of the west wing then down the east wing, across the walkway towards F-building. Students ran in both directions, and without thinking he followed.

As he exited and felt the open air of the walkway, he felt exposed. He glanced down at the courtyard, saw bodies sprinting across the lawn. He'd never seen anything like that before . . . Bang. Bang, bang. The sound came from behind, and when he turned to check, the outline of a dark figure stood on the edge of the roof, a rifle aimed in its hands. The details lost in silhouette from the sun, he raised a hand to block out the light that was blinding. His eyes blinked as his head flinched, slowing to a jog, trying to regain focus.

Pieces of grass and dirt tore and shot up as students ducked behind benches and garbage cans. Some of them lay prone behind the rock wall around the base of the flagpole, covering their ears and shivering.

My locker . . . !

As he stumbled into F-building, eyes still adjusting, the thought entered Evan's mind. To steady himself, he pressed one hand on the wall then crouched down. He glanced again at the figure, still aimed at the courtyard where a girl toppled down on the grass and a boy tumbled over the curb of the cul-de-sac. A few backpacks and binders lined the steps of the wide set of stairs. The statue cracked and chipped.

His eyes clung to the figure. His limbs were frozen, would not move. His breathing grew rapid. The walkway down to the next building, to G-building where his locker was, even more out in the open, even more exposed. He knelt low and braced himself, fingertips on the concrete, a hand on the railing. His chest rose and fell. The walls and floor rattled with each shot, every vibration a shockwave passing through.

If he wasn't fast enough, if he made even the slightest error, it would all be over. Bang. Bang, bang, bang. He flinched, the hollow echoes seeming closer and closer, right behind him, right next to him.

Again, he breathed. Again, he stared at the figure in silhouette. Tightening his grip on the rail, he pivoted on the ball of his foot. Again, he stared down the walkway.

This is it. Shit, shit.

6

9th Grade

Screens flashed and blinked with high scores, short demos, and INSERT COINS scrolling marquee in block letters. His hands dragged across the different machines, over buttons and levers, slipping onto and off of joysticks until one machine in particular caught his attention. Reaching down, Evan touched the gripped handle of the zapper then pulled it from its holster. He dangled it, untwisting the black cable, then picked it up and aimed. Squeezing one eye, gazing down the sight, he pulled on the trigger . . .

There was an unexplainable pleasure in that. Some sort of destructive force inside that beckoned, whether it's squishing bugs or throwing rocks or lighting a match.

As pixelated creatures hopped out from behind barrels and crates in the demo, he aimed and shot, aimed and shot. The clicking noise of the gun was like a wind-up toy unleashed. He wanted to play right then and there but decided to wait, save his tokens for when the others arrived.

Around him, the arcade roared with noise and lights. Tokens crashed down and tickets printed. Behind the counter was stuffed animals of different sizes and different shapes, along with generic toys. There was a row of pinball machines and there was Skee-Ball. Driver's seats of race cars digitally revved. The cockpit of a fighter jet tilted left and right, raised up and down. There were puzzle games and shooting games and fighting games. Also, there was a claw machine off to the corner.

"Ev-an!"

"Yo, E."

From behind, he felt a light shove and turned. It was two of his closest friends. Now, the three friends—three musketeers, three stooges—were back together again. From the playground in the dirt next to the one big tree, all the way to the playground of modern day in the air conditioning. He and Mark clapped palms together then snapped their fingers. Jared held a sideways fist that they bumped then spread with a raspy explosion noise.

"What up, you guys."

"Derek *said* you were back . . ." Mark's big grin made his squinty eyes even squintier, behind his glasses. "Ha, they couldn't keep us apart!"

With arms crossed, Jared stood with a thin smile on his dark face. In his hand was a Coca-Cola bottle.

"So, what? We diggin' up dinosaur bones?"

Evan laughed. "I'm sure Mrs. Nelson would loove that . . ."

"We could just do roundhouse kicks." Jared gave an exaggerated sarcastic nod. "Or, hey, Mark could just get beamed in the face again."

"Shut up, man. Screw you."

They all laughed, inside jokes, a language they alone knew.

"Wasn't even my fault—"

"I think . . ." Jared leaned in, real close. "Yeah, I can still see the etchings from the ball on the side of your face."

"Screw. You."

Laughing turned to playful shoving, and then playful punching. Derek snuck behind and hugged Evan with one arm, then leaned on his shoulder. This was their group. Two friends in classes since elementary school—three musketeers. And one best friend he did it all with outside of school. Over all the semesters and summers, they somehow molded to one.

Straightening their dollar bills, they each lined up to stick them into the slot. A robotic rolling noise was followed by loud clanging from small bronze tokens at the bottom. They then spread into the arcade like hungry dogs. Jared wandered to the fighting game, where he could make two tokens last a half an hour. There was already another kid on the machine, but it wouldn't be for long. Mark walked to one of the puzzle games, where he aimed and shot arrows that popped different colored balloons. Derek went to a racing game in back, adjusted the seat then slipped a token in. Evan sat on the next machine over, leaned in and watched, saving the tokens in his pocket still.

"Look out, look out." Evan squirmed, grimaced. "He's coming straight for you."

"I know!" Derek jerked the wheel left, right, shifted into gear while slamming the brake. "This frickin' bastard!"

Both moved their bodies as if in a real car chase, as if a real car had smashed into their side, trying with deadly force to run them off the road.

"Cut through the grass." He pointed, tapped his friend on the arm. "There."

"La-di-freaking-dah!"

Big numbers flashed, ten, nine, eight, the timer winding down, finish line just out of sight . . . Derek drifted across the asphalt fast as he could, his car spinning out with a loud screech, then crashed into the wall. He slapped the center of the steering wheel, slapped it again. Evan touched him on the shoulder, smirked. They each stood and walked back over to Mark, who watched as Jared was still at it. He took a sip of soda before the next challenger.

He sat almost without expression, effortlessly nudging the joystick and mashing the buttons. Blood splattered, dark red. Bones crunched and flesh tore. Jared kicked, jumped, uppercutted, in a fierce combo that connected. Block. Counter. Special move, with perfect timing. His opponent's body hurled upwards and across the screen, almost like claymation—smack, smack, smack—with each consecutive strike.

After a flawless victory, Mark passed around sticks of gum, the obligatory vice since it was banned on campus. This went on for a few matches. There was a small line, all ready to try and dethrone the new reigning champ. Before they left, the four of them walked around the arcade one last time.

"The hell?" Derek pointed.

"Oh, that's new." Mark chewed with obnoxious and loud smacks, blowing a quick bubble. "Just imported in."

"Like a dance game."

"Hmm."

While the rest gazed at this fancy new machine, Evan headed towards the front doors. He wasn't too interested.

It was bright and sunny back out in the real world, with not too many clouds in the sky. A slight breeze swept through as they walked along the canal on the ocean side, next to a section with chain-link fence. Mark dragged his fingers on each rusty metal diamond as he lectured which superhero could beat up who. Jared was next to him in back, quiet, while Evan and Derek took up the front. They moved from the fence to a bridge that arched its way across the water.

Evan peered down, watched the sun sparkle in each ripple. Grass and bushes lined the banks on either side. He thought he could see something swimming but wasn't sure.

"How come you didn't play?"

"Ah, next time."

". . . You could always just borrow, you know." Derek glanced over, a quick raise of his eyebrow. "No biggie."

Evan didn't say anything, kept his hands in his pockets while facing down to the water. He lingered a second, the others moving past. Then he leaned on the concrete of the bridge, at the peak of the arch, as the water flowed. Blades of grass swayed in the current. Branches swung in the breeze, hanging low. Each tiny burst of light emanated from the surface of the water like lit sparklers. His eyes traced up the canal, to where it flowed, to its vanishing point.

❧

As they approached the entrance, in front of the elevators and the security door, Derek stopped the group and told them to wait. There was a small shop on the first floor that had little snacks, random toiletries. He went in, and there was a light jingle as he swung through the door. Derek liked to stop there first before they all came over. Evan faced Mark and Jared, with his back to the shop.

"I got you in Geometry, y'know." Jared crossed his arms. "I'm always in back."

"Really? I didn't see you. Guess we do all face forward."

"Yeah, you like to take off right when the bell rings." He laughed. "I'm too lazy to catch up."

"Ah, haha. Well, I'll keep an eye out then. Sit next to you since it's not assigned seats."

"Lucky for me, I don't have *any* classes with you." Mark

shoved Evan who shoved him back. "So I don't gotta see your ugly face!"

The laughter died down when the light jingle went off again, and they each turned around. Derek stared past them, pointing with his chin since his hands were full.

"Hey, look who decided to show up."

Jared stepped, gave a fist bump. Mark walked over and forced a limp high five. Derek put his arm around Evan with snacks in hand, hanging it down the opposite shoulder, pulling him in close.

"Evan, this is Max. Max, this is Evan."

He felt his smile fade when he held his hand out, as it lingered there in mid-air along with his lower lip. Standing in front of him, like a ghost, one step further back behind the others, head down low, arms draped half-across his body, was the same kid from the week before . . . The one that was in the middle of the crowd bounced around like a ping-pong ball, laughed at and heckled and taunted, kicked around and stomped and spit on . . .

The images flashed, one by one. His limp body thrown back in like waves crashing on the shore. Every thudded whack. His body falling, eyes shut tight, arms wrapped around himself. The sounds replayed. His scratchy wail. His breathing, his moaning. There he was, almost more scrawny and more pale than he had remembered, with bad acne, and big ol' braces he now noticed up close.

This fucking poor bastard . . .

A long pause, then the kid reached forward, timid, shy, took his hand in return. "'Sup."

&

The rest of that afternoon dragged on. It felt like he was drowning. Guilt set in, from not having said or done anything, of having left him there on the ground, alone, and in pain. Evan thought all this as he leaned forward on the fluffy couch, glanced across at Max sitting on the floor with his hands in his lap. Derek walked back from the kitchen and offered them each a can of soda. Evan took one, turned it over in his hand, put it on the glass coffee table. Max snatched it, snapped open the tab and gulped it down, belching a proud belch. He watched as Max did this, shaking his head.

Jared knelt down in front of the TV on the carpet. Rubber cords were in a tangled mess, plastic controllers and cartridges scattered and strewn about. He sorted through and plugged them into their respective ports. Then he tossed a cartridge to Derek, who took the cap off and blew into its slot as if playing the harmonica, albeit one that sounded like a broken flute or a broken whistle.

"Blow it!"

"Yeah, blow it. Long and hard."

"Man, screw you guys," Derek said in between breaths. "You guys come in *my* house, drink *my* soda, eat my—"

"Shut up." Mark's mouth was full as he reached back into the bag. "Shut up and blow."

"Yeah, blow it!"

Derek tossed the cartridge back. Jared put it in the top of the machine, gave it a good slam into place. He flicked the power switch but all that happened was the TV screen flashed bright blue. The gang booed, threw chips and crumpled paper balls.

"Hey, you freaks!" Derek turned back in faux anger, shook a balled fist. "I'm the one that's gotta clean that."

"Dammit. Let me blow, give it." Mark held it, took a deep

breath as the rest joked more of the same. "Hey. Shut up, shut up. Wait."

Evan watched as Max chuckled a subdued laugh and knocked back a handful of junk food. He felt some relief knowing at least he had this: the group, the boys. More a feeling of home than he ever knew. On the screen, the game logo flashed with a light chime, the intro sequence starting, to which the gang roared. In their celebratory burst of cheers and hooting, a soda can knocked off the table and onto the carpet, in a nice long rolling curve.

"Shit, shit!" Derek grabbed paper towels. "Quick, apply pressure!"

Evan laughed along with the rest, opening his can of soda. He leaned into the cushion.

"Okay, you assholes. No more spills. Carpet's nasty already."

"Your mom's carpet is nasty." Mark forced the food down in a hard swallow. "And by carpet, I mean her vag."

"Screw you guys. Assholes. Let's game."

Jared offered a controller but Evan said he'll take the next round. It was Derek, Jared, Mark and Max—in red, blue, green and yellow blob form in the corners of the screen. They each bent and tilted in place, mashing the different buttons with their thumbs.

Derek squealed as he narrowly escaped a chain reaction of explosions. Mark stuck his foot out, pressed it into Max's side to distract him. Jared stared, almost bored, cool, calm, calculated. His character hovered at deft velocity, zigzagged in and out of spaces, laying intricate traps and wreaking havoc in his wake. Derek squealed again, shouted a long cry as his character burned in a ball of flame.

"Gonna kill you! Gonna kill you!" Max muttered through an awkward smile. "Lemme kill you, bitch!"

For the first time since transferring, Evan felt the thing he had been waiting for. The sense of everyday life feeling somewhat normal and somehow right. This was something familiar to him, essential and nourishing to his teenaged soul. Mark being a jackass. Derek freaking out. Jared whooping everyone's ass in 16-bit.

He gazed at each one of them. And he gazed over at his new friend, too. This was almost more family than his very own. Regret was taken over by sympathy and compassion now, by pity.

You'll be all right, man. I got your back next time. They won't mess with you. Not on my watch. No way.

7

Jan 19th
11:19am

HIS LEGS SPRANG forth with a leap, one hand yanking up on the rail, one hand shoving down from the concrete. The bangs flew out of his eyes, off his forehead, while his shirt tail flapped. Each powerful lunge was unsteady as his feet slid on the floor, his arms swinging at unnatural angles as he struggled to keep balance. Evan flinched, couldn't help but imagine his flesh being torn apart. Bang, a single shot pierced through his chest. Bang, a hole dug into his arm. Bang, bang, holes in each leg. *No! No!!! Oh please God no!* The sound in the air was like billowing smoke.

The soles of his feet slid with the sharp turn. He dropped to one knee, scraping his palm and staggering back up, then ran straight. Through an open door, he saw students hiding under their desks. Ahead, a door slammed shut then another. Inside, he could hear tables screeching, scraping against the linoleum floor presumably behind each door. Cries of panic and shouting for order was flooded with whimpering and gasps, all muffled inside. His legs slowed as he turned backwards to see. With the roof of the admin building obstructed partway at an angle from G-building, he felt some semblance of safety, enough to catch his breath at least.

He knelt over, slapping his palms on his knees. His left side twisted in on itself. Beads of sweat collected in the pores of his skin. Gasping turned to borderline gagging, as a cold pit sank inside him like a vacuum. There was a hard thumping at his chest.

Ahead was the row of lockers to which Evan hobbled over, one arm hugging at his ribs. His hands trembled as he picked up the lock. He turned the dial, spun it back, turned again, tried to click it open but nothing happened. He stopped and glanced down, breathed out through pursed lips. Still trembling, he turned the dial once more, this time a slow and careful touch, spun it back, turned again into place at each marker between each digit . . . Click.

A textbook bound in brown paper from a grocery bag stared back at him. Crumpled balls of folder paper and gum wrappers littered the bottom of the metal space. There were old composition books leaned against the side. He reached in, rifled through these, and took out a small rectangular box. Under the lid was an object wrapped in cloth. Evan unwound the fabric, held it in his hand, squeezed. It was the blade of a knife, and it shimmered through circular holes in the handle.

Oh, man. What the hell is going on?

What am I even doing?

The door creaked as he closed it. He faced down to the floor, took another deep breath, wiped at his forehead with the back of his sleeve. He stared back across the hall, to the open walkway where he knew a figure stood on the roof with a rifle aimed. The shots were slower, a little more distant. He put the knife away in his back pocket.

On the far side of G-building, the same as buildings B

through F, was a stairwell down. There were inner and outer stairwells on the opposite ends of each building. He started in that direction, touching the knife in his back pocket, making sure it was still there. About to turn, he stopped in place when he saw a long dark shadow stretch across the landing between the two flights of stairs. It glided up the wall, step by step. In its hands, he could see it clearly—the distinct outline of a gun.

8

9th Grade

THE NEXT FEW days in Chem went by fluidly, pun intended. On the lab counter in front of them lay the trifold poster board. Sheets of construction paper, scissors, glue, and printed information sprawled out in a rainbow mesh. With the big presentation and the big test coming up, it was crunch time and they had to push to get everything done. There was a small synergy starting to form between them, out of necessity.

"Like this?"

Evan's eyes darted back at her with an uncertain smirk. He didn't think it was possible but she was right, her sense of design was pretty bad. The color scheme didn't match. Her edges were cut crooked. Backs of pieces were overglued, oozing out all over her fingers, with no balance or proportion whatsoever.

He patted her on the shoulder, refraining from laughter.

"See. I told you."

Judith stood, tossed the monstrosity in the rubbish then washed her hands. When she returned, she watched as he cut strips and blocks and glued them together. Complementary colors formed frames and labels around informative rectangles and squares regarding the different bonds and the different reactions. Between certain blocks, he left blank spaces in which he drew small illustrations, further diagramming the information. He first sketched in pencil, then outlined in pen. The outside edge he colored in thick marker, the inside areas he colored in light streaks with color pencil. It was well spaced and well balanced.

"Wow . . ."

She couldn't finish her sentence, shook her head then turned to him, smiling. For the first time, he noticed she had these deep dimples in her cheeks. But just when she smiled a certain way like that.

"Covalent bond is when electrons are shared equally?"

Judith raised an eyebrow, held the makeshift flashcard closer to his face. He rubbed a hand over his mouth, under his chin, then shrugged.

"Oh, come on. We went over this."

She tapped the flashcard, nodded along. Evan scratched his head, gazed up at the ceiling, shrugged again.

"It's polar covalent."

"Wait. I thought polar covalent was when electrons are transferred . . ."

She patted him on the shoulder, showed him the back of the card once more.

It was elegantly written in, with underline and with highlighter. He noticed her pretty fingernail again, smirked to himself as he faced the other way.

❧

The day of the big test, Evan sat there and crammed. He flipped through her flashcards as a half-sheet slid in front of him. When he glanced up, he saw the teacher walking away, handing out more half-sheets one by one. There were positive remarks written in red ink. At the bottom, he saw a sloppy happy face with a big circle around it. They apparently had gotten full credit. He turned backwards in his chair, towards Judith whose face was buried in her notes and textbook, the half-sheet in mid-air between them.

"Oh . . . Oh, no . . ." Judith saw all the red ink. "Please, God, please."

Evan couldn't help but smirk at her desperation. He watched her eyes move as she scanned. It seemed like they were starting to sparkle, like the reflection on the surface of the water from the other day, with just the tiniest drop forming in the corner of what he'd come to describe as her almond eyes. Then those deep dimples formed again, as her smile grew.

"Jude, we did it."

"You know, we're pretty good together."

"We are?" Evan laughed, an eyebrow raised. "I wish we could tag team this test. I'm so screwed."

"Ah, you'll be fine. We went over everything like three times. Then three more times."

"Yeah, I guess but—"

The teacher cleared his throat, pointed to the back of the class where all the different projects were on display. Theirs stood out compared to the rest. He went on to explain the multiple choice, matching, fill-in-the-blank, and short bonus question on the second page.

As the test trickled its way down each column, towards the third column, fourth row, Evan felt the increase in pressure. His nervousness was like a soda bottle that had been shook up, ready to burst, and now felt like a fire hydrant knocked out that sprayed high into the air. His mind was an hourglass but filled with quicksand.

Evan turned, handed the test back to Judith, who saw his face and became worried herself. She mouthed the words, it's okay, it's okay.

He nodded, turned to face forward again with a hard dry swallow. Around him, everyone else had already began. The scratching of lead. The rubbing then brushing or blowing of eraser particles. His paper remained blank except for his name at the top, in the usual chicken-scratch.

The eraser end of his mechanical pencil tapped on the desk, then wedged in the corner of his lips. Some of the others had flipped to the next page. It just wasn't clicking in his brain, from the very first question. No matter how many times he forced himself to graze over it. No matter how hard he reread it and reread it.

A couple of students stood now, walking to the front, putting their tests facedown in the tray. Behind him, Judith also rose and walked past. On the way back, their eyes locked. She smiled, tucked her hair behind her left ear. He noticed her fingernail for a fraction of a second. Evan forced a smirk back. With this, somehow, when he shifted back down to the paper, it all clicked.

The assignment for the day was blind contour drawing, as they had gone over the week prior. When they covered vanishing point, he chose to sketch a train track at a crossroads, with distant buildings in the background. It was some imaginary place he had conjured up in his mind. Evan moved the ruler, drew the line, moved the ruler again, then drew another line. Like spokes in a bicycle tire. Like maybe glints of light from inside the barrel of a gun. An illusion of convergence formed within three dimensions on the two-dimensional plane.

Today, Evan sat with his head on the desk. In part, because he liked to lay his head on the desk whenever possible. If there was ever a video on or any kind of free time, he often did this. In part, because he also was a little nervous about how he did on the test for Chem. He stared down at his feet this time from the edge of the desk. Keeping his forehead down, wrist flat, pencil in hand, he sketched.

He started first with the tips of the toes, the rim of the sole all the way around. Then he focused on the texture. Kind of like diagonal slants in between solid pieces that were stitched together, as well as the stitches themselves. The tongue. The laces crisscrossed. The bunny ears of the loop, swoop and pull, and how they hung down and across. Last, he drew the bottom of his jeans. Wrinkles and creases, and the hem along the inside the pants leg.

When he lifted his head and glanced back up, it was interesting how it turned out. The lines weren't as solid or straight as he normally would draw them. They had kind of a wavy quality to them, unsteady, almost wiggling its way from point to point. Some parts weren't connected, with small gaps. Some parts overlapped or crisscrossed, messy. Overall, though, it turned out pretty cool. He stood and walked to the front of the class, slipping his drawing on the front table next to some of the others in a grid.

❧

Lunch that day, he didn't go to his new hiding spot, although he was tempted. Evan often found himself in the library at Roosevelt at lunch. It just never felt quite right there. He wondered what high school was supposed to be like. Were you supposed to like it? Were you supposed to fit in? Classes, classrooms, even classmates, it was all so strange to him. Almost as if he was a stray cat wandering, scavenging, in the library alone, composition book open and mechanical pencil in hand.

Almost as if he was a ghost glowing translucent, detached, roaming the hallways, head down, hands in his pockets.

Now, though, wandering from behind E-building toward the cafeteria, he felt far from alone. It was noisy. It was hectic. He walked past the line that was forming and wandered in the open space. There were long rows of long tables. Different groups of kids scattered in their different areas, different vibes within each one. He spotted Max walking, tray in hand, bag pulled up high on his shoulders.

Evan walked behind him, jumped at his side matching his pace. Max initially grew tense, seemed nervous, then relaxed when he realized who it was. His lips grew into an awkward smile. "'Sup."

The gang roared in a small cheer as the two of them sat down. Jared handed his chocolate milk to Evan. Derek handed his bread, Mark slid his tray over and offered tater tots.

"Thanks, man." Evan took them.

Why hadn't he come here sooner, he thought. Then again, he just wasn't ready yet, needed that moment to feel like a stray cat or a ghost a little bit longer.

Derek kicked at him beneath the table. "Took you long enough. Mister Loner over here."

Glancing down, Evan swallowed then shook his head with an embarrassed smirk.

"Okay. Gimme the cards." Mark's mouth was full as he nudged the glasses at his nose. "It's that time."

He swirled the cards on the table in a wax-on-wax-off motion then started flinging them out face up. Jared stared at him, shaking his head. Derek got a two. He threw up a hand with a grimace. Jared got an ace. Max, the one-eyed jack. He picked it up and glanced at it. In front of Evan, a joker spun into place.

"A joker!? The hell . . ."

"Damn it, Mark."

"That's not even how you do it. Geez. What kind of shuffle is that?"

"Man, screw you."

Jared took the cards, straightened them against the table-top then split them in half. He flapped the cards down in each hand then bridged back up almost like a machine. In his hands, he pulled from the middle then stacked on top, pulled and stacked, pulled and stacked. Then he handed it to Evan.

Evan positioned the deck between his index and middle fingers, slid his thumb to the opposite side and rotated the top half along his index finger in one smooth motion under the bottom half. A one-handed cut.

"Oh, wow. I got a trick too." Mark stood, stuck out his middle finger, then leaned on Jared's shoulder to get a better view. "Frickin' show-off."

Again, Jared had that cool, calm, calculated look. One by one, starting left of dealer, facedown, he slid each card into place. Jared, Derek next to him, Max in the middle, then Evan diagonally across from Derek. He dealt out all the cards, with the last card landing in his own pile. They each picked up their hands and began sorting.

The game was called Killer. You each took turns, clock-wise, and tried to beat out what was put down in the middle. It could be singles, pairs, triples. It could be a straight. (Straights had to be three or more in a row.) You could beat either by number or by suit. Spades beat clubs. Diamonds beat spades. Hearts beat diamonds. Two of hearts was the highest.

"Okay, who's got the three of clubs?" Three of clubs was lowest so they went first. It went from three all the way up to ace, then back to two. If someone had four twos, you had to reshuffle. "Don't tell me it's a four twos situation."

"Nah, nah." Evan put down the three of clubs.

"Good. Let's get rid of some trash." Jared put his card down over Evan's three of clubs. Then Derek. Then Max.

Jared displayed a perfect poker face, with no emotion, his cards down on the table. Derek hid half his face behind his hand, placing his card down. Max wore an awkward smile as per usual, an excited nod in anticipation. Evan held his cards with an elbow on the table, almost showing his hand.

After Jared won the first round, he put down a triple king. Whoever won the round got to pick what they put in the middle for everyone to try to beat.

They each groaned.

"Pfft . . ."

"Man, ain't nobody got a damn triple, let alone that high a triple. Bastard."

Holding onto control, Jared then put down a straight: five, six, seven. Derek put down a six, seven, eight.

"Ah, you fuckers." Max leaned back, put his cards on the table, then crossed his arms. "Pass."

"El pass-o." Mark popped a tater tot into his mouth. "I didn't know you were from el pass-o."

Sorting the cards in his hand, Evan contemplated, then placed a seven, eight, nine. Jared topped it with a ten, jack, queen. Derek slammed down a jack, queen, king.

They each groaned again.

"Okay, finally. I gotta get rid of these . . ." Derek started a round of low singles again.

It rose, number by number, suit by suit. Until Max again was forced to pass.

"Damn it . . . Pass."

"You put the 'ass' in pass, Max." Mark was especially proud of that one.

Evan rubbed his chin, then dropped a card. Jared, with the slightest hint of a smile creeping in, dropped a high card, jumping the pile.

"The hell, man." Derek faced Jared, faced back down at his hand. "Are you bluffing?"

"I don't know." Jared stared with wide eyes, leaning his face close in. "Am I . . . ?"

"You bastard, pass."

"Pass."

Mark let out an evil laugh. "Ohh, you guys are screwed."

Jared put down an ace, with confidence, just two cards left in his hand which were no doubt high cards. Derek put a two over it. Max then slammed down a bomb—either a four of a kind or three consecutive pairs, in this case three consecutive pairs. Only bombs could beat twos.

"Bomb!!!" Max let out a subdued chuckle. "Haha, bomb you mofos!"

Then he dropped his last card, thus winning the game.

Jared nodded. "Good job. I somehow lost with a two in my hand. See, Derek's was two of clubs so I coulda beat that with two of hearts. The bomb, that's why."

"All right, who's got the junkest cards left?"

They each put down their cards and showed what remained in their hands. After a slight pause of calculation, they pointed and laughed at Derek. They all shoved their piles over to him in a big heaping mess.

"Loser deals."

"Well, la-di-freaking-dah. Bastards."

❧

On the chalkboard in front were the various triangles again from last class. Evan gazed up this time as opposed to drawing in his composition book, stared at the different versions side by side. They were defined by the interior angles and by the lengths of each side. A right triangle could be calculated using a certain theorem, which was interesting. Right triangle had at least one corner at ninety degrees. The teacher added three squares connected to the three sides of the right triangle, explaining how the theorem worked.

Funny. Something as simple as a little shape had so much to it. The world around us, with so much depth and complexity, we all seemed to take for granted. Evan smirked to himself as this realization set in. Three points, the distance and the lines between each of those points. The area within. The angles they formed.

An isosceles triangle had two equal sides. There were two matching hatch marks on the "legs" and two matching concentric arcs at the angles in the base. This one seemed to interest him the most. The teacher went on to show them printouts of historical architecture that used this shape, even flag designs. It opened his eyes. He never noticed before. There it was, in the roofs of old temples and old houses. Etched in the side of ancient walls. Inside old tiles. Even in the beams under modern bridges.

The shapes on the board stirred something in him. They appeared to be staring. Different sizes and shapes lined, like slices of pizza, like paper airplanes. Like the pyramids. Like constellations in the night sky.

Jared nudged him with an elbow, pointed with his chin at the clock. It was almost time. Evan nodded back. He stared at the triangles once more. And then the bell rang.

They walked down the walkway from D-building to the admin building, in front of the library, then down the stairs. Evan tapped on the rail. Jared skipped a step and hopped down onto the landing. A girl passed them as they neared the bottom. Jared glanced with the corner of his eye. Evan turned backward, tilted his head to get a better angle. They each exchanged an excited hormonal glance.

Compared to eighth grade, girls in high school were further in their development. Their shirts hugged tight around their growing breasts. Shorts and skirts curved around their buttocks, highlighting smooth legs. Hairstyles and makeup crept in. Little girls were now becoming young women. Of course, it was observation (and admiration) at this stage in their lives. Look but don't touch.

This coursed through his mind as Jared walked to the vending machine. Evan gazed around them, saw there were many girls. One bent over the water fountain. Two walked in tandem giggling amongst themselves. So many beautiful women. What it would be like to just talk to one of them . . . Just to touch, to have even one . . . One time. For even a short time.

Twisting the cap that leaked a fizzy hiss, Jared took a good long chug. Evan watched him, smirked, shaking his head.

"Man. Long as I can remember, you been drinking that."

Jared recapped the bottle, let it dangle down in his hand. "I'm a Coke addict."

As they pressed out the double doors and down the wide set of stairs, Evan peered at the statue up high on the oval median. It was their new routine to meet after school by the flagpole versus before when they used to meet by the bleachers on the fields. The sunlight reflected off of it with a bright gleam. His eyes focused to the flag waving, then down to the rock wall where Mark stood with arms folded and a big grin on his face.

"What took you guys, huh?"

Max was there, too, and as they all came together, they formed a kind of lopsided polygon. One side was missing.

"Hey, uh, where's Der?"

Both shrugged.

"Hmm . . ." Evan shifted left, right, panned the courtyard. "Well, maybe he had to go do something or something."

"Dang! It was supposed to be cards rematch!"

"Yeah, but you don't get to shuffle. Never again."

A small round of laughter.

"He's usually the first one here."

"Uh, we can go to my house if you guys want." Max's voice always sounded like a low mumble. It was as if he was uncertain of his words, uncertain of even speaking in the first place.

"Yeah, okay. Sure."

The group took up most of the sidewalk as they left campus from the long driveways. It was the opposite way compared to their usual route along the canal. As they walked, they could see the shopping center across the street but continued. Loud, obnoxious, they pushed, shoved and punched one another. With the sun up high in the clear sky, school out for the weekend, they strutted like kings.

Max's house was hidden in the back streets. They cut through a small dog park, jaywalked across a half-busy street, then crossed a long bridge over the freeway. Cars whizzed past beneath them in both directions.

"Jar, I'm lost already. Y'know the way back?"

"Yup." He sipped his soda.

The neighborhood was like a maze with its many twists and turns. Evan swung from the pole of a crooked stop sign, walked just a bit behind the rest. Max took the front. Mark and Jared were in middle, this time debating which anime character could beat up who.

As they neared, Evan saw that the building seemed kind of like Derek's, just smaller and more plain. There was a barbecue area out front. There was a security gate, but no shop. Then there was a lobby area to the elevator. Even inside the apartment, there was a coffee table but not made of glass. A couch lined the wall in almost the same place but it wasn't as fluffy. And not as much junk food there for sure, either.

He had been going to Derek's since he was a little kid so he was used to it there. Again, more home than his own. There was a small tennis court and a pool, and he and Derek would sometimes go and whack a ball around. One time they flung one over the fence and heard a windshield crack and a car alarm go off to which they both bolted. His mom was always nice to them, offering to order takeout or to cook something. She was the kind of mom he himself wish he had. Again, almost more family than his own.

"My mom's not home so . . ." Max said, again in a mumble.

"Just you and your mom?"

He nodded, led them down the hall to his room.

"Ah, I see." Again, kinda like Derek.

Max jumped on his bed. Jared went around and sat on the computer chair, spun in place. Mark sat at the edge of the bed, grabbed a tennis ball from the floor. Evan leaned in the frame of the door for a moment, watched them.

"Whatchu guys wanna do?"

"Game?"

"Nah." Mark bounced the tennis ball against the wall, caught it, bounced it again.

"Watch TV?"

"Nah."

"Oh, wait, I wanted to show you guys . . ." Max went to the closet, rifled through plastic containers and bags, opened a shoebox. "Check this out."

It was a gun.

"Cool, right? It's a Beretta. Like what cops use."

Max handed the gun to Evan, who held it, turned it over, weighed it in his hand. He released the magazine, slammed it in. He pulled the slide back and let go, held it, aimed down the sights. Observing the barrel, he felt the gripped handle. Evan squeezed the trigger.

"It looks so real, man."

"Yeah, just if it weren't for the orange cap. Also, I mean, it is plastic. Heavy plastic, but still plastic. Not metal."

Evan noticed the muzzle where it was painted bright orange, then handed it to Mark.

"What does this thing shoot?"

Max took a bottle of plastic pellets from the shoebox, held it up, shook it with a light rattle. It sounded like Tic-Tacs.

"It won't kill anybody, no, but it does hurt like a motherfucker."

9

Jan 19th
11:22am

Crouching down, he kept his eyes on the long dark shadow as it stretched and distorted. Evan waddled back on the balls of his feet, pulled the knife from his pocket, readying himself. He literally brought a knife to a gunfight. It remained in his locker, hidden, hadn't thought about it 'til this day. And now it rattled in his hand. Whoever it was, right there on the other side of the G-building stairs, inched closer. Evan gripped tighter, watched the tip of the toe, the rim of the sole, the other shoe swinging, then pounced with a forceful thrust intent on injuring or otherwise incapacitating.

Evan rammed into the fleshy torso with his shoulder, hard, pushing them back against the edge of the top stair. The barrel of the gun pressed into the side of his rib. Evan unfolded the knife out to one side—swish, swish, flick, click—and prepared to lunge forward and topple him down.

"What the hell!!!"

"Huh!? Jesus Christ!"

She punched Evan in the chest, punched him again. It was

a mixture of punch and shove. He held a hand up in surrender, put the knife away. A false alarm. A very close call.

"You coulda killed me!"

"Damn it, I thought—"

"Y-you asshole." Part groan, part slur, her stuttered outburst was mixed with heavy breathing. "What the frickin' crap."

"I'm sorry. I—"

"You asshole." She punched him again one last time, this time not as hard. "Glad to see you. I guess."

"I thought your camera . . ." Evan shook his head, caught his breath. "Oh, God. My bad."

"Was that a knife?" She inspected the camera that hung around her neck from a thick lanyard. "You almost scratched it, dude."

"Yeah. It's, uh . . . It's a long story."

"What kind of knife is that?"

Bang. The loud gunshot interrupted their brief moment. Their heads whipped over, both of them glancing down the hall to the walkway. A couple of students ran by, one of them tripping and bumping into the other.

"Listen. Michelle, you gotta get off campus."

"What'd you see? What do you know?" She nudged at her glasses, edged over to the wall.

"I think I saw . . ."

"What?"

"There was, like, a guy on the roof. I think he has a rifle."

She stepped towards the lockers, towards the walkway, as more students ran past and down the other stairs on the far side.

He grabbed her by the arm. "Wait, no. Michelle. Don't go that way."

"Evan, stop. Let go a me."

"Are you crazy?" He shook his head side to side. "You gotta get outta here. Seriously."

She turned, her eyes wide. "Nope. Nuh-uh. This is the story of the millennium, and I'm catching it on film. Not digital but freaking film."

He stared, arms dropped at his sides.

"This . . . This is a huge deal. Can't you feel it?"

More gunshots fired, in a distant echo.

"I feel *that!* Can you feel that!?"

"Listen. Washington . . . 'Washington' is going to become synonymous with this, right here, now. That name. It's going to change everything. Whenever someone looks down at a dollar bill or at a quarter. Whenever someone mentions the capital, or the state . . . This . . . This is going to pop into their minds from now on."

A gulp of air lodged in his throat.

"And we got front row seats. I got the best camera 'round for miles. I got the whole scoop right here on a plate in front of me. I can get his face, get some bullet holes or spent shell casings. I'm on the inside, Evan."

He sighed. "That is insane."

"Well, excuse me, but some of us are actually trying to go places in life! Some of us have aspirations! Not everyone can live off of doodles and daydreams."

Evan glared, fixated on the ground, away from her words and her face. More shots echoed from the courtyard.

"Okay. Okay, I'm sorry. I shouldn't have—"

"It's fine." He held up a hand, pulled his shoulder away as she tried to touch it. "Don't even worry about it."

"What you wanna do then?"

"I just gotta find somebody, and then I'm out of here. You should do the same."

"What? Who you lookin' for?"

He didn't say anything, shook his head with a sigh. His shoulders hung down low.

"Wait. It's her, isn't it? You still like her . . ."

10

9th Grade

THE NEXT DAY in Chem, Evan arrived before the rest of class and sat there waiting in the third column, fourth row. Waited for what, he wasn't sure. Most of the time, he strolled in just before the bell rang or just as the teacher began speaking. Here he was now, writing the assignments on the board down on a piece of folder paper. Taking out his composition book, he rested his chin in his palm and thought of something to sketch. Evan turned and gazed out the window. As he drifted, he tapped his mechanical pencil like a little drumstick.

"Hi."

He faced up, and there she was.

"Oh, hey."

"You're early."

"Well, don't look too surprised." He laughed.

Judith wore denim shorts and a tight top with thin straps over the shoulder. He forced himself to turn away, as not to stare. Evan's dark t-shirt and baggy cargo pants contrasted her bright colors. He swept the bangs out of his eyes. She smiled, tucked her hair behind her left ear, then went ahead and sat down in the desk behind him.

"So, how you think you did?"

"Hmm?"

"The test."

"Oh, right. Like I said, I mean, this class is kind of a joke. It makes me a little mad. I'm here to learn. And it's, um, just way too easy."

Evan smirked, but also squinted. It escaped him how that might even feel. An idea that was foreign to him.

High school really is just high school. Each student was obligated to attend and to participate. Each teacher obligated to direct, to observe and to assess. The different subjects, the timing of the school year, even, all predetermined by some government entity to mold the naive and innocent into a general labor force of responsible citizens who contributed to the system.

A majority of the population did what was asked of them, at least to a satisfactory degree, to maintain a sense of order. In this way, there was the least hassle. Then there were those who rebelled, who did the bare minimum or did nothing at all. And then there were those who paid attention, who engaged, who aimed to excel.

She pointed with her finger to the front of the class, where the teacher was handing back tests.

"Moment of truth . . ." He slouched in his chair, took a deep breath in and out.

"You did fine, Evan. Trust me."

The teacher walked past, slipped the test facedown in front of Judith. Evan raised his eyebrows as she flipped it over and peeked.

Her big smile formed those dimples in her cheeks that he was starting to become familiar with. Her almond eyes lit up as she placed it on the desk for him to see.

"Oh, wow. Look at that. A-plus, nice." Evan nodded. "Well, we already knew that was gonna happen."

"It's still scary."

"I guess. Geniuses have their doubts, too, I suppose."

"Well, it helps when the teacher can actually *read* what you've written."

"Okay. My writing's not that—" The teacher then slipped the test facedown in front of Evan.

She folded her arms, rested her chin on them.

He turned it over. "All right, what's the damage?"

"And?"

Evan didn't respond. She nudged him but still no word. Then he started laughing an almost maniacal laugh.

"What? What is it?"

"Whoo!!!" He slammed the top of the desk. "B-minus, baby! Hells yeah!"

She shook her head, lips stretching in a smile.

Tests and assignments were point-based, thus had a plus or minus. In the end, the letter grade for the quarter wouldn't have a plus or minus. Yet, how important it was for each of them to get that specific grade. Back to least hassle, bare minimum, as opposed to pay attention, engage, excel.

Summing up the chapter, the teacher went over the results of the assignment and test. He introduced the next chapter, which would also have an assignment and test, then returned to reading aloud.

I wonder if we'll be together again . . .

She scooted her desk close. When he turned backward, the textbook was already turned sideways and she already had the page open. Evan leaned in his chair, his eyes tracing where her fingernail followed the words. He glanced at the bracelets on her wrist, then glanced up at her eyes as she read along. Again, she seemed so engrossed.

The bell rang after a while. It was another short day. He

walked with her out the door this time, which he never did, and they headed down the west wing through admin towards her next class. As for him, his next class was the opposite way, the far end of upper campus out in M-building.

"Hey, um, I just wanted to say . . ." Evan cleared his throat, fidgeted with the straps of his backpack. "Just, thank you."

Judith held her books in front of her, faced down as they walked together side by side.

"I didn't know how I felt transferring here, being in a class like that. But, with your help, I feel so much better." He licked his lips, leaned in closer. "I couldn't have done it without you. I don't even have a copy of the textbook if it wasn't for you."

They stood in place like that while the rest of school walked on. The light from the sun hit her face and her hair in a way that he couldn't help staring this time.

"You're welcome." She smiled, adjusted her books. "I will say, class was pretty boring until you arrived."

"Well. I better get going, I'm all the way in M."

She shook her head, laughed. "Are you serious? You even gonna make it?"

"I mean, not like I have much choice."

"Okay, well, hurry up. You better go."

He didn't move from that position. Instead, he stood there and watched as she walked away, her hair floating just out of view amongst the crowd. Evan noticed it was the same spot from the other day where he saw there were many girls, beautiful young women. Except, this time, he only saw one.

By the flagpole, after school, their group again formed a lopsided polygon. Mark yawned an unruly yawn, shuddering with the last of his breath then nudging his glasses into place. Max leaned on the rock wall. His arms were crossed as he gazed up at the roof of the admin building, perhaps daydreaming. Jared popped open the tab of his soda, sipped. Evan kicked at the dirt, turned on the ball of his foot, glanced around the courtyard.

"Um. Where's Der again?"

"Remember? He said he'd meet us at Game Works." Mark let out another long yawn.

"Oh, right. Then what are we waiting for?" Evan shook his head, started walking away. "That guy. He's barely been around the past few days . . ."

Max hopped off the wall, and they began their short migration. Down the long driveways, across the street, to the small shopping center.

Evan hung back a bit behind the others, noticed it was a little cloudy. He faced down to his feet, hands in his pockets. Something was on his mind but he wasn't sure what. Just a little quiet today, just a little tired. Something.

The others attacked the change machine like vultures. Straightening then sticking in dollar bills, they reached into the bottom where tokens clanged down. Evan simply watched them.

"You're not playing?" Jared asked.

"Nah. The last of my change went into the fucking swear jar, man."

They both laughed.

"Here." Jared handed him a couple of tokens. "I won't need that much anyway."

Mark went to the puzzle game. He sat on the stool, rattled the joystick. Jared went to the fighting game, placed a token on the edge of the screen. That's how you marked your turn in line, put your token on display then stand back and wait. Jared watched his opponents with arms folded as the two players mashed buttons. He studied their moves, observed their patterns.

Evan walked with Max further into the arcade. Bright lights dinged and flashed. Loud digital noises and music blared. Other kids laughed, screamed. One of them ran past the two of them chasing another.

"Crazy mofos . . ." Again, Max always spoke in a low mumble.

Evan watched him bend down, slip a token into the machine. It was the same one Evan was at a while back.

"Wanna play?"

"That's what I always play. I love shooting games. But nah, I only got so many tokens today . . ." Evan jiggled the small bronze coins in his hand, ones from last time and the ones Jared just gave him. "Gotta make it count, ya know?"

Evan watched Max squeeze an eye, aim down the sight, pull the trigger. That unexplainable pleasure.

He continued his circle around the arcade. In the row of racing games, he saw Derek then walked over.

"Ha! I found you."

"Eh, what's up, man." Derek jerked the steering wheel.

"Laying low, huh? Hiding out?" Evan nudged him, messed up his hair. "Man, sounds more like me."

Derek laughed. "Hey. I came at lunch, what."

"Uh-huh. Sure. For like a second. What the hell you been up to?"

"Nah, nothing. I just—" He was cut off by a car ramming into his side. He slammed the brake, shifted gears. "There's something I been meaning to—"

"You got this, Der."

Evan tapped him on the shoulder, smirked.

He could see Jared sitting down at the fighting game now, where Mark stood behind cheering him on. He jiggled the coins in his hand again, continued to circle around.

What to play, what to play . . .

I could play two meh games or I could play one good game. A game that costs a little bit more. Hmm.

In the center of the next aisle was a new dinging and flashing of lights, a new music blaring. It was unfamiliar and strange, oddly drawing him in. The machine was different from the other games. At the top was a lit panel with the name and design, colored spotlights on either side. The screen was slanted at an angle, below it were huge speakers with neon rings. Separate from the speakers and the screen was a thick floor piece that was kind of like futuristic hopscotch. There were bright squares with arrows on them, two sets of four, like the directional pad on a controller. In back, a big bar was laid across with cushion.

It was the dance game the others had mentioned. There was a mini-dance stage with mini-stage lights up top. This time, there was a mini-dancer too. Some girl, and she hopped on the square tiles facing forward with her back to him. Her smooth legs were deftly and quick. Evan couldn't help but be mesmerized at her movements, at her body, in the flashing lights—like he was under some sort of spell. He stepped towards the machine, in awe, in wonder. As she hopped, turning side to side, a sliver of her midriff showed between her shorts and her top. He watched as her legs spread with each step, closed, then spread again, teasing him. Her top was just tight enough that he could see the curvature of her chest.

She did a kind of spin move. Right, up. Up, left. Left, down. Down, right. And he caught a glimpse of her face, her neck, her shoulders and hair.

Whoa, whoa. Wait.

He stepped sideways, peered closer. That's when he caught a glimpse of her eyes. Her almond eyes.

No way. Is that—?

Evan did a double take, flinched. It was her. What was she doing there? He peered again, at her legs, at her curves. There was an implosion deep in his bones, in his teeth. A feeling euphoric yet sickening at the same time. He shook his head, smirked to himself. Then he stepped forward, put the tokens away, placed a hand on the cushion of the back bar, watching.

She finished off to the last notes of the upbeat techno song then turned. When she saw him standing there, she blinked, expressionless for a moment as she processed, then smiled. Her cheeks were a shade pink, from the exhaustive routine.

"H-how long you been there? The whole time?"

Evan laughed. "Nah, I only caught the second half."

"Oh, God." She waved her fingers at herself in a fanning motion. "I hope it wasn't too embarrassing."

"You know . . . It didn't look half-bad, Jude." He nodded then leaned on the back bar. "In fact, I gotta say, you were pretty damn good."

Their eyes locked. The lights shined behind her, the screens flashed behind him. It was like the air around them was spinning, roaring with noise, increasing in velocity, starting to hurl debris. He could almost feel the wind blow the bangs out of his eyes. She appeared lighter, adrift, as gravity lessened. Like they were in the midst of a swirling vortex.

"Ev-an!"

"Yo, E."

Mark and Jared walked over, shoved Evan. Derek was just behind them. Mark leaned on Evan's shoulder, noticed the girl.

"Did you play?"

"No, I just . . ."

Evan turned to Judith, was about to introduce her when Derek stepped past. He hopped on the floor piece in front of the machine and wrapped his arm around her.

His mind couldn't comprehend what just happened, in that tiny fraction of a second. Evan was beside himself in disbelief.

"Guys, I got a little announcement." Derek shifted to each face, even Max who joined them now. "This is my girlfriend. Her name is Judy."

She gave Derek a quick look.

"Whaaat?"

"So, *that's* why you been all flaky."

"Hehe. Congrats."

Evan didn't move, didn't say a word, his mouth hanging open. In his chest, there was a sensation like falling.

She shook hands with Mark and Jared from across the bar, then Max. Judith waved and smiled then turned to Evan too. There was a momentary pause.

"Hi. I'm Judy."

"I . . . I'm Evan." His eyes squinted, face contorted in a grimace, mouth open still. "Nice to meet you."

Neither was sure why it came out that way like that. They each noticed the minute it slipped from their tongues and their lips. As the lights flashed around them, and as bells dinged and coins clashed, the vortex slowed. As the music and sound effects echoed, their hearts beat in sync. It would be the first of many little secrets between them.

Their group was no longer a lopsided polygon, now full, now expanded. And, within that polygon, a small triangle was embedded. Nobody realized at the time but it had begun that day. It transformed from a simplistic two-dimensional shape to a three-dimensional object, vast and complex. The tornado had spun. They were now in the vanishing point.

PART TWO
THE BUTTERFLY KNIFE EFFECT

1

Jan 19th
11:23am

THERE WAS DEAD silence, as the two stood facing one another in the hall still. Evan glanced down, couldn't answer her question. His eyes grazed the cracks in the floor as he began to shuffle on his feet. Michelle watched him, waited, shifted the other way. In the distance, there was more echoed gunfire. The shots cut through the air between the two of them as they each turned backward and stared, on instinct, like small rodents in the wild.

"Let me get one shot, one good pic."

He gave a stern look in return. "Just from the walkway then. Over there."

Michelle ducked low and walked forward. Evan was right behind, his hand hovering near his back pocket where the knife was. In the closed doors to their side, they could hear the worried cries of students hiding and teachers trying to calm everybody down. One classroom was mixed shouting and arguments. The other was silent, whispers, speaking in low voices.

"Right there. If you look at the top of admin, you should be able to see."

God . . . Please.

Michelle took off the lens cap, knelt in position, aiming around the wall and over the rail up to the roof from the corner of the walkway.

Through her lens, she traced the roof of the building with one eye closed. It was the third floor, right above the library, where Evan saw a figure standing with a rifle aimed. However, there was nothing. There might have been slight movement but it was hard for her to tell.

"I don't see anything." She pulled the camera from her face. "Did he move?"

"Crap . . ." Evan stepped closer, his hands on the wall.

"Not sure, but I might've caught a glimpse. I think something moved. The damned sun."

The two turned, sat with their backs against the wall, breathing. There weren't any shots. From where they were sitting, they gazed at the inner stairwell. Evan ran past it on the way in, almost didn't notice, but now sitting on the floor, he stared into it.

"Isn't there a fire escape in back of the building. Like, that big ladder, right? Maybe he went down?"

Michelle's eyes widened.

"It could be dangerous, but if we headed that way . . . Between admin and the auditorium, I don't know, maybe you could get your shot."

"Let's hurry."

Already, she was on one knee ducking down. Sneaking to the inner stairwell, she peeked out from the edge of the walkway to the roof again. Nothing.

"W-wait. Michelle. Aren't you scared?"

"Of course. I'm terrified. We should all be inside, hiding, cowered under our desks. We should be running away, off campus. But I'm assuming I'm out here just like you're out here . . . It's something we *have* to do."

For a moment, crouched near the top stair, the two of them locked eyes with a look neither of them had seen on the other. A reminder of the dire circumstances.

"In and out, okay? No games. This is a matter of life and death here." Evan sighed, swallowed. "We don't know what's gonna happen, but I don't intend on losing anybody today."

2

9th Grade

It was like that moment was frozen in time, like they were in suspended animation. Her eyes gazed at him from across the way. She seemed so far, with that arm around her. His eyes continued to linger. The lights, the flashing, piercing a hole through his heart. Like an incendiary bullet lodged into him, and he was bleeding out dark red. The universe had torn, the bubble had popped. Evan wanted to clutch a hand to his chest but couldn't.

There's always one girl. One girl that comes along and changes everything. Boy meets girl. Hormones raging in the angst, the awakening of adolescence.

With a quick playful shove, all that faded. He was back in the arcade again, next to his friends, in the expanded polygon they formed. Evan glanced at Judith who glanced back, for just a moment, then down and away, tucking his hands in his pockets.

"You guys gonna play?"

"Uhh, nope. Hell no." Derek pulled his arm away, stepped down from the floor piece, raising his hands up. "That game is stupid. I'm gonna look dumb."

"So . . . pretty much the same, then." Mark grinned a big grin as the others laughed.

"Anyone?" Judith's eyes scanned the group. Each shook their head, stepped backward.

Again, the two locked eyes.

In his pocket, Evan's hand grazed the small bronze tokens. His mouth open, brow furled, he took them out in his hand.

Mark shoved him. "Oh, I gotta see this."

Jared pointed with his soda bottle to the floor piece, nodded. Max inched closer with arms folded, an excited awkward smile spreading across his face.

Evan stepped onto the floor piece, turned towards Judith who smiled. They both knelt down in unison.

The sound effect blasted as the tokens dropped in. A bold text reading 2 CREDIT(S) flashed at the bottom of the screen, while the 1P and 2P start buttons illuminated.

"Hold on, let's switch sides." She grabbed him by the hip behind his back, an electricity in that brief moment.

"What does it matter?" He laughed.

She shifted toward him, smiled. "Oh, it matters."

Judith pressed the 1P button. Evan lingered a second, then pushed the 2P button also.

He watched as she navigated the screen with the two arrow buttons, scrolled between her choice of song. She told him what options to pick, what level of difficulty.

"Ready?"

Ah, geez . . .

The song blared on, the upbeat techno, as they both faced the screen and stood with their feet on the square tiles. The arrows slid up. Their feet stomped the corresponding squares while the group cheered on.

Up, up, down, down, left, right, left, right.

Now there were two arrows at a time on his side, three in a row on her side. As the music built up, so did their movements. He jumped. She did a triple step. They exchanged a quick glance as they did so, both smiling, different colors shining on their skin and on their clothes.

Judith again did her spin move. In the corner of his eye, Evan could see her legs and her midriff, the curvature of her breasts and buttocks. He watched her shoulders, the slender of her neck and back, as she switched sides with her right foot in front.

With the last few arrows to the beat, they each stomped down, until they ended in their last positions. She blew the hair out of her face while he wiped the sweat from his brow. They both smiled, and when he saw her dimples, he felt a small flutter in his chest.

"Nice, nice." Jared laughed, shook his head.

"Judy! You *kicked* Evan's ass!" Mark yelled through cupped hands. "Evan, you got beat by a girl!"

Oh, she kicked his ass, all right, in more ways than one.

The next day in Chem, another short day with all their classes, was of course a little bit awkward. Judith walked past holding her books in front of her, with a smile. Evan smirked, nodded. The exchange seemed forced on both ends. The teacher asked for the assignment and each student unzipped their bags, unclipped their binders. He reached back, took her paper with elegantly written ink and placed it over his chicken-scratch in pencil, handed them both forward.

Before the teacher read aloud, he wrote a few lines on the board. Judith scooted close, turned the textbook sideways. Evan turned around. This time he found he didn't glance at her fingernail—didn't watch her eyes, didn't notice her bracelets or her perfume—no, it was just the reading. Or, rather, it was just the staring at words on the page.

In his boredom, he gazed out the window. It was cloudy out. He rested his chin in his palm, turned sideways to the chalkboard where the lines were written. Evan observed a symbol that the teacher used. Although he'd seen it before, quite a few times, it was as if it was for the first time.

It was a triangle. The little shape scribbled in chalk, right there in front of him, simply matter of fact, representing "change." Evan didn't realize but he clenched a fist then, grinded his teeth.

Keep your damn triangle.

Keep your damn change.

Why couldn't things just stay the same? Anger and frustration simmered in him, turned to melancholy. Things were fine. He was almost starting to feel normal, almost starting to feel at home, and then all that happened. Why did that have to happen?

Chemistry, the study of change. Reactions, bonds. Atoms and molecules and the sharing of electrons. All the different elements. Pouring powder into a beaker with liquid, swirling it around at heated temperature, as the effervescence built and built. The splashing and bubbling in the centrifugal force, like a tornado.

With the sound of the bell, Evan shoved his things in his backpack, yanked the zipper, stood, and hurried out the door.

"Evan!"

He cringed at the voice.

"Evan, wait . . ."

Although he kept walking, she circled around in front of him.

"Please. Wait." She faced down, tilted her head at an angle. "I . . . I feel like maybe you're mad or something."

"Why would I be mad?" Evan tried to step past. "I gotta go to class."

"Hold on." Judith shook her head. "Please, just one minute."

He sighed, turned. "Okay, what?"

"I just . . . I'm sorry if things are, like, weird now."

"It's fine. I'm fine."

The sound of his words startled him. He didn't realize he raised his voice, that he sounded angry. Evan took a breath, calmed himself.

"Things are fine. Okay, Jude? We're okay."

"I hope so. 'Cause . . . 'Cause . . ."

He waited for her to finish.

There was a pause. No words, it was just their eyes speaking. Her eyes blinked, in an intermittent flutter. His eyes traced her face, her lips, her hair down to her shoulders. Around them, the hall grew quiet in anticipation of the coming bell.

"I don't want anything to *change.*" There it was again, that dreaded word. "I like sitting next to you, I like talking to you. You're fun. You're funny, different."

"I like all that too, Jude. I do. And you're . . . You're so cool. You are. Really."

She smiled. He smirked.

"Can we work together again?"

Evan was quiet, licked his lips. "You're my best friend's girlfriend . . ."

"Do you want to pass this class or not?"

He shook his head, faced down.

"Let me help you." She stepped closer. He could see a slight shimmer in her almond eyes. "Please."

❧

The assignment was clear, yet he sat there staring at the page. Or perhaps the page was staring at him. Evan's mind was as blank as the off-white piece of sketch paper, he just didn't know what to draw. He nibbled on the eraser end of his mechanical pencil, then banged it on the desk like a small drumstick. Beneath the desk, his feet fidgeted in place.

He realized the teacher was watching. Compared to his chem and geometry teachers, his art teacher was pretty cool. She was younger, mellow, just a little bit hippie. Evan turned away, gazed out the window where he watched the clouds, which appeared a tad darker.

I don't know what to do . . .

Of course, he was referring to the assignment, to the blank paper in front of him. But he also meant in his life in general, and the new dilemma that had formed.

Evan placed the pencil sideways, slouched in his chair. It was the short day so the bell would soon ring. There was not one etching. There was not one curve, not a single trace of lead. Nothing. His body was in that chair in that classroom, but his mind was elsewhere.

❧

Walking along with the crowd, he felt like a zombie. The other kids laughed and joked and talked. Evan followed them, with a blank expression across his face. In their usual spot in the cafe, there was just Derek. Evan paused for a second, but continued forward, sitting next to him.

"Hey, what's up." Derek glanced up with his usual goofy smile. "You all right?"

"Yeah. I'm fine." Evan put his backpack under the seat. "I'm just tired today, lazy."

Derek laughed. "That's me every day, pretty much."

"Where is everybody?"

"Ah, they're all stuck in line." Derek slid his tray over. "I think they were late doing cafe duty or something."

Evan took a piece of bread, bit into it. "So . . . You got a girlfriend now, huh? Congratulations."

The words were dull, empty. He wasn't sure why. Derek didn't seem to notice, continued to smile.

"Well, tell me about her."

"Ah. What can I say? She's sweet, and kind, and pretty. I don't really know how else to put it. All just sort of happened, I guess."

"I'm happy you're happy, man." He meant it, although it might not have seemed. "That's so awesome."

"Remember in summer fun there was that one girl we all thought was so hot, so cool?"

"Hehe, yeah. And one time she wore a dress that was kinda see-through? Oh, man."

"Yeah!"

They both laughed.

"Polka dots."

"Well, she kind of . . ."

Evan couldn't help but smirk at his friend's excitement, his difficulty forming the words.

"Like, she kinda gives me that feeling. You know? Not the sexy part, no, but like, someone that's . . . well, amazing. 'Cause that girl was way too good to have been in the same summer fun as us."

He nodded.

She is *that amazing. She's more than sweet, kind, pretty. She's smart. She's beautiful.*

"Hey, Der. Do me one favor."

"Yeah?"

"Treat her right, okay?" Evan put a hand on Derek's shoulder as he said this. "She seems like a . . . like a really good girl."

"I will. She is. La-di-freaking-dah."

⁂

The group didn't play cards so they had a little extra time left in recess. They migrated to the east wing of the admin building. Evan followed Derek who chose a spot, marked it by leaning on one of the pillars. Evan stood next to him with his hands in his pockets, kicked his shoe at the concrete. Mark leaned an arm on his shoulder while Jared joined in. Max was lagging somewhere behind. The four of them stood together in a semi-circle while they waited for him.

Evan peered up at the gray sky, panned around the courtyard. It was that small moment between classes, the middle of the day when kids gathered. Each respective clique in each respective territory discussing the usual things. And this was his, this was theirs.

Jared took a sip of soda. "Mark said there's this new game coming out that might be kinda cool."

"Yeah. Arcade. Up to four players. It's like a beat-'em-up RPG, if that makes sense. We get to pick characters, like one of us can be a mage, one can be a archer—"

"Was it a mage?" Jared interrupted. "I thought you said it was a wizard."

"Mage, wizard. Whatever. Is there even a difference?" Mark shook his head with a sigh. "Not even important. Can we get to the game please, and strategy. God."

"Or, wait, was it magician?" Evan added on, to which Jared chuckled. "Sorcerer?"

Mark continued, despite his annoyance. "And then one of us can be warrior—"

"I thought there was two warriors?"

"There's one male, one female. Female has better armor, I think. Male better attack."

Jared chugged the last few drops from the can then threw it in the garbage. "All right, it's decided then. Derek can be warrior, I'll be wizard . . ."

"I call archer." Evan smirked then covered his mouth, fighting back laughter.

He glanced over and noticed Derek hadn't been paying attention, seemed distracted.

Hmm.

Probably thinking about you-know-who.

Evan thought of her then too, just for a moment. Her circling around in front of him. Her head down, tilted at such an angle that he almost couldn't see her face. And the way she pleaded with her eyes . . . her almond eyes.

He blinked, shook his head, faced Jared again.

"Which leeaves . . . Mark to be *female* warrior."

Mark hesitated, glared, then spoke. "Hey. I am not being female warrior. Max can be female warrior!"

They each turned, noticed he wasn't there.

"Max?"

Derek stepped past, walked up the hall of the east wing. Evan stared, saw there was a small huddle.

Oh, crap.

"Hey!"

It was the two punks from the other week. They held Max by his shirt and his backpack, trying to lift him and throw him in the garbage can. His eyes were wide. His skin was pale. A couple of spectators stood nearby heckling and taunting, until they saw Evan and Derek approaching. Evan ran up alongside Derek with both fists clenched.

"Hey! Assholes!"

"Yeah, you! Pieces of shit!"

The two punks noticed, let go. The one kid glared, shot a look at his friend. They shoved Max one last time into the wall, then took off laughing.

"The fuck, man?"

Mark and Jared checked on Max, made sure he was okay. His shirt collar was stretched out and the loop of his backpack was torn. Jared stood close, with arms crossed. Mark leaned in, put a hand out on his shoulder. Max nodded back, shook his head. His eyes were teary.

Derek and Evan watched as the spectators dispersed and as the punks disappeared around E-building. Evan's fists were still clenched. Derek grinded his teeth.

"The hell was all that about?" Derek turned to Evan.

"Ah, probably just two bastards." He didn't bring up what he saw before, not sure why.

"Well. It better not happen again."

"I'm with you. We ain't no pussies. I frickin' dare them."

On the fifth floor of Derek's building was a tennis court and pool area. The pool was lined with long chairs to lie down on, from the shallow end to the deep end. To one side of the pool, there was a wide space with artificial grass for barbecues and birthdays. There was a grill there, and a bench and a table. Max, Mark and Jared sat on the fake grass facing forward while Evan and Derek stood in front of them in attack positions.

Max rubbed at his eye. Mark scratched the back of his head then his ear. Jared covered a long yawn with his palm. For a quick second, they resembled three monkeys on the ground.

"Okay, guys. Me and Der used to go to the Y when we were little. Took a couple martial arts classes there."

"Yeah. We're gonna practice some moves, show Max how to fight if anybody ever pulls some crap again."

Mark leaned over and punched Jared in the arm, hard. Jared elbowed him back, in his side, drove it in with his other arm.

Again, that unexplainable pleasure, that destructive force. It could be whacking a stick against a tree trunk. It could be banging two plastic toy cars together. And, like this, it could be hitting your friend for no apparent reason.

"Keep one hand by your face, keep one hand down. Ready to block either high or low. Make a fist with your thumb like this, not like this . . ." Evan showed Max who nodded with his arms crossed. "Your body's kind of turned, like, at an angle. Stay light, kinda bouncy almost."

He gave a similar speech to his little brother after he was ganged up on by the playground. Although he arrived in time, broke it up and scared them off, it was still best to teach a thing or two.

Evan punched Derek, who punched him back in the chest.

"If he hits you, you hit him right back. Right away. Fast. It's a counter." Derek bounced on his feet, switched sides, then stepped up. "A quick switch like that can throw the guy off."

Evan switched sides, stepped, kicked him in his left butt cheek. The smack was so loud that it echoed up the side of the building and throughout the complex. Derek squealed in pain, hopping on one leg.

"Ow, man! The fuck!!!"

The group howled in laughter. Jared keeled forward, Mark fell backward. Max snorted and couldn't breathe.

"Shit, man. I'm so sorry." Evan laughed. "I meant to hit you only lightly."

"Asshole."

They both got back into attack position, bouncing barefoot on the grass.

"Here's how you block." Evan let Derek throw a punch, let Derek kick. "Move with the hit, use your forearm. Like Derek said, you can counter . . ."

Evan punched forward and upward, right into Derek's stomach. Derek toppled down in pain.

"Son of a BITCH!!!"

The group roared again, tears in their eyes, cheeks sore and sides aching.

"I'm so sorry, man." Evan laughed, knelt with a hand on Derek's shoulder. "I think you were too close."

"Oh, so it's *my* fault you kicked me in my ass then punched me in the gut." He closed his eyes, rolled over on his side. "Damn that hurts . . . Stings like a scorpion."

"My bad. I feel like crap now."

"You should."

Derek hobbled over to Max then sat down. Evan motioned for Mark and Jared to come join.

"I don't really like to fight, but I'll defend myself if I have to. Me and my grandma live in a pretty sketchy neighborhood." Jared put down his soda.

They kicked off their shoes, faced each other.

"Just trip 'im, I say." Jared put his foot behind Mark, pushed him to which he teetered. "They never expect that."

Mark went behind Jared, wrapped an arm around his neck. "Yeah? And what about this?"

"Same thing. Trip 'im, get him down, then that's your chance."

Jared wrapped his foot behind Mark's, pushed backwards causing Mark to buckle.

"Ah." Mark let go.

"Oh, and even if you're down, too, check this out . . ."

Jared got on the ground. Mark stood near. Jared scissored his feet around Mark's lower leg.

"In front of the ankle. Back of the knee."

Evan watched as Mark wobbled then regained balance. He helped Jared back up.

"Nice. Got anything, Mark?"

"At the end of the day, it always comes back to this." Mark held up a tight fist. "If you can punch, you can punch. End of story."

Mark arguably had the hardest punch of all of them. Pretty tough for a skinny kid with glasses.

"Like Evan said, don't tuck your thumb. And put your whole weight into it. Plant your feet. Drive it."

With a quick jab, Mark hit Jared on the arm. The smack was audible and loud. Jared rubbed at his upper arm, glared at Mark.

"Damn it, Mark."

Evan laughed. "You wanna try?"

Max shook his head, folded his arms tight.

Derek leaned in towards him. "C'mon, man. Give it a shot. This is all for you."

"If you don't want to, you don't gotta. It's cool. Point is, you have to stand up for yourself." Evan stepped forward, got on one knee.

With a hand on his shoulder, Derek nodded.

Evan looked Max in the eye. "The plan is for you to stick

close. We're not gonna let anything happen to you. But, if you ever need, you can't be afraid to punch . . . You can't be afraid to punch back."

3

Jan 19th
11:26am

FROM THE WALL of E-building, on the ground floor, Evan strafed the corner and peeked. Students ran from the back entrance of the administration building. He could see the mural on the back wall facing the auditorium, its hopeful images seeming out of place. A circular monument gleamed in the sun then dimmed with the cloud cover. He saw the portables on the far side, over by D-building. Behind him in the other direction was the cafeteria.

"Come on. Quiet."

Evan waved his hand, put a finger to his lips. Michelle snuck up, leaned on the wall. They both glanced at the ladder.

He felt his heart thumping, a cold sweat on his neck and palms. Michelle crept forward, pulling in front. They walked into the open space between the admin building and the auditorium. Evan tilted his head to one side as more students ran in spurts.

Again, Evan noticed the mural closer up. A big bold eagle flew overhead as boys and girls stood holding hands along the edge of the globe. The eagle, the designated mascot of the school, represented "freedom." The figures holding hands, the student body, represented "harmony." It was the so-called American dream personified.

He didn't realize but it had become eerily quiet. The ladder was so far away, so high up, but they kept walking towards it, keeping crouched. They stopped in place when a sharp high-pitched scream broke the silence and swept through the open area like a tidal wave.

Evan turned to the back entrance where a flock of students ran with tears in their eyes.

There was the sound of shattering glass then a loud whooshing noise. Before him, a fireball mushroomed with thick black smoke.

Is that a . . . ?

As if from out of nowhere, he was forced to step back from the heat of the flammable liquid, one hand over his face.

Boom. Some of the students fell down to the concrete. Michelle tried to step back as the students ran toward her in a stampede. Boom, boom.

This sounded different than the other gunfire, stronger, deeper, and more loud. Michelle was engulfed by the herding mob, cut off from Evan as he stood by the fire that burned on the ground.

Boom. Boom.

She got her one shot.

The blood splattered upward and at an angle like a large truck running through a pool of rainwater. It was a red mist that floated in the air, every droplet of blood like aerosol spray. Her eyes closed, she gasped with her cheeks drenched in what appeared like red paint. The paint dripped from her chin, streaming down her neck.

"Michelle!!! Get out of there!"

In front of her, the student's body convulsed with a gagging noise then fell to the ground.

Behind them, with the last of the stampede, the shooter reloaded the shotgun. First one shell, then the other.

She could see it all: the mask, the messy short hair, the double barrel. Michelle was frozen, in fear, in disgust, but somehow jerked backward. One of the students running past knocked into her, turning her around, but she was still stunned.

"Run! Michelle, run!!!"

Evan jumped up as he yelled, lashing his arms out, as another fireball then emerged between them. The bright orange and dark black appeared like a carved pumpkin.

Where did that come from? He was confused by what just happened but there was no time to think.

Boom, boom.

He peered through the smoke, saw Michelle running along with the crowd towards the portables.

The shooter now turned towards him, as some of the students ran in his direction. Between the two puddles of fire and the two plumes of smoke, Evan shifted. He ran in back of the monument, with two other students following him. Huddled together, they glanced at the cafeteria, but it was too far away, too out in the open. Evan faced each of them, shook his head.

What to do?

Where do we go!?

Behind them were the doors to the auditorium but they were almost never unlocked. Evan ran over to the first of the big doors and jiggled the handle.

He stepped over to the next one, jiggled again. The other students got up and tried the same. One of them banged on the door, pleaded, jiggled the handle hard then kicked at the bottom. The one all the way on the end swung open and the student ran in. Evan followed, then the other.

Boom.

Evan and the last student skidded inside, closed the door, fumbled to try to lock it.

Evan stepped back, to the left of the other two, a guy and a girl. The handle rattled as the door shook in place. There was loud pounding. All three turned to one another.

Boom.

The middle of the door blasted apart. In the air, falling splinters and little planks of wood spiraled like dust. Evan felt a warm spritz on the right side of his neck and cheek, on his right forearm. He darted his eyes sideways, saw the guy next to him hurtling towards the back wall, the girl past him covering her mouth with both hands. From the hole in the door, an arm poked through, in it what appeared like a large handgun but with an extended magazine from the barrel.

4

9th Grade

IT WAS ANOTHER day lost in thought. There was a lot on his mind, yet, there was nothing at the same time. With his cheek in his palm, Evan sat at the table, watched the different kids stuffing their faces, chewing, talking. He listened to all the noise occurring around him and observed all the movement. The white table in front of him was so empty and open, as he stared and drifted along the periphery of consciousness and daydreaming.

"Hey, you okay?" Her voice was comforting, a much needed familiarity. "You got that look again. Did someone die?"

Evan smirked, shook his head. "Oh, hey."

Judith put down her tray, put down her bag, sat down next to him. She turned, leaned with a hand on her cheek, waited. Her eyes opened wide and her eyebrows raised.

"It's nothing. Just . . ." He drifted off again, to some distant place.

Her eyes searched his. Both were together in a space between spaces, away for a brief moment.

Evan gazed in her almond eyes, eyes he couldn't deny. "You remember Max, right?"

"Yeah. Kid with the braces?"

Evan nodded, adjusted in his seat.

"Well, these guys were messing with him yesterday. We scared 'em off, but . . . I'm still worried." Evan cleared his throat. "Like, I can't be there with him every single second. What if something happens?"

Judith touched his arm. "It's okay."

"I hope so." Their eyes met again, lingered. ". . . So, what, you sitting with us for lunch?"

"I'm not studying today, so sure, why not."

"Right, right. Where's Der?"

"He's over there, stuck in line."

Evan lifted his head, glanced over. Derek then turned and glanced back.

"Speaking of which, where's your food?"

He tilted his head, scrunched his lips and squinted. "Uh, I don't really eat. Just, it's kinda the only money I get if I ever wanna buy a CD or something. You know?"

A bit of a sore subject for him. He always tried to avoid the topic of home, of family and money.

"But don't you get hungry?"

"Well, the guys usually got me, gimme a piece a bread or something."

Judith slid her tray over.

Evan leaned in with a smirk. "You sure?"

"Oh, I hate carrots, so."

"Fine. I guess. I'll just take one . . ."

"Have them all!" Her smile grew wide, until her deep dimples were exposed. "No, take that one too."

"Ew, it's an ugly one."

Behind them, Mark and Jared walked around and sat down on the opposite side of the table. They also slid their trays and Evan took some of their food. Jared pulled the tab up, opened his can of soda.

She narrowed her eyes. "What's with the soda?"

"Oh, Judy, Judy . . ." Jared chuckled, wiped his mouth. "You have much to learn."

"Don't mind us." Mark slapped a hand on Jared's shoulder. "These guys are rude, loud, obnoxious assholes."

Jared stared at him.

"Nah, but seriously. You'll have to get used to our swearing, dirty jokes, and overall dumbness."

Judith turned to Evan for confirmation. He nodded.

Derek sat on the other side of Judith, put his tray down and then his bag. Evan faced away as he kissed her on the cheek. With his back turned, he bit into a carrot stick.

"So, you're part of the group now?"

As Mark asked this, Evan watched Max in line, kept his eye on him. He wanted to make sure those punks weren't anywhere near.

"If I'm not studying or too busy, yeah."

"Why? You study that much?" Jared swilled the can around. "I barely study."

"She's tryna get into a good college." Derek twirled the fork, held it up. "To become a doctor."

Really? I didn't know that.

The fact unveiled caused him to drift for a brief moment, and it was unclear whether it was the fact itself or the fact that he didn't know until now.

Mark struggled to open his milk. "A doctor?"

"Yeah. I mean, my parentals are pushing me."

Evan shifted back, still half-watching Max. "Why? You don't want to?"

"Kind of . . . But then again, no . . . Maybe. I don't know, I'm not sure." She shrugged, inclined her head. "Is that weird?"

"No, it's cool. Totally fine. But, I mean, the rest of your life's a pretty long time. If you're gonna do something, it should be for a reason. A good reason."

Judith gazed downward with a slight nod. Evan watched her as she blinked, then shifted again towards Max.

His backpack high up on his shoulders, Max walked, unsure of his step, holding the tray tight with both hands trying to balance it.

"Well, I just want a job. Just to be comfortable, do whatever." Derek laughed, stuck the fork in his mouth. "I'll be a bus driver or something, it doesn't really matter."

Mark turned the milk around, still struggling with it. "This fricking thing . . ."

"Really, a bus driver?" Jared chuckled.

"Yeah. Who even cares." Derek shrugged his shoulders, shook his head as he stabbed into his food. "Something. Anything. I'll stock boxes in some back room."

Putting the tray down, taking his bag off, Max sat down near Mark. Mark sipped from the carton which was horrendously torn.

"It's just a job. This whole 'idea' of go to school, get some degree . . . Punch a clock. Put on a uniform. Nah . . . Life sucks and then you die." Derek laughed again. "What's the point?"

"What do you guys wanna do?" Judith asked.

Jared took a small bite, chewed then swallowed. "I wanna work in computers."

"I don't know, maybe be a math teacher or professor or something . . ." Mark said, unaware of his milk mustache.

"And you?" Judith turned to Evan.

"Uh, I'm not sure. I kinda get what Derek's saying. Who

cares. And I get Jared, too, do what you're good at, what you kind of like. I get Mark and you, that maybe you should try to get that 'good' job and all that . . ."

Evan held up another carrot stick, faced Judith.

"But I do got dreams, I guess. I can't seem to help it. I wanna do something kinda crazy. Like, I think it would be cool to work on movies or music or something. Something fun. Something big like that, that lasts. I know that's probably stupid but . . ."

"It's not stupid." Her voice was again comforting, again familiar. "That's not stupid at all."

Evan smirked, noticed Max spill some of his food. "Max. You okay over there?"

His mouth full, he just nodded and gathered a wad of napkins.

Shaking his head, with a silent laugh, Evan glanced at each member of this new group. Derek and Judith playing with the food on each other's plates, giggling. Mark and Jared bickering and arguing until Mark punched him on the arm. And Max, wiping away at the spaghetti stain on his crotch. The polygon now full, now expanded.

I guess I can be okay with this . . .

This ain't too bad.

❧

Leaning back into the fluffy couch, Evan kicked his socks up on the glass table. Max sat on the floor at the base of the couch with his arms crossed. He gazed over at Max then forward to the TV, at their own reflection floating in the glass. Jared and Mark grabbed sodas from the fridge in the kitchen, double fisting with two in one hand. Derek came from his room down the hall with a big box and sat down on the carpet.

Mark handed Evan and Max a soda each, then hopped on the couch. Jared handed Derek a soda, sat down on the floor next to him.

"All right. Listen up. Me and Evan been talking . . . Y'know, it's not really just Max. Any one of us could get in a fight at any time." Derek looked each of them in the eye, pushing the box forward in the middle. "It could be walking home. It could be right on campus, at the arcade even. Anywhere. Any time."

"Yeah. I mean, we'll all stick together. We're a group." Evan reached forward, grabbed chips from the open bag. "But, you just never know."

"We need to be able to defend ourselves."

Derek tilted the box, showed various tools inside.

"I'm getting us something *real.* 'Til then, this will work. Max, you get to pick first."

Getting down on both knees, Max waddled forward, reached in and pulled out a box cutter. He nodded to himself, clicked the blade into place, turned it over, clicked it back.

Derek tilted the box again. "Mark . . ."

Mark scooted forward on the cushion, reached way forward almost losing his balance, pulling out a pair of scissors. It was sharp and sturdy.

"Ooh, the good kind." Mark spun it from his finger like a cowboy gun.

Turning back, Derek offered the box to Jared, but Jared shook his head, raised a hand up.

Mark stared at him, still spinning the scissors. "Lame."

"Fine for now. But, like I said, I'm getting us all something, one for everybody, and you gotta have one."

Derek took out the two last tools, giving one to Evan. Phillips and flat-head screwdrivers.

Evan stabbed it down in the air, stabbed it forward.

"Now, don't just go off attacking somebody. No. But if you're ever in trouble, like real deep shit, some desperate situation, this could help. Maybe just to scare 'em off." Derek held the screwdriver tight, pointy end up.

Evan scooted over, close to Mark, glanced at Max on the floor who glanced back. "This is for you, man."

Max nodded, stared at the box cutter in his hand.

"Listen. Don't be scared. You stand up. You fight. Fight back. These assholes had it coming to them. Punch 'em. Kick 'em. Bite. You got that with you now. And you got us right here."

5

Jan 19th
11:29am

BANG, BANG, BANG, bang. The arm poking through pulled the trigger and aimed sporadically. Pieces of the back wall crumbled and tore apart. The girl flinched and turned away. The guy slumped over on the floor. Evan pulled the knife out from his back pocket—swish, swish, flick, click—held it at his side then lunged at the door.

He swung left, right, slicing at the forearm, then stabbed downward. There was a demonic squeal on the other end as the hand retreated.

Evan stumbled backwards and fell. The girl sobbed into her hands and covered her face, hunching over. The guy groaned in pain through gritted teeth. Evan stared at the two of them, at the knife in his hand covered in what seemed like red paint. His head arched back, his mouth flung open, as he turned and dry heaved over the beige carpet.

Michelle . . .

He thought of the red paint all over her face. He thought of the puddles of fire. He thought of the baseball diamond and then the football field past the portables.

I hope she made it out.

Don't be stupid, just get off campus.

He wiped sweat from his forehead, cleaned the knife on the floor, staggered to one foot.

"Hey. That, over there. Quick."

Evan got on one end of the long table. The girl wiped tears from her face, got to the other side.

They moved it down and placed it sideways, covering the door and blocking the hole.

"How 'bout those things." Evan pointed to metal poles with red rope attached. He grabbed a nearby chair, set it against the table. "I think that's all we got."

An odd and unlikely combination. The guy had a blue bandana on, another bandana hanging from his pocket, a denim jacket, and baggy jeans with one side rolled up. The girl had a pierced nose, a pierced lip, dark lipstick and dark eye shadow, wore a thin white shirt with no bra. You could see her pierced nipples beneath the fabric.

"You okay?"

"Nah, dawg . . ." A drip of blood trickled from the corner of his lip. "God . . ."

Evan knelt, opened up the guy's jacket. "Lemme see."

He turned away as dark crimson soaked into his wife beater, a mangle of cloth and flesh.

Oh my God.

"It fuckin' hurts."

"I know, I know." Evan nodded, looked him in the eye. "All right. Okay. We're gonna get you outta here."

She put her hands on her knees, sniffled and gasped.

Evan reached for the bandana on his head, to which the guy grabbed him at the wrist.

"I gotta, man. We need—"

The guy then let go, faced away, like a pouting child almost. Evan also grabbed the other bandana hanging from his pocket and pressed both against his abdomen, motioned to the girl with a nod.

She pressed her hands on his stomach, over the two bandanas, held them down in place as he groaned.

"What about that thing?" The girl's voice was quiet.

Evan shifted, saw there was a rolling cart for supplies. It was metal and wide, perfect. He jogged over and got it.

The guy nodded. Evan knelt to one side, wrapped an arm around his neck and shoulder. Hissing in pain, grunting, the guy pivoted onto the cart lying down flat. The girl tried to hold the cloth against his torso.

Jude . . . Hang on, all right?

I'm coming.

I won't let anything happen to you.

"Okay, now just lay still." Evan glanced at the girl. "Keep talking to him."

They rolled the cart around the corner, down the hall to the inside of the auditorium. There were long rows of red cushioned seats in front of the big stage, curtains pulled back to either side, lit like a special premiere showing.

Students stood there on the stage, staring at them with horrified faces. An ominous dread blanketed the dimly lit space between them. It was going to be one helluva show. Knock 'em dead. Break a leg.

6

9th Grade

FIRST, FROM HER fingernail, then to her wrist, up to her neck, his eyes wandered. They meandered all the way to her lips and her eyes. When she lifted her head, he faced down. Evan kept his eyes on the page with a half-embarrassed smirk, as the teacher finished reading. Judith scribbled the details of the assignment in her binder as soon as they were announced. She glanced at the board as the teacher wrote, copied it all in a precise and timely manner.

As the bell rang, Evan turned to the front, put all his things away. He then stood, waited for her.

"So, we'll work together?"

He nodded, let her walk through the door first.

Out in the hall, with the rest of the school in motion, they walked side by side. Again, his eyes wandered, this time to the contour of her cheek and ear, at the way her hair bounced, having to stop himself.

"You know, I only been late once in my life."

"What?" Evan laughed.

"Yeah. Last time, when we talked after class like this, I was late." She tilted her head to one side.

"Oh, I'm sorry." He shook his head, fought back his smirk creeping into a little smile. "Well, we'll keep it short this time. I'm all the way in M, anyway, remember? I got Art."

"Do you think . . ." She pulled the strap of her backpack, aligned her books tight against her body. "We could, like, meet after school? Get a head start."

Evan paused, thought about it. "Uh. Sure, okay."

"Let's meet in the computer lab since he wants us to make a website or whatever. Kind of dumb for an assignment."

"I know. Trying to stay with the times and all that." He shook his head.

The world was beginning to change, in many ways. In terms of technology, it was both the window to and the engine driving a lot of the change, which was on the brink of revolution. Now, with a dial-up connection, a keyboard, a mouse, you could connect to the world wide web. The information super highway.

She glanced to one side, sighed. "I don't know anything about that stuff."

"I actually know some HTML."

"You do?"

"I post some of my drawings online, just little things, for fun. It's nothing."

Judith smiled. "Really? What a relief again. Hmm. I'm kinda interested to see."

"No, no . . ." Evan gazed down, kicked at the ground.

"Okay. I better go. You, too, don't be late." She turned, walked across the west wing, shifted back. "I'll see you after school."

"See you after school."

The words spilled out of his mouth, a whisper, as he watched her disappear into the crowd. His eyes traced her hair, her shoulders, her legs, even the air around her with each movement. He breathed in and breathed out, facing down then away.

He brushed the eraser particles with the back of his hand, blew the lead dust away. The assignment for the day was to draw a portrait referencing a photograph, but it just wasn't coming to him. The lines were askew. The proportions were obscured. The very style of it seemed hollow and empty. He couldn't tell why. This kind of thing always came easy, without much thought or effort. But, today, for some reason, it was like putting together puzzle pieces without the picture on the box.

Evan felt fatigue in his fingertips, on the side of his wrist that landed on the paper on the desk. He shook his hand out, gazed again at the photo, wondering why he chose that particular one. He had rummaged through the pile of magazines, some of them news, some entertainment, choosing a fashion magazine and tore it from the spread. The woman's lashes were pretty. The woman's hair was flawless. In theory, the cheekbones and the slender line of her jaw were the perfect subject to capture. Yet, somehow, he just wasn't inspired by the face in front of him.

Peeping out the window, Evan sighed. He glanced at the time on the clock. It was almost recess so he decided to just wait it out. Instead, he took out his composition book, where he was free to draw anything . . .

The tip of the pencil dragged and swirled on the paper like a figure skater on ice. Lines came together and formed images on the surface. Darkening, shading in, even dotting it.

A metal cylinder. A missile. A small flame burning and

a long trail of smoke winding. An explosion. A fireball with cinders, with embers, debris flying in the shockwave.

"Evan?"

He faced up, saw the teacher standing there. The other kids were already getting ready to leave.

"Are you okay? You seem a bit distracted lately."

"Yeah, I . . ." He shook his head, put the pencil down. "Just tired, ya know? That's all."

She nodded, unconvinced.

"Really. It's nothing."

Evan smirked. He closed the composition book, put the rest of his things away in his backpack.

"Okay. Well, I'm telling select students about an upcoming art contest." She handed him a rectangular flyer on pastel color paper. "It's not until the end of next quarter so you have time to come up with something."

"Hmm . . ." Evan took it but just stared. "Um, I don't know. You think I should?"

"Why not? Nothing to lose, and hey, you never know." She had light freckles on her face and arms. He noticed freckles on her chest too. "I chose to tell you, out of everyone in your class. You should really try."

"Okay. Cool. Thanks, miss. I'll think about it."

It was on the second floor of the library, third floor of the admin building. Evan walked up the stairs, step by step. His hand bounced off the rail as he peeked through the glass panel down to the first floor in its entirety. He walked past the slanted shelves all the way in back, to the far corner. He pushed the door open and peeped in the computer lab. It was cool, quiet, even more than the library itself. Judith spotted him over the row of monitors and waved.

On one of the screens, he saw a rectangular blinking cursor slide right as letters and words populated. There was scattered clacking as kids backspaced, double-clicked and right-clicked. Another screen was blank with a square dragging to specific size, a floating paint can icon about to fill in the shape. Games were technically not allowed, against the rules, but one screen had a pixelated wagon rolling that was pulled by an ox, about to cross a river.

"Can we even talk in here?" He said this leaning close to her ear.

"Of course, you silly. Just not all loud or anything, like your friend Mark."

They laughed a hushed laugh.

"So. Where's this webpage of yours? I wanna see . . ."

"Ah, geez."

"Come on. I just want an idea of what it might look like. Our project."

"I mean, it's the same as the poster before pretty much, just internet format. Right?"

Judith turned to him with pleading eyes, her lower lip curling.

"All right, all right. Fine."

Evan slid over onto her chair as she stood back. He held the mouse, pointed, clicked, typed in the address.

Judith leaned over. "Wow . . . Let me."

Her hand grazed over the top of his, as she slid the mouse on the mousepad. The skin of his hand tingled against her palm. He could feel her breasts against his neck, her chest against the back of his head. There was a slight warmth from her breathing and the faint scent of her perfume.

Evan closed his eyes, couldn't move, willed himself to scoot forward.

"I-it's not much."

"No way, look. Headings. Different color backgrounds, fonts in different sizes and italics, underline. And all these pictures look great."

"You think?"

"This is super good. If you could do even a tenth of this, we'll get an A-plus, easily."

He laughed. "You and your A-plus."

"What? I need the perfect GPA, perfect SAT score. I need extracurricular. The best schools are all competitive. You know?"

"Eh, I'm sure you'll get in. I just know it."

She smiled, turned to the screen. She sat on the next chair over and pulled out paper and her Hello Kitty pencil case. "Let's do planning for today, and we'll start next time."

"Okay. Cool, cool."

"I really like this layout, maybe just different colors? Yours is kinda dark, and bleak. And you think you can do, like, diagrams again?"

"It's not dark, it's cool . . ."

He raised a brow.

She shook her head.

"Whatever. Sure. And you type the info again?"

Judith nodded, jotted down. She leaned and reached in her bag for the textbook. He could see a sliver of her lower back as she bent down.

From the science lab to the computer lab, they had spent quite a bit of time together. In that quiet room on the top floor, back row in front of the monitors, their knees touched. When she had a full page of elegantly written notes, they gathered their things. Side by side, they walked down the stairs, through the turnstile and sensor, and back out the automatic doors.

"You know . . . I never got to ask."

He stopped, waited, while she turned to listen.

"How come you never said anything? That we knew each other? Back at the arcade."

She stared down, kind of laughed. "I don't know. It just didn't feel right or something."

"I see. Hmm." He faced away. "Uh, do you live far?"

"Pretty close. But I'm actually not going home yet."

"Oh. Where you going?"

"I got piano practice . . ."

Evan adjusted the strap of his backpack. "No way. You play piano?"

"Sadly, yes. Ever since I was little." Judith rolled her eyes. "Parentals."

"That's pretty cool."

Judith swayed on her feet, held her books tight.

"Hey, you need me to walk with you?"

"You'd do that?"

"Yeah. Just wanna make sure you're okay. You know?"

"Uh, one thing. We gotta be careful. If my parents see us, I might get in trouble."

He almost did a double take. "Wait, what?"

"Yeah, I'm not supposed to talk to boys."

"But you have a boyfriend." Evan laughed, shaking his head.

"Funny, we never technically put a label. If that makes sense. He told me he liked me. He asked to hang out. Next thing I know I met all you guys at Game Works."

"You like him, though, right?"

She gave a slow nod. "Of course. He's nice."

"Good, good. 'Cause he really likes you. And I want to see him happy. You're a good girl. He's a good guy."

Glancing up at him, her lips stretched to a thin smile.

"Like, he let me steal his favorite toy. I borrowed his tapes and never returned them, they're still in my house. I ate all his Halloween candy without asking, and he didn't even care. You know? *Good.* The best."

Evan laughed, watched as her dimples appeared.

"All right, well, we better get going. I know you don't wanna be late. Miss A-plus over here, even though I'm pretty sure piano lessons don't give grades."

7

Jan 19th
11:34am

Struggling to shove the cart onstage from the side ramp, Evan recognized some of the faces closer up. One kid was wearing a JROTC uniform. He joined in and helped pull the cart up, then knelt down, seeing the bloody cloth. Another was a short girl with glasses, a quiet girl who always sat in the front row. She covered her mouth with one hand, stepped backwards. They both were in a couple of his classes, not friends, per se, but friendly.

The short girl moved her hand, pressed the glasses to her face. "What happened? W-we heard gunshots."

"Outside, near admin, there was like an explosion. The shooter was coming so we ran in here." Evan stared at the girl with piercings, who still held the bandanas in place. "The door got shot out, and then he was hit."

"You okay?" The girl with piercings asked, gazing at her hands on the cloth.

With eyes closed, the guy on the cart nodded back, leaning his head.

"Explosion?"

"It was kind of like—"

"Molotov cocktail."

The group turned to the cart, where the guy spoke through gritted teeth.

"Molotov, gasoline in a glass jar."

An intensity spread through the quiet auditorium, between this randomly mixed group in hiding. Stage lights shined at different angles. Mismatched ropes hung down from the rafters. The orchestra pit was like a moat. And the non-existent audience sat on the edge of their seats in the dark and empty rows.

This scene, reserved for theater productions, for show, for illusion, now was realer than the real world had ever been. Where a certain magic happened, spectacular moments, after hours of practice, words and actions that collided together in a suspension of disbelief, now was the eye of the storm—the tornado—and was a small seemingly safe haven.

"I know he had a rifle, a shotgun. There was some other gun too."

The girl with piercings shifted, faced up from the floor. "It might've been a TEC, I think."

A slight pause, as the severity sunk in. Some of them glanced around the space. Some glanced at one another.

"A-anyone else hurt?" Evan asked.

One of the kids in back raised a hand up, wrapped in a makeshift bandage.

"Got lucky," the kid in uniform said. "Barely grazed him."

"You do that? The wrapping?"

He nodded. "I'll go get the first aid."

"I saw there were teachers and students hiding in the classrooms, back at G-building." Evan scratched his head, dropped his arms at his side. "We can't stay here, though. He knows we're in here."

The girl with piercings stepped back from the cart as the kid in uniform took over. "I don't think it's safe to hide, anywhere. We've got to make a run for it."

"I agree." The short girl with glasses placed her hands on the back of her hips.

The kid in uniform shook his head as he layered the gauze. "No, we stay. Hide. Police will be coming. Fire department."

"Where are they? Do you think anyone's even called?"

"There's pay phones at the front of the school. I know they have phones in admin. Someone's gotta have one of those cellular phone thingies—"

"I overheard somebody say the lines aren't working." There was hesitation and apprehension in the short girl's voice.

All of them felt it, knew it right then. That this wasn't some postal worker gone berserk but a planned and premeditated attack. As if they were mice in a cardboard maze for a science experiment in class.

Jude. Be careful.

Evan turned side to side. "If that's true, there's still a way. Has to be."

"W-what about the stores across the street?"

The girl with piercings faced down. "I mean, unless the lines are connected . . ."

"No time." Evan sighed, peered at the guy on the cart. "We gotta do something."

"Should we split up? Take a vote?" Another girl in back spoke up, her voice frustrated and scared, with droopy eyes and long dark hair. "What are we supposed to do?"

"And what about him?" The kid in uniform turned the guy on his side, wrapped the gauze. "What, just roll the cart? It might as well be a bullseye."

"Maybe we shouldn't move him in his condition."

"You gonna leave him behind like this?" The kid in uniform raised his head, adjusted on one knee. "Frickin' animal."

"Hey, hey." Evan tried to interject.

"That's not fair." The girl with the droopy eyes stepped forward with her arms crossed, leaning in. "I'm sorry but I am not gonna get shot. I don't care if that makes me *insensitive.*"

"C'mon, let's talk through all the options." The short girl shook her head.

The kid in uniform finished the dressing, angry, annoyed, stared back up from the cart.

"We don't have much time. What if he comes back? Did you hear us?" The girl with piercings stood close to Evan now, wiped her hands clean with a wad of napkins.

She handed one to Evan that he dabbed at the skin on his neck and forearm. "He has enough weapons to blast that door down, easily, for sure."

"The police. Are. Coming." The kid in uniform stood, too, starting to bite his lower lip.

"Oh yeah? Where? Where are they?" The girl with droopy eyes shook her head, her long hair shaking with it. "It's been way too long, and we can't sit here waiting for those incompetent pigs."

The kid with the bandaged hand gazed down, turned away with a sigh. The short girl rolled her head back and let out a guttural moan.

The girl with piercings faced the guy on the cart, glanced over at Evan who glanced back.

"We fight back . . ."

Everyone turned to the cart once more, where the guy spoke again through gritted teeth, this time between breaths.

"Fight . . . Fight that motherfucker. It's the only way. No hiding, no waiting around."

The girl with the droopy eyes hung her mouth open, almost laughing. "Are you crazy?"

"You know, he has a point. Whether we run or we hide, we need to be prepared." The kid in uniform scanned around the stage. "There's gotta be something we can—"

A loud banging pierced through the dark, from the front of the auditorium back by the big doors.

Each kid shifted with startled wide eyes. They stepped back and gasped with the pounding. One of the girls let out a scream with the sound of ambiguous metal clanging on the floor.

"Come on. We gotta go, now. That thing ain't gonna hold. I know a way through the back."

Evan turned to lead them backstage but stopped.

From behind the curtain, the barrel of a gun pointed at him and floated closer. It was steady and raised to meet him face to face. One hand up in surrender, he backed away, with the other hand down to signal the others who did the same.

Behind the gun, an ominous mask came into focus. The mask was like a black and white swirl with a splash of red . . . Not unlike the tornado. The tornado mixed with red paint, red paint that sprayed and splattered and filled the auditorium. A red painted gun. A red painted mask. Along with a big black duffel bag.

8

9th Grade

A LITTLE EXTRA time left in recess, the group lingered by the east wing of the admin building. There were certain spots they liked to inhabit. At recess, their spot was often the side of the cafe by the inside wall. If there was extra time, like today, then this spot by admin. Like before they met by the flagpole after school, they used to meet by the bleachers. Evan had suggested it once and it just stuck. Creatures of habit. Set in their routine. Institutionalized.

Half on the concrete, half on the grass, Mark leaned on Jared's shoulder. Max stood next to them, his arms crossed, facing down to his feet. Judith was close to Derek who leaned back against one of the pillars. Other side of her, Evan glanced out at the courtyard. The group. The polygon.

"What you guys doing after school?" Judith held her wrist with her other hand.

Jared untwisted the cap. "Why, you free?"

"For once, yes, actually. Tutoring got canceled."

"So funny you do tutoring . . ." Jared shook his head, Evan and some of the others holding back laughter. "Like, of all people."

"Hey. You don't make honor roll by doing just the bare minimum."

Mark pressed the glasses to his face, raised one hand in the air. "Bare minimum, ha."

"Game Works?" Max's voice was almost inaudible.

"Hmm, maybe."

"Nah."

Max cleared his throat. "Uh, Jam Comics?"

"Yeah, maybe, haven't been there in a while. We really should go to the mall or something. Or like an internet cafe."

"Ah, we gotta take the bus, though."

"Maybe tomorrow." Derek, who was quiet throughout the conversation, spoke up. "End of the week. And we'd have extra time if we ditched the assembly."

The group was a mix of laughter and silence. Judith didn't make a sound, and Evan matched her.

"You guys wanna ditch? I don't know . . ."

"Oh, come on. It'll be fun." Mark began handing out sticks of gum. "Not like they take attendance. No one'll notice."

Evan stared at her face, saw her discomfort. Her cheeks flushed the faintest touch of pink.

"Hey. You don't gotta if you don't want to. Nobody here cares. We're not pressuring you."

Judith shifted back, with a soft smile.

Evan blinked, smirked.

"Really, it's no big deal. Totally fine."

After school, the day seemed stretched out thanks to a fire drill, and the group walked from the courtyard down the long driveways. Judith lingered close to Evan, both of them behind the others. Derek was out in front, led the group towards the shopping center, walking with authority and confidence. Mark and Jared followed close, while Max tried to keep up. Evan and Judith dragged just a tiny bit, enough to widen the gap. He could tell she wanted to say something.

"You think I should ditch?"

Evan laughed.

"Still thinking about that, huh? I mean, hey, you already were *late* for the first time in your life. Why not add this."

"Shut up . . ."

Her cheeks were pink, with a soft small smile, as she tucked her hair behind her left ear.

"I'll think about it."

He glanced sideways at her, as she glanced back. Their eyes locked for the briefest of moments.

"You should."

The group gathered again at the crosswalk. Derek attacked the button, pressing it over and over.

"Why don't we just jaywalk like normal people?" Mark chewed his gum. "This thing's gonna take forever."

Jared chuckled with arms folded.

"Like, seriously."

"You all right?" Evan asked, leaning towards Max who nodded in return. "Okay, cool."

As the light changed, the group crossed. Derek again took the lead. Mark and Jared followed, then Max. Judith hung back a little, drifted close to Evan.

She leaned in, whispered, her lips next to his cheek. "You know what. Yeah. I'm gonna ditch too."

Evan turned to her, smirked. "No way . . . Haha."

Judith nodded. "Why not."

The hands of the clock glided, swinging around in a taunting manner. Evan already pre-packed his bag, sat there with his hands on the desk, jittering on the balls of his feet. Jared had his bag zipped, already wore it on his back, a can of soda at the ready. They exchanged a quick glance with mutual determined nod. A cold weight sank in then, shallow in their skin. Extra oxygen pumped in each breath. Adrenaline rushed. The thrill of mischief.

For the same reason that they chewed gum—because it was against the rules, it wasn't allowed—they were on a mission now to escape another boring assembly. It was the force inside that beckoned. That unexplainable pleasure. Every adolescent's urge to be wrong, to do bad, almost as a rite of passage.

With the bell, they both stood and walked out. They circled the corner of the walkway of D-building, went down the west wing of admin across to the east wing, waited at the top of the inner stairwell.

Evan darted his head left then right, as kids walked past. "We doing this?"

"Yup. No turning back now." Jared sipped, wiped at his mouth. "Let's go."

"Give the others some time."

"Not too much, though. If they take long, we just go. Remember the plan?"

"I know, I know."

"We don't wanna look too suspicious just standing around like assholes."

"But that's what we always do."

A quiet laughter between the two.

Max appeared first, his backpack high up on his shoulders. Evan clapped him on the arm, nodded.

Jared stared down at the courtyard. "Looks like security's gonna be in full force today."

"Ah, shit . . ." Max glanced down too.

"Golf carts and everything."

Evan sighed. "That gonna be a problem?"

"Nah, but that means they're definitely on the lookout. Only bust those things out every now and then."

Mark and Derek appeared next, from opposite ends of the walkway. Derek from the corner of E-building, Mark from the inner stairwell down by G-building.

Derek was out of breath. "Where's Judy?"

"Uh, I don't know."

"We didn't see her yet."

Evan was quiet, gazed around, scrunched his lips together and threw a hand up.

"Crap . . . We'll give her another minute but then we really gotta go." Derek leaned down, a hand on his knee.

"She'll be here." Evan furled his brow, nibbled at his lower lip.

The crowd thinned out with the final few students making their way to the gymnasium.

"Okay. It's time." Derek stood, exhaled.

"Wait, wait." Evan held a finger up. "Just one more minute."

The halls and the walkway were quiet, still. The campus became a ghost town. Derek shook his head as Evan nodded with his finger still up. Mark and Jared stared down, around. Max tapped his toe.

They could hear the security guards starting the cart, ready to begin their patrol. Waiting, breathing, they stood together in their semi-circle.

Evan lowered his hand, nodded.

Derek tapped Mark and Jared on the back, pointed down the hall of F-building.

Where are you, Jude . . .

As they walked past the inner stairwell, Judith appeared, almost tripping and dropping all her books.

The group turned with wide eyes and open mouths, in a subdued cheer. Derek hugged her then walked to the front. She adjusted the strap of her backpack, as Mark and Jared followed Derek. Max took the middle.

Evan leaned in. "Glad you made it."

She blew the bangs out of her eyes with a single puff, smiled with her head arched back.

"Whatever happens, stay close. Okay?"

Derek strafed the wall, turned, signaled with a wave for the rest to follow. Mark and Jared ducked down, crouched. Max walked on tippy toes, wobbling.

Evan let Judith walk in front of him, put her books in his bag which was pretty much empty, then went in back. He licked his lips, facing down to his feet as he stepped, passing by a closed door.

The group was about midway through the hall to the outer stairwell when one of the classroom doors ahead flung open. From inside, a teacher came out with a set of keys in her hand.

Derek and Mark hesitated, then continued forward.

"Excuse me . . . E-excuse me. Where do you think you're going? You two."

Breaking into a full sprint, Derek and Mark disappeared down the hall into the far stairwell. Jared turned back, pushed Max who staggered on his feet.

"Hey!" The teacher's voice echoed through the hall.

Evan grabbed Judith by her hips, turned her around, as Jared and Max ran past them down the inner stairs. Evan took her by the hand, turned the corner, passing the east wing of the admin building, headed down the walkway to E-building.

"Evan! Where are we—!?"

"We gotta split up!"

They could hear security guards shouting in the courtyard, followed by scattered footsteps. He held her hand tight as they rounded the corner, plopped down the inner stairwell back out into the open.

Evan shifted, peeped at Judith who smiled a wide smile. She bounced on her feet, her hair flowing behind her.

Judith gripped his hand, stared at him. Evan smirked then faced forward again.

To their left was the cafeteria, beyond that the last droves made their way inside the gym. Hand in hand, they went between the auditorium and the tennis courts, onto the baseball field. From the edge of the bleachers, they slowed to a jog then a hurried walk.

Both let go and walked now side by side, catching their breath. Smiling, they gazed across at one another.

"This is so stupid . . ."

"I know." Evan laughed, gasping in between breaths. "Welcome to being a regular kid, Jude."

She pouted her lips, hiding a smile, then nudged over to the right.

He watched as she fixed her hair and fanned herself by flapping her shirt. Evan could see the top lining of her panties. He faced away, instead toward her legs.

"Y-you okay?"

"Yeah." Her voice was soft as she breathed.

Evan could still feel the warmth on the inside of his palm where her hand had been, where their skin had touched. He lifted his hand and stared at it, glanced across at her as she breathed in and out.

"Oh, this is so stupid . . ."

"Hey. It's gonna be okay. That teacher doesn't know us. No one knows we're here."

She nodded, trying not to hyperventilate.

"It's just me and you now. We're okay."

"Okay, Evan. Oh . . ."

He led them further down the field. She followed, staying close. From the bleachers between the baseball diamond and the football field, they crossed the lines of the track that circled around.

With the gentle breeze, it was somehow peaceful. Not far from the goal post, it was just the two of them alongside each other in the open grass. A flock of birds flew overhead.

"Wait a sec." Jude stopped in place, knelt down. "I need to tie my shoe."

"All right, but make it quick. I'll keep watch."

"So stupid . . . This is so stupid."

Evan held back a smirk, touched a hand to her shoulder, as he faced the fields by the gym.

It was empty. The last of the students huddled inside, seated and listening to the marching band, watching as the cheerleading squad hopped and cartwheeled and posed in their respective routines.

No, no, no . . .

A white blur moved from behind the tennis courts along the bleachers to the far end of the baseball diamond, circling around to the main field. It was the golf cart.

"Jude. Jude."

She stared up, stared to where his gaze remained locked.

With a quick gasp, she scurried to her knees like a frightened animal.

"We gotta go." He took her hand again, helped her up. "We need to get out of here, now."

"Oh. Shit . . . Shit! What do we do? I can't get busted, I can't blow it all."

"We're not gonna get busted." Evan turned, peered at the far end of the football field. "If we can make it off campus, they can't follow us."

Judith glanced at him with worried eyes. He glanced back, nodded along convincingly, touched her on the arm, felt light goosebumps on her skin.

"You can do this. We have to do this." He licked his lips, shifted again. "Ready?"

She nodded, swallowed.

"To the end of the field, hurry."

The white blur began to take on squarish form, with a looming cloud of dust rising behind it.

Evan could see her smile now faded. He darted his head back, saw the blur take a sharp left. Slowing, he turned to a side step. The cart revved up from the red dirt of the circular track onto the grass field towards a different group of kids running in the opposite direction.

He bent, slapped his hands down on his knees, howled in exclamation. She turned, saw, raised her hands up in a small cheer, stepping back to join.

She put one arm around him, plopped down, and the two hugged on their knees half on the ground. As they embraced, their bodies shuddered and writhed as their laughter grew. Evan fell onto his side, knocking Judith backward, both of them rolling in the grass coughing from the laughter.

Judith breathed out a long sigh, leaning her head to

glance at him. Evan did the same, rolling onto his side. They both smiled.

Her cheeks were a touch red from the sunlight. There was a fluttering in his chest from the exhilaration. The light breeze again swept through, waving the blades of grass amongst them like a whisper. That whisper in the wind told them something, something only the two of them needed to know. Behind her hair with its fiery sheen, the clouds began to thin and scatter, changing in shape. He lay there a moment, breathing, temporarily lost in her dimples and her almond eyes.

❧

Stealing a glance, Evan watched while she played with her hair, turning down with a smirk. Judith smiled, too, faced the other way. She sat on a bench by the bushes. With her hands in her lap in between her legs, she fidgeted with her fingers. Jared stood off to one side. Max was in the middle. The air seemed still as they all waited. It was quiet in the area in front of Derek's, outside the small shop in front of the lobby on the first floor.

"That was pretty close," Jared said with a chuckle.

Max shuddered at the shoulders, snorting as he struggled to contain his laughter.

"Like, waay too close. There were other guys running so we got lucky. Real lucky. How 'bout you?"

"Yeah, we had to split up, but we made it somehow. Man, Derek and Mark just taking off like that . . . Geez."

"Frickin' Derek." Jared shook his head.

Max let out a loud whine, like a hyena, with his head tilted back. "Ha, I know!"

"You guys are crazy." Judith rolled her eyes in faux annoyance. "And I put my life in your hands?"

"For all this effort, maybe we shoulda just gone to the mall already. Damn."

"Ah, I know, but it was too risky."

"I guess." Jared peeked around to the front gate. "What's taking them? I need my soda."

Max let a loud whine again, snorted.

"Think they got busted?"

"Nah, I don't think so . . ." Jared turned to Evan then to Judith. "You guys took long, too, and you still made it."

Evan raised an eyebrow. Judith squirmed on the bench.

From behind, on the other side of the bushes by the front gate, Derek and Mark appeared. Mark was cleaning his glasses with the bottom of his shirt, plodding with a slight limp. Derek wiped a hand across his forehead dripping with sweat, ran his fingers through his hair.

"'Ey!!!"

"There you are!"

Everybody roared in laughter and applause. Jared bumped fists with them one by one. Max turned to face them, Judith stood from the bench. Mark clapped palms with Evan then wrapped around for a bro hug. Derek hugged Judith and spun her in his arms.

Evan gazed at each member of the group, watched them laugh and smile. Max had an awkward smile and an awkward nod. Jared had his arms folded, shook his head. Mark was excited, animated, gesturing with both hands. Derek put an arm around Judith's shoulder as she hugged him around his torso. Evan then turned back to face Mark.

As the laughter died down, Derek walked around in front, took out his key to open the security gate. Moving through the lobby to the elevator, down the hall, into the apartment, the commenting and jokes continued.

Stealing another glance, Evan watched as she again played with her hair. He noticed the contour of her cheek and ear, then noticed her hand holding someone else's. With this, he stared down at his shoes, tugging on one strap of his backpack, falling further behind the others.

Mark and Jared raced one another to hop onto the fluffy couch. Max followed, sitting down on the carpet, leaning back against the base of it. Derek pulled Judith by the hand down the hall to his room then closed the door.

Circling the living room, Evan peeked down the hall to the closed door. He could see the light on through the crack, and a shadow moving along.

"Whoa, whoa! Get-tin' freaky over there!" Mark yelled through a cupped hand.

Jared chuckled, stood to walk to the kitchen.

"Remember to use protection!" Max added, snorting again.

He would laugh along as well, at least smirk. But these jokes seemed to leave a small wound. An abrasion somewhere deep in his chest, perhaps on one of his organs or the connective tissue. It was an ache unfamiliar, not sharp, but dull.

With an icy cold tap, Evan turned away from the hall. Jared stood in front of him holding out a soda.

"Thanks." Evan took it, walked over to the couch.

Max held his can up. Evan tapped it with his own as he passed, clinking in a rated PG-13 cheers. He sat with his legs stretched forward near Max on the floor.

Mark stared out the window down to the fifth floor area where they practiced fighting the other day. "You know, we never go swimming. Like, in the pool. We should."

"Uh, we didn't bring any trunks."

"Ah. No need. Just go in my underwear."

"But your underwear's white!"

This turned into a small slap fight over by the window. Jared shoved Mark, who wrapped an arm around Jared's neck in a headlock. The two rotated counterclockwise as they wrestled. Max stood, jogged over and tackled them both against the wall messing up the curtain. Evan stayed on the couch, sipped, didn't smile, didn't laugh. He again glanced down the hall to where the door remained closed.

9

Jan 19th
11:38am

Ushered in to the center of the stage before the empty rows, each student got down on their knees with their hands up. The shooter gestured with the chin of his mask, pointed the gun, poked it into Evan's back. Turning around, Evan put both hands in the air, let the barrel of the handgun nudge him forward. He took his place on the hardwood floor next to the others. Forming two squiggly lines, with the cart on the far end, they faced one another like slaves. Some began to sniffle and cry. Some began to beg, plead.

There was more banging and pounding then a final loud clang on the ground back by the front doors, followed by slow footsteps. Evan turned, stared at the far corner of the auditorium where another shooter appeared. He could see the large handgun with the extended magazine held up by an arm wrapped in cloth . . .

Shit. That's the one.

Could one of them have still been on the roof, and threw that Molotov down?

A high-pitched cackling echoed through the auditorium, like a witch in the night.

"Well, well."

Evan blinked, glanced across at the short girl with glasses, glanced over at the kid in uniform. He wondered what they were thinking.

All this time, he was so concerned about Judith. But now, his friends came to mind as well. He thought about Mark and Jared, about Max, about Derek. Images of all of them in similar horrifying situations flashed one by one. His worst fear was anything happening to them.

God. Please.

Please, please tell me they're okay.

Step by step, the second shooter walked past each row, along the side of the open theater down to the ramp. Both arms open, wide, almost above their head, they seemed like a magician stepping into the spotlight—like an opera singer, like a ringmaster.

"Just wish I had some POPCORN." Again, the voice was higher in pitch, whiney, just a touch nasally. "For the BIG SHOW, our lit-tle mat-i-nee."

To Evan's side, the girl with piercings and dark lipstick whimpered, slumped forward on one hand to maintain balance, her body beginning to shudder.

Almost like a ballerina, the shooter stepped lightly and whimsically up the ramp to the stage, waving the gun from side to side. He could see the mask: feathery, colorful, with rhinestones. Like at a masquerade ball.

Evan studied the face . . . her face?

Crooked teeth and thick lips were exposed under the mask that covered the upper half, on top of the brow and nose and forehead.

He noticed the short messy hair, the blonde highlights flared out with spikes. He saw the neck and limbs past the cuffs and collar of the leather jacket, thin and gangly.

"What do you want!" The girl with droopy eyes slammed a fist on the floor, blurted out, tears gathering in the corners of her red eyes.

The kid with the bandaged hand turned, tried to shush her, but she ignored it.

Her lips quivered as she lifted herself high up on her knees, yelling even louder and more desperate. "Let us *go!* Leave us alone!!!"

The first shooter hovered from Evan to the girl, pointed the gun to the back of her head. He tilted his neck, framing the kabuki mask just behind her as tears streamed down her cheeks. The kabuki mask—with its black and white swirl, with its splash of red—was like the head of a puppet, moved as if controlled by strings.

All were too young to deal with the scenario occurring. All in adolescence and puberty, angst. Too young and naive to experience this level of sheer terror. Too innocent to be taken before prom, before graduation, before a first kiss.

God. God, please help us.

Between the two squiggly lines, pointing the gun at the ground in front of each student kneeling, with delicate yet deliberate steps, the second shooter walked through.

"Are you on your PERIOD or something?"

The girl with droopy eyes faced down, but the shooter grabbed her by the chin.

"I get it. I just got off my PERIOD. But, listen, you need to SHUT the HELL up. Ya hear me?" The way the shooter spoke was again whiney, nasally. "Can you do that for me, sweetie? Huh? Can you?"

Smack.

Hitting her across the face with the back of their hand, the gun still in it, the shooter again cackled. The girl fell onto the hardwood crying out.

“Pleease!!!”

As Evan stared at the back of the shooter’s head, in horror, at their movements and their voice, he noticed pale skin beneath fishnet stockings like porcelain. With a slow turn, from that angle with the shadow from the dim lights, the mask with its feathers and rhinestones was reminiscent of a jester.

He realized there were goosebumps on the skin of his forearms, his fingers starting to tremble. A tingle radiated through the crowns of his teeth. Water gathered in the corners of his narrowed eyes.

The first shooter, quiet, smooth, like a puppet still, yanked the girl upright, while the second shooter stepped on the balls of their feet back in front.

Dancing, swaying, the jester stood at one end of the two lines. Tilting his head, pointing the gun, the puppet stood on the other.

“I gots a ques-tion for yoou.” The voice was high in tone, as if at a tea party on the playground. “Which one of you PRICKS cut my FREAKING arm? Hmm?”

Peeking sideways, Evan saw the girl with piercings begin to sob, unable to control herself.

The jester stepped close, crouched down.

“Aww . . . You afwaid?”

“Stop! You bitch!”

Each kneeling student glanced over, their eyes wide, their mouths open. The kid on the cart rolled onto his side, shouted through gritted teeth with a hiss.

“Leave her alone!”

A light snicker from the puppet beneath his mask, as he hovered on the other side. He stood without moving, like a gothic statue.

His mask covered the entire face, skin and hair obscured by the hood of a black hoodie pulled tight.

Who is that?

Who's behind the mask?

The guy on the cart pushed off on one elbow, firm in his words with a steady glare.

"Just, leave her alone. Okay? It was me."

What? No.

The high-pitch cackling sounded again, as the jester hopped to the cart, lifted the gun, pulled the trigger.

Bang. Bang.

"I could end it for ya, oh, I could, but why spoil the fun. I'll just let you BLEED." The jester kicked the cart, lifted a leg then pressed down on his torso with the heel of her foot. "Yeah. That's more like it . . . Now, sit back. Enjoy."

The jester lowered the wrapped arm that pointed to the ceiling, leaking a smoky fume from the barrel of the gun. One of the lights sparked then fizzled where she had shot.

It was almost worse that she was toying with them, taking her time and dragging it out, waiting for the precise moment, timing it, all on a whim.

Kneeling low, with their heads down in humiliation, the crying and sniffling grew more pronounced. It spread through the stage out into the dark and empty rows.

From the front of the line, the puppet grunted, pointed his gun at the girl with the droopy eyes.

"No! Please, let us *go!*"

"What did I say!? HUH???"

The jester rushed forward, aimed, pulled the trigger without hesitation. Gasps and screams from the kneeling students drowned out the loud echo. Each of them squirmed on the floor, reeled, swayed. The kid with the bandaged hand groaned in disgust, in fear, curled his lower lip in a desperate whimper. A puddle of blood spread from the pile of long dark hair sprawled out on the floor.

Her droopy eyes now dead, now lifeless, stared up at the stage lights and the hanging ropes.

"Fuck you! You whore!"

The guy on the cart yelled through gritted teeth, fighting back the searing pain in his abdomen.

"You goddamned bitch!"

The jester smiled. Again, crooked teeth and thick lips showed through the open half of the mask.

"You knoow, let's make this a lit-tle more INTERESTING." The jester turned to the puppet. "You gots the bag?"

He nudged with the chin of his mask, pointing to the floor.

"Now. Lookie, lookie."

Rummaging through the duffel bag, the jester leaned and placed the bulky handgun down on the floor. In one hand, she held a pump-action shotgun but put it back, over the top of the double-barrel, held a glass jar with flammable liquid but also put it back. She took a regular handgun and stuck it in back of her shorts, then continued to reach around the bag.

"Ah. Here we go. Ooh, LOTS a FUN."

Evan fixated on the fishnets again, around the thin shins and thin calves, the bony knees. Hanging from the skinny fingers was a hammer dangling down. He glanced at the short girl, at the kid in uniform, nodded a slight nod.

The short girl shook her head, nibbled her lip. The kid in uniform signaled back with his eyes.

Gotta do something . . .

"Who's it gonna be. Hmm?"

On the balls of her feet, the jester stepped past each kneeling student, swinging the hammer.

"Let's see. How 'bout the goth?"

The girl with piercings bawled, facing up in desperation, hanging her shoulders down.

"Aww, that's so precious."

Step. Step.

The jester twirled the hammer.

"Not the goth. Not the gangsta in the cart."

Evan watched the knee bend, watched the fishnets contort as the jester bent down in front of him. The mask came into view and lurched toward him, causing him to flinch backward. Light and shadow across the hollows of the eyes, from the curves in the cheekbones, appeared terrifying and ghastly.

"Maybe the pretty boy? Huh? Yeah, the pretty boy. BASH in those pretty BRAINS of yours all over this pretty wittle floor. All those pretty wittle pieces of skull . . ."

Evan closed his eyes with a shudder. He could feel the weight of the hammer near his ear, then over the top of his head. The breath beneath the mask in front of him was like a bloodthirsty creature in the night.

Please. Please.

I need to see my friends again. I need to see Jude, at least one last time . . .

"No, sadly. I don't think so. It's your lucky day, pretty boy. Your. Lucky. Day."

Opening his eyes again, he watched as the thin legs turned and walked over to the girl with glasses.

"Hmm? No. No, no."

Step, step. Step.

"Ah. Yes. . . . How a-bout yoou, army boy?"

The kid in uniform darted his eyes up, glared with utter malice, lips forming into a snarl.

Squirming, adjusting on his knees, Evan stared. The jester's shadow slid up the kid's torso then up his neck and face. A sinking in his teeth, a twisting squeeze in his chest, Evan's breathing grew heavy and deep as the jester held the hammer way up high.

Each bony finger wrapped tight around the wooden handle, knuckles white, the metal head rattling.

"Ar-my boy."

There was a gleeful squeal, then a quick rough grunt.

Thwack!

10

9th Grade

After a nice long three-day weekend, it was back to school, back to Chem II. During the teacher's monotone rambling, Evan stared with his cheek in his palm, drifting off in that space between consciousness and daydreams. He blinked as he noticed the lines being written down. He felt helplessness linger and spread over his skin, sadness. It was that small dreaded shape again, scribbled in chalk on the board, taunting him . . . representing "change." The triangle.

There was a light tap on his shoulder. Evan faced up, saw all the other students getting up and splitting into partners and groups. He shook his head, got to his feet.

Judith watched as he stood. They then both walked around to the lab area in back with the sinks, taking up a counter near the window. He put down his composition book and took out his mechanical pencil. She put the textbook and her elegantly written notes near, slid the worksheet in place. It was a small chapter assignment between stages in the computer project, before another big test.

"Did you hear that? What he said?" Her voice was soft, her eyes narrowed.

Evan shook his head. "Oh. No, I didn't. I'm still waking up, I guess. What is it?"

"The teachers might go on strike . . ."

He inclined his head, squinted. "Really? I never heard of such a thing. I mean, it's common knowledge they're all underpaid and underappreciated."

"Yeah, he said classroom size, salary, the amount of instructional days, number of standardized tests . . . It will be statewide and could go on indefinitely."

Any kid would feel elated to hear such news. To get a break from the mundane routine. But she seemed perturbed at the notion. Evan himself didn't mind. As he traced his eyes over her chest that rose and fell, over her lips and her eyes that appeared just a touch worried, he reached forward, put a hand on her arm.

"Lemme guess, you hate it."

"Of course I do. I don't want to jeopardize my grades, any chance of getting into a good school."

"I get it. But we don't know what's gonna happen. This could be a bluff. We'll just have to wait and see. For now, we got this . . ." He tapped the worksheet with his finger.

She was still worried, glanced down, didn't move, didn't say anything.

"Actually, know what, maybe let's just take it easy. Get our mind off things. Me too. I'm all . . ." Evan motioned with a wave in the air, shook his head. "Like, we don't need to jump into things right away."

"Okay."

"I was gonna show you some diagrams I'm working on, but let's take a break from chem, from 'school' in general." He opened the composition book, took the rectangular flyer out and handed it to her.

"What's this?" Judith held it with both hands.

"Yeah, my teacher gave it to me. Just me. Some kinda art contest or something. She said I should try, but I don't know. What you think?"

Judith turned to him. Evan found himself mesmerized by her almond eyes, just for a moment, the way the morning sun hit them from the window. It was like they were gazing right through to his bare soul. They had the ability to soften him, to make him speak truths.

"I think you should try, Evan. Why not."

"Ah, I don't really got any ideas or anything. And I kinda don't see the point. They're not gonna pick me. I'm not that good."

"You should still try. You should always try." She stepped closer, put one hand over his. "There's gotta be something sometime that important, that's worth chasing after."

Their eyes locked. For a brief few seconds, the counter and the sink, the notes, the worksheet, it all faded away. No longer were they in a classroom, no longer were they on campus, but floating in space or maybe underwater.

At least she's smiling again, he thought to himself.

"Actually, I saw this too. It was posted in the admin building like last week, but I never got to mention . . ." She lifted the cover of the textbook, showed him a crinkled poster.

He gazed at her with a smirk. "A talent contest?"

"Hey. Extracurricular, right?" She smiled.

"Totally, yeah. Great idea. You gonna play piano?"

"I don't have anything else. I'm a little nervous, but it could be good. You think I should?"

"Of course. Absolutely." Evan stared at the poster again, nodded. "Yeah. You'll do great."

"I'll tell you what. If I try for this, then you gotta try for that art contest. Deal?"

Evan laughed to himself. "Fine. Deal."

ᔕ

After school, the group walked along the canal with the running path towards the ocean side, the way to Derek's house. It was always a pleasant walk, versus the route to Max's on the other side of campus over the freeway overpass. Derek stopped, pulled back from the front, letting Mark and Jared pass then Max. He waited for Evan, walked with him in back behind the others. It was just the boys today. Judith had tutoring.

"Hey. What you thinking about? You seem . . ." Derek nudged him at the elbow.

"Ah. Nothing, man. Just tired."

In truth, he was thinking about a lot of different things. The triangle. The tornado. The talent show and the art contest.

It was a pretty ordinary day. Evan stared at the surface of the water that shined bright on most days, but today was dim from the clouds. A gray sky hovered over the green water.

"How 'bout you? Things good?"

"Yeah, I think so. I mean, we just had a nice three-day weekend. School is out. I'm hanging with my best friends. Got the best girlfriend in the world. And, there might even be a teacher's strike." Derek laughed aloud up at the sky. "I feel like I just won the freaking jackpot at Game Works."

Evan laughed as well. "Kinda like when you get all the Lego pieces to fit together perfect, and you didn't even use the instruction booklet."

Derek's eyes widened, with a big grin. "There ya go! That's the Evan I know."

"Yeah, yeah."

"I actually, uh . . . could use your advice with something. I was thinking about getting a gift for Judy. Like, a present. I'm not good at that kinda stuff. Expressing myself, being all sentimental and crap. You know?"

"What's the occasion?"

"Nothing. She's just amazing. She just deserves it."

Evan nodded, with a half-smirk.

"Think you can help me pick something out? Piece a jewelry, maybe."

"I can try." He laughed, facing forward. "Ironically, you're the one who's got all the experience here now."

Derek leaned in. "Y'know, it should have been you. You're the deep one, all artsy. I'm not sure what I'm even doing, if I even deserve—"

"Hey, don't say that." The response was genuine. "You're one of the best guys I know. You gotta have confidence in that. You lucked out, you did it, got the best girl, and you can't go doubting yourself."

He nodded, breathed. "Thanks, man. See."

They both glanced sideways at one another. Derek shoved Evan who shoved him back, and they then started to punch and kick. After a good couple hits, they walked with their arms around each other's shoulders.

Ahead, the others stood near a bus stop. Jared bent down to tie his shoelaces. Mark and Max faced the other direction, one of them pointed while the other shook his head. Somebody stepped past Derek and Evan, towards the others, but they didn't notice. Another person followed.

With a good hard shove at the shoulder, the first of them bumped into Max, while the other laughed. It was the two punks from the other week.

Fists clenched, Mark stepped forward. "Hey, man! What's your problem!?"

The one punk backhanded him across the face sending his glasses flying. Mark stood with the guy chest to chest, about to throw a fist, but Derek hurried over, grabbed him, held him back.

Jared walked up, handed Mark his glasses, as the one punk glanced at his one punk friend.

Max stuck a hand in his pocket, felt at the box cutter hidden there. Evan tapped him on the small of his back, nodded as he passed by. He stood near Derek and Mark in front.

"You're lucky I'm holding this guy back," Derek said with his brow furled. "Because he'll knock you both out, easy."

"Oh yeah? I'd like to see him try."

"Hey, shit-for-brains." Evan chimed in. "There's five of us and two of you. Just make your move."

Derek held a hand to Mark's chest, who glared with two hard fists at his sides, his skin flushed with red. He almost teared from all the rage inside him.

Evan stepped in front, arms out, daring the punk to try something. Jared stood close behind. Max lingered in back, his hand still on the box cutter.

The punk stared with arms hanging at his side, nodded. "You know, most of you guys are all right . . ."

He peeped past the others to the back, to Max.

"But then you hang around *losers* like that. Pitiful." The punk shot a look at his friend, spit at the ground, turned and then walked away.

The two glanced back, saw the group still standing and watching. Derek held Mark who still had his fists clenched. Evan raised both arms out again, daring them once more. Jared had his arms crossed. Max kept his hand in his pocket.

As the two disappeared, the group each turned to one another and laughed.

"Man. Start shit but can't end shit." Jared shook his head.

"Told you. We ain't no pussies. Right, Der?" Evan tapped Derek on the arm. "Hells yeah."

Derek nodded, let go of Mark. "You okay?"

"I think so . . ." Mark lifted his glasses, showed a small scratch on the bridge of his nose. "Fricking asshole's lucky I didn't break his jaw."

Evan turned back. "Max?"

He nodded, took his hand out of his pocket.

"See. Didn't even need the screwdrivers and scissors. Jared could just brain the guy with his soda."

⸙

On the day of the sleepover, the others splashed about in the pool, tossed and spit water. Derek was floating on his back until Mark snuck up and dowsed him in a relentless bombing. Max pulled himself up onto the side, ran around the outside edge then jumped back in with a cannonball motion. Jared sat on the edge dangling his feet beneath the surface, shirt still on. He watched all the bubbles gather and rise from the commotion, flinched as some of the white water sprayed his way.

On one of the long chairs by the shallow end, Evan laid down and gazed up at the clouds moving in the sky. Their movement against the side of the apartment building was like staring into those trickling oil knickknacks in the counselor's office when you got in trouble. A silhouette blocked out the clouds to one side, and he turned over to see.

"Not going in yet?" He could just hear her voice.

"Yeah, I wanna relax for a bit first. You?"

Judith adjusted her clothes, her hair, then laid on the next chair. "Well, I ate. It was only a snack but you're supposed to wait before you swim, right?"

Evan smirked to himself.

Although, in her, he found this endearing, to him, rules were always meant to be broken. Like how running along the outside rim of the pool was forbidden—right there on the sign that Max ignored. Like how playing games in the computer lab was against the rules, playing cards in the cafe was against the rules. Or chewing gum on campus. But, with her, there was an innocence and a purity he couldn't help but appreciate.

Evan shifted, glanced over. Now he could see her since they were level. She was on her side, wore a t-shirt that covered her swimsuit underneath. He could see one of the straps, a bright yellow.

"Did you sign up for the talent show?"

"Yeah, I did actually. You enter into the art contest?" She smiled.

"Not yet. I told you, I need an idea. There's still time left. It's gotta be a bold striking image for me to really get behind it."

"You're pretty into that stuff, huh?"

He didn't respond, instead stared down at the pool. Mark continued to splash the others. Derek squealed, rubbing his eyes that stung from the chlorine. Max let out a whining screech like a hyena, dunking his body in then coming back up. Jared sat on the edge in silence, annoyed he got sprayed.

"You know, I saw the sign. For the talent show. There was one outside the cafe."

She rested her chin on her hand, listened. He could see the curvature of her cheek.

"It's like next week already. That's so crazy."

"I know. I'll just do a song I know."

"They said they could use help with production and set design. I was thinking about maybe looking into it."

"That's a great idea."

"I mean, unless you think I got a better chance doing tricks with my gyro ring or tending my Tamagotchi."

"Mine always died." She shook her head, smiled. ". . . Hey, I been wondering. What were you like? You know, at your old school."

"At Roosevelt?"

She nodded.

"I actually didn't quite fit in there. To be honest, I'd just hide in the library most the time. I'd draw, maybe read a comic book. If I wasn't doing that, then I liked to find a nice quiet stairs and just sit."

"Hmm. I can't imagine you doing that." Judith's eyes lingered then she sat upright. "Okay. Ready?"

"Sure, I guess. Haha."

With a smile and a blink, she lifted her shirt from her torso to the top of her head revealing the bright one-piece underneath. He could see the shape of her body, her breasts beneath the thin yellow layer of fabric. Every inch of her smooth legs right there in front of him, he struggled not to let his mouth hang open.

He sat up, eyes now grazing over her chest, her shoulders and neck. Her cheeks reddened the longer his eyes remained glued. Taking off his own shirt, he stood, glancing down at her with a smirk.

The two walked over to the shallow end. The others waved to them from the deep.

Judith held the rail, stepped down the submerged stairs while Evan walked around to the side. She dipped her feet in one by one, waded until the water was waist level. He walked around the edge matching her pace. They both continued until the water was right beneath her bust. Evan gave her a look then jumped in, with a pencil dive.

Under the water, he floated, watched as she dropped her body in with him. He smiled, blowing out bubbles, while his arms treaded water. She covered her mouth with one hand, pedaled with her feet.

As waves of light glided on her face like neon leaves in the wind, her hair floating, she appeared angelic. He stared into her almond eyes, watched as her dimples appeared. She stared back at him, blinking. Her lips appeared like candy in the water. He just wished he could hold his breath longer.

When he came back up, with a gasp, he was tackled from behind by Max who wrapped an arm around him and gave him a hard noogie. Judith had her hands around Derek's shoulders as he held her at the waist. Evan watched as the two twirled, their eyes meeting again when his back was turned. Mark snuck around the side while Jared was distracted, pulled him down into the pool.

"You douchebag!" Jared resurfaced, spraying water from his lips as he yelled. "You frickin' ass!"

Everybody burst into laughter that echoed up the side of the building, to the clouds in the sky that thinned and scattered and changed in shape. The pool and its white water splashing was like a chemical reaction in a beaker. The clouds in the sky was hot steam rising from the effervescence. If you took the contents of that beaker and shook it, spun all the different elements and the steam, it would surely resemble that of a tornado.

❧

Her hair was still messy, still wet, but she wore different clothes that were nice and dry. Judith walked in front of the group next to Derek, the two of them giggling. Evan was behind, could see the contour of her ear, the slender of her neck. Next to him, Max tried to keep pace. They were heading to the shopping center. It was later in the afternoon already, and the sun was starting to go down.

"We should've just cut through campus," Mark yelled from the back. "Lot quicker."

Jared walked next to him, quiet, shirt still half-soaked.

Derek turned backward. "Yeah, but you never know. The gate might be locked or something."

"Right, right."

The shopping center had everything they needed: snacks, drinks, movies. Derek's mom gave him twenty bucks. She had to work late so it was the perfect night to do the sleepover. A nice little swim, a nice little hangout.

"Let's stop by Jam Comics first. I wanna pick something up, if it came in." Derek put his arm around Judith.

"What are we getting again?" Max's voice was a mutter.

Derek furled his brow as Judith pulled away, took his arm off her. She glanced around to make sure nobody saw.

Evan watched this occur, stepped over a wide crack in the ground, which was bad luck.

"Uh. Chips, soda. We already got pizza at home. Gotta pick up a movie."

The group passed through the swinging double doors. Jared stood by the long table in front as a small group of kids played some card game. Mark went over to the glass display case on the side with different trading cards. Derek continued to the back of the shop, in search of collectible figures. Max hovered first by the long table, then followed Derek.

Judith seemed upset. "I told him . . . We have to be careful . . ."

"Ah, he probably just forgot." Evan touched her on the arm, turned, moved to the stacks in the shelves.

She walked close, watched as he ran his fingers across the different covers highlighted. He then went to the bins laid out, started flipping through them.

"What are you looking for?"

"Eh, just looking. Gotta save money first."

There was a cardboard cutout of a femme fatale on the side of one of the shelves. Her hair was styled, costume skintight, hugging at her breasts and her legs in an exaggerated jump pose. Evan traced the lines and the curves with his eyes, then moved from the comics section to the manga.

Judith followed, tucking her hair behind her left ear. Above them, scrolls hung down from the ceiling. She stared up at one of them, stepped to get a better angle. Evan picked up one of the volumes, read the summary on the back, put it back. He watched as she gazed at the different scrolls.

"What are you into, Jude?"

She paused, her eyes meeting his from across the bins. He leaned forward, lifting an eyebrow.

"Hmm. Lemme guess. Like, cutesy anime."

"Yes . . ." Judith laughed, clicking her tongue. "Why?"

Evan shook his head, smirked.

"Like this one." She pulled a manga from the shelf, showed the cover. "I watch it every week, even the reruns."

"Really, half-dog demon?"

"What? It's adventure, it's romantic."

"Uh-huh. Yeah. Now, see, this one, right here . . ." He pulled a different manga, this one a magazine, turned it over and tilted it. "This one is freaking amazing."

"Bounty hunters in space? Seriously? Come on."

Both laughed, each turning to the shelf that transitioned from manga to anime.

From around the corner, Max appeared with Derek who held a small blind box. That was a series of figures you could try to collect, not knowing which one was inside. Derek motioned with his head as he walked to the register.

They got in line. Mark waved to them from the long table, near Jared who watched the game rubbing his chin. Max crossed his arms, stood next to Derek as he examined the box. He rattled it, listened inside, felt the weight of it.

As they swung back out the double doors, Derek opened the box. It was already turning dark.

"Was it the one you wanted?" Jared peeped his head over his shoulder, chuckled. "Nope."

"The hell. Course not." Derek threw the box in the garbage, held the small figurine in his hand. "Bastard. It's the fricking one I least wanted . . ."

Mark laughed, slapped a hand on Derek's shoulder. "It's the odds, man. Like one out of eight. And, really, it's more like one outta eighty."

"I know, I know. La-di-freaking-dah."

The group continued forward past a small fast food joint, up and behind the bend in the parking lot. From there, the group split in two: Derek and Max went to get snacks and soda, the others went to go find a movie. Derek turned right to the grocery store. Max glanced back, followed. Evan led the rest of the group left to the DVD rental place.

Out front, there were big movie posters on the wide glass pane. He pushed through the door, held it open for Judith, then for Mark and Jared. Inside, a couple of big cardboard displays from popular movies welcomed them. There was candy and microwave popcorn for sale by the front counter in the impulse section. All along the outside walls were the new releases. In segmented sections throughout the inside were shelves with the different genres.

"Here. This one." Mark held up the case, tapped it with his finger. "A killer in a ghost mask. You gotta guess who the killer is."

Jared continued. "Eh, seen it already."

"What? But there's hot chicks in it." Mark put it back, followed along.

Evan walked near Judith behind them, perusing at their own pace. Most the time, someone was partial either to sci-fi or to fantasy or horror, but she didn't seem too interested. He wondered what kind of movies she did like.

Tapping Mark on the arm, Jared showed a different movie. "Okay. How 'bout this?"

"Is that part three?"

"No, part four."

"Part four? I thought she kills herself."

"Well, yeah, but they cloned her DNA."

"What?" Mark stared at him. "What's next? A crossover, a prequel? Where does it end, Jared? Where does it end? Before you know, there'll be like seven, eight movies . . ."

"Okay, okay. Sheesh."

Evan spoke up from behind, took one of the cases off the shelf. "Ah. I got one, you guys."

It was a movie about an intergalactic war between humans and evolved insects. On the cover was the heroic leader ambiguously grunting, with armored soldiers in back.

"Nice. I heard that was good." Jared nodded in approval.

"I don't know, man . . ." Mark walked over, took it in his hand. "Is there hot chicks?"

Evan tilted his head, nodded. "I think there's nudity, actually."

Judith rolled her eyes.

❧

Bent forward, reaching back behind the small TV and the table, Derek squirmed in place fumbling with the different cords. For some reason, the DVD player in the living room cut in and out, rolled, was fuzzy with static so they decided to swap the cable with the one from his room. Jared and Max were in the kitchen. They popped frozen pizza in the oven, threw sodas in the freezer and fridge. Evan sat on Derek's bed, leaned against the wall. On one side of him, Judith sat with her hands in her lap. He could feel her close. Opposite side, Mark rolled his head backward, annoyed.

"Hurry up already. Damn."

"Kiss my ass! You try it then!"

Mark hopped off the bed, about to, but then Jared called out from the kitchen. He went down the hall to check.

It was just Evan and Judith on the bed now, behind Derek who had his back turned. He could feel a light electricity to his side where her knee was next to his thigh, their arms close together. In the glass, he could see their reflection staring back. He wasn't sure but it appeared like she was staring too, right at him, right through him. Evan watched as the reflection of her head tilted, nestled on his shoulder.

He could feel the warmth, could feel her shoulders rise and fall with each breath. He could smell her hair.

Ah, she's just tired. It's just late. That's all.

Doesn't mean anything . . .

He tilted his head back towards her, touched his cheek to the top of her head. Again, their eyes met in the glass, or at least seemed like they did. Then he stopped himself while they each straightened up, right as Derek returned from the jungle of cords.

The movie had been the perfect choice, when they got it to work at last. It was fun, funny, with lots of action and, indeed, some nudity. Derek reached forward, put down a piece of bitten pizza crust. He sat in the middle of the couch, holding Judith's hand. Next to him, Evan stretched his feet out near Max on the floor, who sat with his back against the base as per usual. Mark took up the armrest near Evan, one arm out over the top of the cushion. Jared sat on the carpet close to the TV, popping his second can of soda.

Mark breathed out a sigh, peeped at his watch. "Man, I'm not gonna get to finish the movie. Better not be another nude scene."

Little did he know, there was. A full-blown make out scene, with spectacular topless close-up. Of course, it wouldn't come on until after he left the building.

Judith let go of Derek's hand, turned. "Yeah. I better get going too. My parents are gonna kill me already as is . . ."

"Not even a little longer?"

"No, really, I can't."

Sliding off the armrest, Mark tapped Max on the shoulder. He went to Jared who bumped his fist. He waved to Derek and Judith. Evan stood and joined him by the kitchen. They clapped their palms and did a bro hug.

"You going home too?"

"C'mon, Jar. You know I don't like being at home. My parents don't care about me, haha." It was a joke but a lot of truth is said in jest.

Judith kissed Derek, stood, waved to Max then to Jared. She walked over and joined Mark and Evan.

"Hey, Der, you not gonna walk her?" Evan glanced back toward the couch.

"Man. I can't just leave you guys all alone here with my stuff. Don't trust you freaks." Derek laughed, grabbing another slice of pepperoni.

Evan turned to Mark, who had a hand on the doorknob. He leaned in, whispered.

"Hey. Think you could walk with her? At least halfway? It's kinda dark already."

"Sure, man. No prob."

Judith stepped close. Evan faced her, smirked. There was a pause as they both leaned in. Both began to raise their arms then their hands, in uncertain and uncommitted spurts of motion. At last, they each waved a small wave to one another. Mark opened the door, let her pass through. Evan nodded and they clapped palms again.

11

Jan 19th
11:44am

Some of them watched with wide terrified eyes, unblinking, as the hammer lingered in place, with a slight rattle, high above the jester's head. Some gazed down and away, and some covered their faces. Some began to cry, to cry out. From his place kneeling on the floor, Evan just stared with his mouth hanging open. Each bony finger wrapped snug around the wooden handle. Each feather wafted, each rhinestone on the jester's mask shined prominent as the jester smiled, showing crooked teeth.

The puppet watched motionless from the other side, from behind the vague black and white swirl, the ominous splash of red. Facing up, glaring, the kid in uniform awaited his fate. As the hammer came crashing down he scrambled to his feet, braced for the pending impact while lunging forward. With a dull hard thud, the hammer smashed into his side cracking his upper ribs. Thwack! He grunted as he tackled into her and knocked her back onto the floor.

"Oh, my God!"

"No!!!"

When the hammer bounced on the hardwood and into the orchestra pit, Evan hopped up and ran towards the puppet. The muzzle of the gun shifted in his direction. He slid down to the floor, rolling to his side ready to dodge the coming bullets, but the puppet didn't pull the trigger. The short girl got to her feet as the kid in uniform wrestled with the jester on the floor, reaching for the gun tucked away. He grunted in pain with each movement, gasping as he struggled. The kid with the bandaged hand tried to run at the puppet but stopped when the puppet turned and aimed.

This is it.

Go, go.

Quick as he could, Evan got back to his feet and rushed forward again. About to pull the trigger aimed at the kid with the bandaged hand, Evan grabbed the puppet by the arm, pointed it up at the ceiling. Bang, bang, bang, bang. Some of the lights cracked and exploded, darkening the stage halfway.

There was a sharp scream, then the rest of the group scattered. Most of the others left the stage, raced down the side ramp to the hall back towards the front doors. The girl with piercings hurried to the guy on the cart.

"T-the gun, the bag!" Evan turned and shouted, fighting back the puppet's hand. "Hurry!!!"

It didn't register right away. The kid with the bandaged hand darted his head around, saw the duffel bag, and saw the bulky handgun.

"Come on, ar-my boy. THAT all ya GOT."

The jester kicked at the short girl, shoved her away with the heel of her foot. The kid in uniform continued to wrestle until she clawed her fingernails down his face then kneed him in the groin. She reached behind her, touching the handle of the handgun.

Face to face with the kabuki mask, one on one, Evan tried reaching a hand back for his pocket with the knife but couldn't. He meant to get it earlier but it all happened so fast.

The kid with the bandaged hand stomped over, kicked the bulky gun away beneath the curtains, then picked up the bag. He swung around and hurled it out into the empty rows. He glanced back at Evan, nodded.

Bang.

Holding the bandaged hand in front of his abdomen, the gauze which was once clean now was covered in fresh blood. His eyes moved from his hand to the front of his shirt. It was leaking red. He stared up at Evan, dropping to his knees.

Evan opened his mouth to say something but no words formed. It was a mere shallow breath, and shock and disbelief.

Behind him, the jester stood with the gun still pointed, smoke wafting, as she smiled through sharp and crooked teeth.

A long rope coiled onto the floor, the end of it slapping down from the ceiling. With that, the kid in uniform rolled and staggered up. He hobbled to the side ramp. The short girl followed, running alongside him. The jester turned and shot at them in the dark. Bang, bang.

Bang, bang, bang. The jester chased after them, as they disappeared in the hall toward the front doors.

"Oh, we were JUST getting STARTED."

A loud cackle echoed through the auditorium.

Evan twisted the puppet's arm at the wrist, sending the gun sliding across the floor, pushed him away with a good hard shove, turned to the others. "Run!"

He hurried to the kid with the bandaged hand, wrapped his arm around his neck and shoulder. The girl with piercings shoved the cart. Evan led them backstage behind the curtain towards the dressing rooms and equipment storage. He shifted back, watched as the puppet walked over and picked up the gun. The puppet tilted his head to one side, cracking his neck. From on the stage now half-lit, the mask in the darkness stared back like an apparition.

12

9th Grade

FACING UP AT the asbestos in the ceiling, Evan yawned then adjusted the pillow. He pulled the blanket to his chin, slid over, away from Jared who slept with his back turned. Max was near his feet, like a dog, sleeping horizontally. The coffee table was pushed aside by the TV. On it were open cans and an open bag, an open box—leftovers from their massive feast. He tucked both his hands behind his head, glanced at the glass on the TV, which was blank, empty, then wondered if she made it home okay.

"Can't sleep?"

Evan turned, saw Derek laying on the couch.

"Yeah. Me neither." He sat up, leaned forward. "Wanna go get some fresh air?"

"Is it safe to leave all your stuff?" Evan teased.

Derek laughed. "Shut up, man. Come on."

They took the elevator down to the fifth, went and sat on the long chairs by the pool.

Evan stretched out, gazed up the side of the building with its reflective glass shining against the night sky. He could see many stars twinkling, a few clouds gliding, behind them the bright orb of the moon.

Derek crossed his legs, interlaced his fingers on top his chest and stomach. Evan glanced down to the deep end of the pool, to where the light from the water reflected on the wall like little crinkles in time.

So much of adolescence and high school, of growing up, is noise and chaos. So much of it is a cram of stress and scrambling, of overthinking, of overfeeling, with this general lack of control. But, a lot is also just basking in a particular moment, enjoying, living, whether it's a water balloon war or a food fight or a triumphant dodgeball tournament. Or this, right here, now—two best friends together under the stars late at night, in the quiet, in all the stillness, forgetting anything and everything else.

As kids, they had sleepovers but just the two of them, never a big one. They would sleep on the same bed, and like tonight, often couldn't sleep. For some reason, instead, they talked about ghosts or aliens, what it would be like to have superpowers, about different martial arts systems, about secret government agencies, or time travel. Sometimes they talked about the female body. Their minds were curious and racing, expanding, absorbing. Add to that hormones and angst, and being forced to grow up in a world changing so fast.

"Der?"

"Yeah."

"Remember what we wanted to be when we were kids?"

He laughed to himself. "Well, you always wanted to dig up fossils like Dr. Grant."

Evan smirked. "Yeah, I meant after that."

Again, Derek laughed. "Pilots."

"That's right. We were obsessed with our toys, your model

airplanes. Holding them in our hands, running, making all the swooshing noises. Sonic booms and jet thrusters. Shooting bullets, firing missiles. Being high up in the air, free, flying through the clouds."

Derek licked his lips, swallowed.

"Last summer, or was it the summer before, all we did was play that one game over and over. Every boss. Every level. We took turns. Doing barrel rolls and somersaults, and all the dogfighting. It was like our dream come true."

"Never did find that black hole, did we?"

Evan blinked, shifted from the sky to the pool then back to the sky again.

"You know, we'll never gonna get to do that, huh? In real life, I mean."

"Unless it's an analog control stick, trigger buttons and a rumble thingy, prolly not . . ."

"Now, I don't even know what I wanna be, what I even wanna do. And you, you want to be a bus driver?" Evan laughed.

Derek turned, threw up a hand. "Hey, what's a pilot, anyway? Just a bus driver in the sky."

"I wonder what we're all gonna be when we grow up. I wonder if Jared's actually gonna go into computers, if Mark's actually gonna teach math."

"Judy's gonna be a doctor. I'm pretty sure of that."

"I think you're right." Evan sighed. "Hey, what does Max wanna do again?"

"Pfft, I don't know. Be a weirdo."

They both laughed, perhaps a little too hard. It echoed up the building into the darkness.

"Hey, uh, I been thinking about . . . sex."

"Well. What else is new?" Evan smiled.

Derek shook his head. "No. I mean, since I got, like, a girlfriend now. You know?"

Evan was silent, laid flat on his back.

"All we done so far is kiss. But you always gotta be ready, right?" Derek rolled onto his side. "It might not always seem like it. But I really, really like her."

He breathed in and out. "I know, man."

"That's why, like I said, I gotta get her something. Like a necklace or a bracelet. She's just so . . . so awesome. You don't even know."

There was an ache in his neck. His back was sore. Waking up from the sheets laid out on the carpet was agony. Not to mention, as Evan awoke, Mark was sitting over the top of him, tapping his cheek with a big ol' grin. Jared sat on the couch with a coffee mug filled with soda, seeming miserable, lines from the carpet fibers engraved on his cheek and forehead. Max was still sleeping, with some shaving cream on his hand and face. Mark had been busy that morning.

"Hey, he's just lucky I couldn't find a Sharpie." He grinned a wider grin.

"You're back?"

"Yeah. My mom and dad only said I couldn't *sleep* over. Funny, right? They're even more strict with my sister. Anyway, Derek wanted us all to hang before his mom woke up."

Evan sloshed his tongue around in his dry and sticky mouth, covering a yawn with the back of his hand. He was about to ask where Derek was, but then he appeared from the hallway. Derek carried a shoebox, sat down on the carpet by the TV, crossed his legs, motioned to wake up Max.

Evan leaned over and shook him. Max shuddered awake,

glanced around, sat up and rubbed his eyes. He noticed the shaving cream and flinched, to which Mark laughed, then wiped his hand on his shirt and pants. Jared moved from the couch to the carpet.

The five of them sat in a circle.

"All right, you guys. Like I been saying for a while now, I got us all a little something. This is a pact, a bond, between us. My gift to you, each one. Okay?"

Derek lifted the lid from the shoebox, looked each of them dead in their eye.

"What'd you get? What did you do?" Jared was joking but almost sounded afraid or concerned.

He smiled, reaching in. In his hand was a knife. Max blinked, scooted closer. Mark gazed at it with mouth agape, nudging his glasses. Evan narrowed his eyes with his head inclined.

The first was a combat knife, fixed blade. It came in a sheath with a strap. Derek handed this to Max, who snatched it, almost giddy.

"Now, when I first got this for you, like, I just wanted to make sure you were okay. You know, from those guys . . ." Derek leaned forward, facing to the floor then up at Max. "After we pretty much proved we could take on those bastards, though, I don't think we need these."

Max nodded, took the knife from its sheath, held it tight in his hand. It was black metal with a gripped handle, serrated teeth along a portion of the edge.

"In fact, we never *needed* it really. I don't know what I was thinking. I wanted you to feel stronger, braver. You know? Don't carry it on you or anything. That's kinda nuts, keep it home. It's a gift. Nothing more. Think of it almost like a collector's item."

Evan watched Max stare into the blade as if in a trance, hypnotized. He turned the knife in place, watched the matted sheen respond to the light. He touched his fingertip along the edge, to the serrated teeth. Max had just woken up, technically, but somewhere else deep inside him, another part had also just awakened. In his hands, for the first time in his life, he felt something he never had.

There was something unnerving about that scene. Evan could sense something was wrong, off. Any normal kid played with matches, squished a bug, threw rocks or sticks. Any number of boys practiced fighting, played with knives even. But there was something that day as Max stared into that cold steel. Evan kept his eye on him—his face, his eyes—felt a slight shiver down the hairs of his arm.

Is this going too far?

Derek lurched forward, handed Jared the second knife which was a utility knife with a folding blade. Jared hesitated at first, but eased when he saw its practicality in design. It was the kind of knife he might use in the future when he worked with computers, for removing panels perhaps. He could also use it as a letter opener if anything, cut a box or a sandwich, although that would be major overkill.

"Mark, I got you kind of a cool one."

The third was a switchblade. It was smaller than the others. Mark jutted out his lower lip, raised his brows, as he took it in his hand and nodded to himself. He undid the metal clip at the end and slid the button up. Out protruded the blade, with one good click into place.

"Holy damn that's badass." Mark grinned a big grin, shook his head. "I better hide this thing good. If my parents ever find it, I'm dead."

Jared put his away in his pocket, sipped from his coffee

mug full of soda. Max continued to hold the knife, weighing it in his hand.

Evan drew his gaze from Max back to Derek. He couldn't help thinking there was something in his eyes, or maybe a lack thereof. Derek pulled the last two out from the box. Evan leaned closer toward him, peeped in his hand. The fourth and fifth knives were butterfly knives.

"I got us matching ones." Derek took one, handed Evan the other. "One for you. One for me."

They were simple. Black handles and a silver blade. Derek unfolded his, held it up. Evan felt the circular holes in the handle with his thumb, then flipped it open, flipped it closed.

"See. Now we're one. We're a group, a gang. Forever. It doesn't matter what happens today or tomorrow, or even next week. We'll always be together. No matter what."

Five boys, five knives.

More than a pact or bond, it was a blood oath. Before the events that would transpire, tiny variables had been pieced together and placed in motion. There, on the carpet in front of the TV, with Derek's mom asleep in the next room, the friends had crossed a very fine line. One that would be impossible to uncross.

Evan glanced over again at Max, who nodded back with an awkward smile. He saw the pale skin, the acne, the braces. He glanced at Jared, at his dark round face, at Mark and his squinty eyes. He then glanced at Derek who had a goofy look on his face, with a poof of wavy hair. He faced each one of his best friends, as they sat together in a circle on the floor.

These friends were always there for him. Friends who were his home, his family, who fed him. Friends that he would rush into the face of danger for. Friends that he would put it all on the line for, everything. Friends he would die for.

13

Jan 19th
11:48am

Navigating through the halls, Evan struggled to balance the kid with the bandaged hand who felt more limp, wobbling with each step. *Come on. Stay with me, stay with me.* He pulled his arm tight around his neck and shoulder. They took a sharp turn then another, stepping past two dressing rooms, coming to a fork where they could either go left or right. To the left was the music room, and to the right was the meeting room for rehearsals. Evan turned right, saw boxes filled with wigs and costumes, with various props. The girl with piercings struggled to keep up, pushing the cart with all her might. The guy on the cart grunted with every hard bump. From behind, the puppet—like an unholy ghoul in the darkness—stalked them, barely visible as they twisted around the next corridor.

Ahead was an open room, with tables and stools, with a rolling chalkboard. There were large painted set backdrops and smaller wooden stage pieces scattered about. Evan started panting, felt sweat beads on his skin. From behind, he heard a loud crash and turned back. The cart caught its wheel then hit the wall and the door frame. As the girl with piercings tried to dislodge it, the puppet appeared from the far end of the corridor.

"Forget the cart. We gotta ditch it."

She turned back to where his eyes stared, letting out a sharp scream. The guy on the cart sat upright, held a hand against the bandage.

The slow and steady waltz of the puppet towards them in the dark was mesmerizing and strange.

"Hey. I'm gonna need you to walk. You can walk, okay? The door's right there." Evan faced the kid with the bandaged hand, who now had a growing wet stain down his front. "We are so, so close. You can do this. Okay?"

He struggled to keep his eyes open, nodded. Evan watched him walk forward, unsteady.

Ah, shit . . .

The girl with piercings stepped over the cart from out of the doorway and into the room. She got on one side, Evan on the other, and together they lifted the guy from the cart.

"Go, go."

Evan took a quick peek behind, at the puppet stepping towards them, handgun at his side.

Why wasn't he running? Why wasn't he shooting?

Why didn't he pull the trigger the first time back on stage, when Evan first ran toward him?

It didn't make sense but there wasn't time to think. The kid with the bandaged hand hobbled through the room and out the door, held it open for the three of them: Evan, the girl with piercings, and the guy who was on the cart.

They zigzagged down the ramp from the southwest corner of the auditorium toward the portables. Their legs moved at different speeds and different angles, bumping into one another almost tripping all of them. It was like a bad three-legged race, but with more legs.

"Wait! Don't go that way!"

Evan shouted backward as the kid with the bandaged hand turned and headed toward the tennis court instead, away from the three of them.

The puppet appeared from the door, staring in Evan's direction. Again, he didn't shoot, didn't even lift the gun, just tilted his neck in place. When the puppet turned, the kid with the bandaged hand just got to the chain-link fence. He then raised the gun and aimed.

"NOOO!!!"

Each shot was slow and deliberate. Bang. Bang. Bang.

As the three of them turned behind P5 and P6, the two portable buildings nearest to the auditorium, Evan shifted back one last time.

The puppet stood like a marble statue. His mask wore a blank expression similar to the face of a mannequin or the head of a doll. Unnerving to see, Evan felt a shiver down each hair on the back of his neck. He wanted to bend forward and vomit in the grass but resisted the urge. Ahead was the bleachers, the baseball diamond beyond that, football field on the other side, and then freedom.

14

9th Grade

SHE WAS UPSET but he couldn't tell why. Evan put his mechanical pencil down over the top of his composition book, scooted closer. He was about to touch a hand to her shoulder but instead just stared in her eyes. Judith glanced up, blinking, fighting back tears. She pushed aside her elegantly written notes, put the flashcards near the textbook, leaned forward on her arms and started to sob. Her shoulders shook as she sniffled, as she started to whimper on the table in the study room. It was quiet, cold.

"Hey, hey . . ." Evan put an arm around her. "What's going on? What's wrong?"

She didn't respond, but lifted her head and buried her face between his chest and shoulder. He could feel his shirt become warm and wet. He dazed out the small window in the door, to the first floor of the library.

A single image flashed through his mind: her head on his shoulder, in the reflection of the TV on the bed, with Derek's back turned.

"Jude . . . What is it?"

Her voice was soft, almost cracking, as the words formed. "Y-you're gonna think it's stupid."

"Come on, Jude. Tell me."

"It's my fucking trigonometry class." Judith buried her face deeper, sobbed a little more. "That f-fucking asshole."

He could smell her hair, almost intoxicating. A slight puff of her perfume wafted. Evan wrapped his arm tighter around her, rubbed at her far shoulder, rocking her.

"What happened?"

"No, it's just . . . He gave me an A."

Right then, he understood. All the effort she put in, all the extra studying, the tutoring even, she always aimed for the highest perfection in each one of her classes. The goal was clear in her mind. Not just an A, but an A-plus.

"Oh, no. I'm so sorry." Evan leaned the side of his cheek against the top of her head. "It's okay."

Judith sniffled, nuzzled her face. "I'm so stupid. I'm such an idiot."

"No. No, you're not. That . . ." Evan shook his head. "That teacher's just a jackass."

She lifted her head up, breathed. "I'm sorry."

"Hey, don't be. I totally get it. I do. It's fine." He stared in her almond eyes.

"I mean, it's just one assignment, but it still sucks. I talked to him but he won't do anything."

"Ah, just forget it. You'll do better again next time. Kind of like my drawings. I mean, not every piece of paper's gonna turn into some masterpiece. But I always do try."

Judith raised her arms, wrapped them around his torso. Evan leaned his head onto hers, closed his eyes.

"Thank you, Evan." Another soft sniffle. "Why couldn't you have transferred sooner?"

He wondered what that meant, if anything.

Ah, she's just upset.

That's all.

"We're supposed to be studying and yet here I am . . ." She pulled away with a quiet laugh, wiping at her eyes. "God. I'm so sorry."

"No, it's all good. Don't worry about it." He sighed. "You know, let's take another break again."

Judith nodded, cleared her throat. "I, uh, picked my song. For the talent show."

Evan smirked. "Oh yeah? I signed up too, to help with preparations. I'm going tomorrow after school."

"Cool. And what about the art contest?"

"Well, like I said, just waiting for something to hit me. A little inspiration. I need my muse."

"I see. I'm sure it'll come." She wiped her face once more, tucked her hair behind her left ear. "Did you hear about the strike?"

"Yeah, sounds like it's actually happening. Ten more days." Evan smirked, watched her fix her shirt and straighten back up. "Most people are excited about it . . ."

Judith smiled, pushed him at his chest. "Shut up. I know, I'm weird."

"I'm not really looking forward to it, either."

"Why not?"

"Just, 'cause I won't get to see you."

He swallowed, blinked, cleared his throat. He squirmed in his chair, faced down. Evan regretted saying those words, wasn't even sure why or how they came out. He hung his head low, then his shoulders.

"I know. Me too."

Surprised, he perked up and turned. Judith smiled. Evan

smirked. Her cheeks were just a touch pink. Their eyes locked for a few seconds then broke away. She grabbed the notes and the flashcards. He reached for the textbook.

The sky was blanketed in a splotched dark gray, one big blob of cloud. As they walked in formation taking up most of the sidewalk, Evan glanced up at the vast stretch of sky. His hands were deep in his pockets as he wondered various things. The talent show. The art contest. The triangle and the tornado. With the weather above as it was, something was sure to be on the horizon. To the side, the canal water seemed to flow slow and steady. There wasn't a shiny reflection on the surface like usual, just plain murky ripples.

Mark and Jared walked in front of the group. Mark hopped up on a concrete bus stop then back down, scuttering around a garbage can. Jared chuckled, shook his head, a bottle of soda dangling from his hand. Next to Evan, Derek kicked at the ground. He knocked a snapped twig into the grass then a small rock onto the dirt. It was just the four of them that day.

"You said Max was busy?"

Derek nodded, kicked again. "Yeah, he said he had something to do. I don't know. We'll see him tomorrow."

"And all of us are going? To the talent show?"

"Just gotta come up with the entrance fee. I mean, that's my girlfriend and all, so I kinda have no choice."

Evan shifted. "Why? You don't want to?"

"Well, I'm sure she'll be great. No doubt about it. But then all the other guys . . ." Derek shook his head, laughed to himself. "Gonna be a disaster."

"Ah, I'm sure it'll be okay."

"You really signed up to help with set design?"

Evan smirked, took his hands out of his pockets to shove Derek who shoved him back.

"Just, doesn't seem like you."

"I know. This week went by pretty quick. You'll see, but I did the cloud pieces. I also did a couple backgrounds that come in later on, like halfway through."

Derek leaned close, wrapped an arm around Evan.

"Nah. That's cool, man. I wish I could do that kinda stuff. Draw, paint. Be all artsy."

"Yeah, I kinda liked it. I'm more into drawing, never really paint 'cept when I'm forced to for class."

As the two walked together in tandem, Derek with his arm around him, Evan felt a crumbling pit inside his chest. He remembered sitting close to her on the bed, her head nestled on his shoulder, just before the sleepover. He remembered their arms around one another as she cried, the smell of her hair, in the study room just the other day. A whole slew of images flashed through his mind. Their hands touching over the mouse in the computer lab. Her fingernail. Her ear, her lips. Her almond eyes. The clouds looming above them darkened. Again, he returned his hands to his pockets, returned to wondering various things. The triangle. The tornado.

15

Jan 19th
11:54am

As THEY CARRIED the guy that was on the cart through the baseball diamond, Evan gazed down at the dirt. The three of them buckled, almost fell, but regained their balance. Beneath their feet, the dirt turned to grass as they transitioned to the football field. Each green blade crunched beneath the soles of his shoes. With the sound and feel of it, his mind drifted off. He remembered hugging on their knees, her laughter, as they rolled together on the ground. He remembered holding hands running down the walkway then down the stairs. He remembered how she appeared so beautiful in that dress, the night that would change his life . . . Staring up, he adjusted his grip, wrapped the guy's arm tight around his neck. The girl with piercings panted, limped, as they continued to the end of the field towards the back fence.

I'll find you, Jude.

I promise.

Evan peeped over his shoulder to the school. The bleachers, the portables. The gym on the far side. He could hear distant gunshots, but barely audible.

"You guys shoulda just left me."

"No. We're in this together." The girl with piercings tripped but caught herself. "Almost there, c'mon."

The guy's voice crackled. "This is so messed up. What just happened."

"I know." Evan spoke the words but wasn't all there, still lingered in that place in his mind.

"Am I gonna make it?"

The girl with piercings darted her eyes past the guy, to Evan who faced ahead.

He'd been shot in the stomach with a double-barrel shotgun, had been bleeding for almost half an hour, struggled to walk or stand. The one thing holding him together was a makeshift bandage put together by some kid who might've slept through the drill during JROTC training. Fair to say, his chances were seeming pretty slim.

"W-we get you off campus, then we get you help. It's all gonna be okay." Evan wasn't sure who he was trying to convince.

The back fence grew in sight, with each slow hobble, and with that Evan thought of Michelle. He wondered if she made it this far. Last he saw, she was headed in this direction. Evan then thought of the kid in uniform, the short girl with glasses, and the kid with the bandaged hand. Whatever forces had brought them together now ripped them apart—not unlike himself and Judith.

He thought of each and every one of his friends. Their squinty eyes. Their soda can. Their awkward mumble. Shoving each other and skipping stones by the stream on his first day. And, to his surprise, he thought of his family. His parents who fought too much, who yelled too much. His little brother who he didn't pay enough attention to.

I'm so sorry.

If I live through this . . .

They made it to the fence, passed through and stood on the curb. Evan grunted as he pulled the guy up, who became heavier and heavier. There weren't any cars on the road, which was odd for the intersection that was almost always busy. No pedestrians running errands, no joggers en route. No bicycles riding. Nobody walking their dogs.

Where were the authorities? By now, there should have been a flood of police cars, fire trucks, ambulances and news reporters.

"Keep going. Other side of the street."

They stepped down the curb onto the empty road to the other side, near a slanted tree by the arched bridge. They helped lay the guy down on the dirt. He stared Evan in the eye, nodded, closed his eyes. Evan glanced down the gulch to the canal water.

It occurred to him then, that maybe something happened. A couple of years ago, a bad wreck on the freeway caused traffic in the area to be clogged for hours.

Perhaps that was the reason no one had arrived yet. Perhaps that was the reason that, even now, these very streets were empty. This wasn't natural. Maybe they were in fact on their own, and would have to fend for themselves. An already impossible situation made that much more difficult.

"You just rest, man. Hang in there. Okay? Help is on the way." Evan stood back up, turned. "Can you stay here with him?"

"Wait. Where you going?" The girl with piercings furled her brow, crossed her arms over her chest as she stood with him. "We're supposed to stick together."

"I . . . I have to go back."

The guy on the ground swallowed, breathed. The girl with piercings sighed, put one hand on her hip.

"Thank you." Evan wanted to say more, but there was just too much.

How do you explain it? That the three of them needed to run into one another by the monument, needed to run inside the auditorium, needed to help each other through that whole ordeal, then needed to make it to this place. These two, this guy and this girl. This unlikely pair.

Evan gazed at each of them one last time then turned to cross the street. The girl with piercings grabbed him by the hand, pulled and turned him around. She pressed her body close to his, pouted, leaned her lips in.

"H-hold on, I—"

Her eyes searched his, that blinked, that hesitated. He pulled away, shaking his head.

Perhaps this was a way for her to process the trauma.

"I like somebody."

Those three words, that idea, he had repressed for such a long time. Now, like the canal water, like a fountain, they came flowing out of him. He didn't want to admit it but it was true. As true as the sky, as true as the earth. As true as the gunfire in the distance.

Evan could feel warm tears gather in his eyes, and the breath in him about to be stifled. He turned, hopped off the curb into the empty street. Glancing back, the two waved to him with uncertainty. He took a deep breath in and out, then headed through the fence back onto campus.

16

9th Grade

STARING AT THE canvas and at what he'd painted, Evan stood back and smirked to himself. He peeked from behind the curtain out into the theater, watched the rows of seats filling up. It was intermission and almost time to change the background piece. Two kids rolled a piano over, which was the cue for Evan and the others to carry the canvas down to the middle of the stage. He could hear somebody shouting something as he stepped into the light, which he assumed was Mark. They put the new piece down in the designated spot, carried the old piece to the other side. Then he walked back across, taking his place behind the curtains again.

"You painted that?"

He turned, saw her standing there with a big smile on her face. Judith had makeup on, had her hair up, pulled back with a twist held in place by chopsticks. She wore a fancy evening gown, which was light teal with small floral patterns. It was lower cut so he could see just a sliver of her cleavage, which was milky smooth. Evan flinched, swallowed, almost speechless as he traced her up and down. She was astonishing.

"Uhh, yeah." He let out a nervous laugh. "I was only joking when I said I was gonna do stick figures in crayon."

Her dimples seeped through. Her almond eyes shined with the faintest sparkle.

He scanned his eyes across her face, at her eye liner and mascara, at her lip gloss. He shook his head, fighting back a smirk.

"Jude. You're beautiful."

She faced down to her feet as her cheeks reddened. He couldn't take his eyes off her. The hair, the dress. From her fingernails to her toenails. She was perfection embodied.

The two stepped close together behind the curtain as the stage darkened. Evan licked his lips, Judith bit her bottom lip.

"Shit. I'm nervous now . . ."

Evan leaned in, whispered. "Hey, hey. Don't be. You can do this."

"I mean, I just don't wear all this . . . I don't do this whole kind of . . ."

"Come on, Jude. You look amazing." Evan touched her on the arm, opened his eyes wide. "You go to practice like twice a week. You been doing this song, know it by heart."

He glanced at her collar bone then her chest, where her bosom raised from her heart beating.

"You know, I actually couldn't think of what to paint before too. I was blocked. But then I dug deep down, to what I really cared about, to what really matters. I painted from the heart."

The emcee finished welcoming everyone back, finished a few announcements. Then her name echoed through the speakers, followed by applause.

"You too, Jude. You play from the heart."

He smirked. She smiled.

Judith grabbed his hand, squeezed it, then walked onto the stage in the light. Evan watched her from behind. He could see the slender of the back of her neck. She took her place on the small bench, stretched her arms out and brought her fingertips to the keys. Their eyes locked from across the stage, before she faced forward again and committed to the act.

The sounds spewed from the instrument and floated through the air. One by one, the ascending notes and light chord was just a tad melancholic and somber. With the spotlight hovering over herself and the piano, an aura appeared around Judith in her dress. It was as if she was a comet passing through the upper layers of the atmosphere. As if the stars had aligned, and just the exact timing and placement brought Evan to witness this rare cosmic event. She had such focus and concentration with each press of her fingers. Her wrists danced along the keys, down the whites, dipping up into the black. He could feel his heart unraveling, feel it softening and shrinking, slipping onto the floor.

He was experiencing something magical. So beautiful, so flawless. Her hair, her face, her eyes. The slender of her shoulders. The elegance in her wrists. The light as it shined on her, shined all around her in almost a halo. Each sound, like they were plucking at his very soul, deep in his bones and in his teeth.

Against the backdrop of his painted canvas, it was almost otherworldly. Framed from where he stood, the lush green mountains and the cascading waterfall sprayed a misty haze that enveloped her. Every droplet of water was like early morning snowflakes that drifted. Every crag in the mountain was a historic land undiscovered, majestic. Like her song choice had been waiting to be part of that art piece. Like that painting had been waiting to accentuate her music, her being, in that specific moment in space and time.

Oh, no . . .

From the blurred black and white swirl back at the beginning, to that day in the arcade as they danced, until now, this very night, the tornado had caught up to him. In fact, he stood in the eye of it staring up at the sky. Walls of cloud spun amongst the darkness of the vortex. Continual flashes of bright lightning blazed. Diagonal raindrops fluttered and spread in an explosion almost like sprinklers going off.

Oh, no. No.

No. Please.

Do I . . . like her?

As the revelation he had been denying shot across his brain throughout his torso and limbs, from his eyes and his ears all the way to his fingers and toes, the music changed in tone. It became more upbeat, lighter yet somehow still daunting and dire, a vast spectrum of different notes and chords that built up in rapid succession.

Evan stepped backward, brought a hand to his forehead. He felt faint. He felt sick. The music took him on a journey through the memories and the moments that led him here. Every instance of electricity between the two of them. Every ambiguous grasp, every accidental graze. Each word in each sentence in each conversation. Each breath in between each pause. Just as the piece and the piano belonged together, complementing one another, now Evan too realized he longed for Judith. He stared again across the stage at her as she played. There was the light that shined onto and all around her, sure, but he also saw the light that shined inside of her. It was a light he had caught glimpses of before, but now could see all at once in one breathtaking sweep. He wanted it. He needed it. But it wasn't his, and it could never be.

PART THREE
STRIKE A MATCH

1

Jan 19th
12:02pm

Returning to school was like entering a different plane of existence, an alternate version of reality that had been uprooted when the first shots fired. No longer were there students running up and down the halls in a frenzy, in and out of each stairwell panicked. Now it was quiet, empty. Now it was still. Evan strafed the walls between the portables, making his way back towards D-building. He could see the monument behind the admin building, with the two light pillars of smoke still fuming. One of the auditorium doors hung crooked, one of the door panels lay shattered on the ground with an open hole. The image flashed through his mind—the arm poking through, the finger pulling the trigger. He could hear the cackling, the nasally voice—felt the masks staring at him, felt the hammer hover over and around his head.

There were charred markings on the walls. It wasn't smoking like over by the monument, instead just blackened streaks like charcoal powder. Evan reached one hand forward, touched at round holes dug into the concrete, and little cracks and chips crumbling.

Holy fuckin' shit . . .

Evan turned, stepped towards the nearest pillar and put a hand on it to lean on. He gazed down at the ground, breathed in one deep breath, swallowed a hard swallow. With the others in the auditorium, and then through the field, he was able to be brave, able to find some sort of inner strength. Now, however, all alone by himself, he felt afraid.

Boom.

Flinching in place, he glanced around trying to locate the source. This sounded different than any of the previous gunshots, different than the Molotov cocktail even.

He ducked low and jogged from D-building between the admin building and auditorium, making his way by the monument. He crouched behind it, waited, listened.

Boom.

There it was again, this time, just a little bit louder. Still distant, still soft, but close enough to be worried. Evan peeked his head out, checked to see if it was clear, ducked low again. He snuck over to the inner stairwell of E-building.

Nothing. In the courtyard, he saw a small group of kids, about three or four, running past the oval statue towards the long driveways. That was the first he'd seen anybody in a while. Evan stopped, faced the nearest pillar closing his eyes, pressed his fists against it in frustration, overwhelmed.

Jude, please . . .

Please be okay.

There was another boom, louder. And, with that, he forced himself to continue. From the bottom of the stairwell, he could hear pounding from the second floor. A pounding, then a crash, and then that loud boom again. Evan walked up, step by step, reaching one hand around to his back pocket hovering over the knife.

He peeped from the corner of the stairs into the hall, where he could see the puppet towards the farther end. The puppet lifted one foot up, kicked at the classroom door, lifted, kicked again. Evan saw the door past him already broken in. With one final slam, the door flung open. The puppet stepped into the door frame, pointed the shotgun, fired. He pumped the slide, ejected the cartridge.

Evan watched in terror, helpless. The puppet reached into his pocket, pulled out what appeared like a small PVC pipe with two end caps and a single fuse. In his other hand was a lighter flickering with a small flame. *Oh, no.* It sparked as he held it out to one side. With a slight tilt of his head, the puppet seemed almost robotic, then tossed it in the classroom. Evan could hear screams and scrambling, could hear desks being turned over . . .

Boom.

That was the sound he heard. It was more than just guns now, more than just fire and gasoline. Within the walls and the concrete, he could feel vibration from the explosion. He had to do something.

Crouching down, Evan took the knife out—swish, swish, flick, click—held it in his hand. He leaned towards the wall, peeked around the corner once more, breathed. About to hop the step and run, he was stopped in place as an arm grabbed him and shoved him sideways against the wall.

In front of him, face to face, for the first time in a very long time, his best friend raised a single finger over pouted lips, motioning with a slow nod. The two of them stared back at one another, eyes not blinking, bodies not moving, both quiet, both still.

2

9th Grade

CONTINUING TO STEP back and away, Evan brought the hand from his forehead to his mouth then down to his chest. He could feel the curtain brushing past his other arm. She was so astonishing, the music flowing from her fingertips so soothing and brilliant, but he could no longer remain there watching and listening. Evan stared one last time, deep, longing, at Judith again in the light on the stage. Her aura glowed in a halo around her, framed by the painted canvas in the background. The mountains and the waterfall, in dark green and vivid blue. The floral patterns on her dress, light teal. He turned, shut his eyes, hung his head low with his mouth open.

He walked behind the curtains, past ropes and ladders, through to the back corridors. The music followed him, haunting him, taunting, in amplified echoes that bounced off the walls ringing in his eardrums.

No . . . !

The walking turned to a hurried jog, then a full sprint. He turned, went into the rehearsal room with set pieces, paint and supplies, plastic tarp on the floor, other equipment.

Why? Why did this have to happen!?

Grabbing a paint brush, he spun around and flung it at the back wall. The smack was loud upon impact as well as the sound of it bouncing off the linoleum. He punched a nearby closet door then pounded a fist against one of the tabletops, kicking over a stool. Then he fell onto his knees, knocking into boxes, covering his face with both hands. He rolled onto his side on the plastic tarp letting out a guttural moan.

Please, God.

Don't let it be true.

When Evan opened his teary eyes, he rolled on his back, gazed up at the pipes along the ceiling. There was a spiderweb by the vent in the corner, a cone shape resembling a small tornado. He shook his head, felt the corners of his lips curl downward in a desperate attempt not to cry. He leaned his head back, letting out a slow breath.

From the moment he walked on campus, into that classroom, on that desk . . . To the minute they scooted close with the textbook turned sideways between them . . . Her pretty fingernail that glided along with each sentence. His eyes that wandered, that glanced up at hers. Working together, studying together. Her elegantly written notes with highlighter and underline. His tiny messy chicken-scratch. Walking down the hall, meeting in the computer lab. Sitting in the long chairs by the pool, sitting on the bed against the wall. Their paths intertwined and revolved towards one another like gravity. Like two magnets sliding together across a smooth marble countertop. But no, he just couldn't do that, no way, not to his best friend.

3

Jan 19th
12:05pm

Someone who once was so familiar, now was like a complete stranger. They had grown up together. They had laughed and played and shouted and joked. Evan remembered walking to the mall, remembered ditching martial arts classes at the Y. He remembered playing on the sand on the beach, remembered wrestling, remembered sharing blankets when they slept over. Staring at Derek now, he was so different than before. He had a hat on backwards, had little stubbles of facial hair growing under his nose and around his chin. He even had a gold chain on. With his hand holding him in place against the wall, both Derek and Evan gazed into the open air at the top of the stairs where they could hear pounding again.

"Derek . . ."

Evan watched as his eyes darted down to the knife in his hand, a strange look forming on his face. Perhaps he was surprised he still had it.

"We have *got* to get outta here." Derek shook his head. "The hell you thinking."

They kept their voices down as the pounding around the corner continued.

"Listen. We gotta stop that guy. He's got, like, a pipe bomb or something. People are gonna die."

"What?"

There was a loud crash. The door must have broken in. With that, Evan pushed Derek off and hopped into the hall from out the stairwell. Knife in hand, he ran towards the puppet. The puppet turned towards him, reached behind, taking the handgun from the back of his belt.

Bang, bang, bang.

Evan fell down sideways on the floor. Derek rushed past him straight down the hall.

The puppet paused, lowering the gun, stepped backward. Derek tackled into him and the two rotated clockwise slamming into the wall by the ledge.

Evan tapped his stomach, felt around but there wasn't anything there, felt the bottom of his shirt tail at three dry circular holes.

Damn, that was close . . .

He turned over on his side, saw Derek grapple with the puppet, struggling to contain the hand holding the gun. He staggered to his feet, ran down the hall.

Bang.

In front of him, the two bodies crashed down hard onto the floor. Both remained still. Evan felt cold air inside of him as he stepped closer, fighting back tears.

"Derek? Derek!"

Evan's eyes opened wide as Derek popped his head back up, hunched forward.

"Holy shit, man! Are you okay!?"

"I . . ."

A small puddle of blood formed. Derek slid to the side, got up to his feet.

Evan joined him, faced down to the ground where the puppet lay. His limbs were sprawled out, one hand by his head where the gun plopped down.

"You killed him."

Derek turned, started walking away. Evan followed, tried to grab him at the shoulder but missed as Derek shifted. He grazed a hand over the top of his hat, paced back and forth as Evan put the knife away.

"Hey. Should we take the—"

"No, leave it."

Derek closed his eyes, hung his arms low. He clenched his fists and shuddered.

"Do you wanna check—"

"No." Derek raised his voice. "Let's . . . Let's just get out of here."

Evan leaned in the open classroom. "Everybody, it's time to go. Now. Keep an eye out. Be careful."

The students faced up, unsure, even the teacher, then went out single file. They each walked past Evan and Derek in the hall towards the inner and outer stairwells. Some of them glanced down at the puppet as he lay on the ground in a puddle. When it was just Evan and Derek in the empty hall again, he stepped closer, put one hand on Derek's shoulder. It was something he hadn't done in what seemed like ages, like eons. In fact, they never spoke a single word, didn't even exchange a glance. Yet, somehow, after all this time, here they both were, back together once again.

4

9th Grade

AFTER LYING ON the tarp staring up at the ceiling, Evan wiped away the tears. He stood, sat on a stool in the dimly lit room. With his hands in his lap, he ruminated and dwelled. Then, he went outside, leaned on the wall at the top of the zigzagged ramp in back of the auditorium. He peered out into the darkness, into the pitch black night, as leaves in the trees rustled with the wind. Evan arched his head back, tilted up at the stars where he saw many triangles twinkling like from inside a kaleidoscope. He let out a long breath then buried his face in both palms. Around him, he could hear chatter beginning along with muffled footsteps as crowds gathered. The talent show must have ended. He didn't realize how much time passed.

He sniffled, wiped his face with the back of his wrist, stuck both hands in his pockets. Evan walked down the ramp and blended into the crowd. He turned right, headed towards the front entrance with the monument behind the admin building. He stood at just enough of an angle to see past the corner, but to remain hidden still.

There, he could see the group standing in a lopsided polygon without him. He could see Mark and Jared laughing. He could see Derek standing next to Judith, Max next to them.

Her parents must have been somewhere nearby because she kept a reasonable distance. Evan watched as Judith faced down to her feet and swayed, glanced around at the crowd with a slight furl in her brow. Again, he found himself astonished at her beauty.

Evan had seen her, had gazed at her many times before, but never like this. It was more than just with his eyes. It was deeper, more intense. He watched as she inclined her head, panned one way then the other. Just before their eyes met, Evan turned and walked the other way.

His hands deep in his pockets, he waded in the dark through the fields alone. It was quiet, cold, still. His feet crunched in the patches of grass, peeking up at the road where headlights drove past in a flurry. Clouds overhead now blocked out the stars, hid the triangles in the kaleidoscope lens, as it was about to drizzle. A tiny raindrop floated down and hit him on the side of his cheek. The tornado had officially manifested.

5

Jan 19th
12:07pm

The touch on the arm became a tug on the arm, as Evan turned Derek around. When the two looked each other in the eye, something clicked. Sure, maybe they had a falling out. Maybe all around them, the world had changed. Maybe, even in that moment, it was as if tectonic plates of time had shifted, causing all living things to lose traction. Evan wanted to wrap his arm around Derek, wanted to hug him, but just couldn't. He kept one hand on his shoulder, each of them standing together in silence, staring at one another, staring at the ground, staring out over the ledge of the second floor.

"Y-you okay, Der?" Evan hadn't said that, either: Der. It was kind of a funny thing to have uttered, after such a long time.

He nodded back, swallowed. Derek touched at Evan's stomach, felt the three holes in his shirt tail where the bullets just missed his torso.

"Listen. I gotta find Jude."

There it was. The elephant in the room, er, hall. Derek's

somber, sullen look turned to a slight glare, as he raised his eyes up.

Evan could feel Derek tighten up, shake as he breathed, facing him.

"Mark and Jared. Max."

Derek arched his head back with a long sigh. "You . . . You better find her."

Evan half-smirked. "I will."

"Okay. I guess I'll see if I can find Mark, Jared. Can you look for Max?"

He licked his lips, swallowed with a slight nod.

"I think Mark and Jared might be in N-building, around there, maybe H-building. I'm not too sure. I gotta think where Jude is. I have no idea about Max."

"Evan . . ." Derek shook his head.

"Yeah, Der?"

"You know, we might not find them, they could be—"

"Hey. No, no. Don't think that." Evan pulled his hand away, stepped back. "They're fine. Everybody's okay. Maybe they already got off campus."

"I guess, try to look, but don't linger. We'll meet on the fields in like twenty minutes. Thirty, tops." Derek exhaled, swallowed. "If the other's not there, just take off. It's way too dangerous."

There was silence between the two old friends, the situation unfolding around them. It was all so much for each of them to take in. Derek let out a sigh, glanced up at Evan once more, then turned to walk to the inner stairwell. As he stood there watching him leave, Evan felt as if the ceiling above was beginning to crumble. An aching in his chest stirred, and a pulsing tingle surged throughout his limbs.

"Hey, Der!"

Derek turned, listened.

"Just. Be careful, okay?"

"Of course. La-di-freaking-dah."

6

9th Grade

It was a long weekend followed by a long Monday. Evan tried to distract himself but it was all he could think about, the one thing on his mind. What should he do? Realizing his feelings for Judith was a bitter curse, total agony. Food had lost its taste. TV shows lost all humor and excitement. He laid in bed or on the couch, stayed inside at home. Then, through each of his classes the first day back, he dazed out the window with a cheek in his palm. It was cloudy out with scattered showers, dark, gloomy and gray, just like he felt inside. He sketched but only dismal and morbid things. A raging fire, with every flicker of ash and cinder. A skull and crossbones. A man jumping from a building, jumping off of a cliff, which felt especially cathartic.

I . . . I just don't know.

Sigh . . .

He avoided the cafeteria, and the spot by the pillars between admin and E-building where the group sometimes gathered. Instead, he found himself in his old hiding spot in the library. Like he was back at Roosevelt.

Evan walked up each carpeted stair, dragging his palm

on the rail, gazing through the glass panel beneath it. On the second floor, he went past each slanted row of shelves to a far cubicle tucked away in the corner with no one else around. He plopped his backpack on the floor, opened his composition book, took out his mechanical pencil. The walls of the cubicle were like a prison cell, a literal box he felt trapped in. With the blank page in front of him, he sat there and stared.

After school, Evan took the long way home to avoid the guys. Instead of passing by the flagpole where they often gathered, he went around the outside of buildings D through A, then down the long driveways off campus. He just wasn't ready to see them, didn't know what to say or do, couldn't bear to see her face. Not to mention, if she was going to be holding hands with, going to be kissing . . . you-know-who. It felt as if an entire boulder pressed onto him, and he buckled under the weight of it, gasping for air, muscles shaking from fatigue. Hands in his pockets, backpack over one shoulder, he glanced up at the branches in the trees. Against the gray sky, they seemed almost lifeless.

The bell already rang so he knew he was late. Down the walkway from C-building, Evan dragged his feet. Nobody else was around in the hallway, all the other kids in class, sitting in their assigned seats taking out chapter questions and handing them forward. He stopped in place, both hands tugging on the straps of his backpack, shifting his weight between his toes and his heels rocking back and forth. He stared at the door, saw her face flash through his mind: her almond eyes, her dimples, her hand tucking her hair behind her left ear. Evan shook his head, turned and started walking away.

He just couldn't go in there. He couldn't sit on that desk,

scoot close, with the textbook turned sideways. Her pretty fingernail would mock him. If he caught a whiff of her perfume, he might lose it. Evan continued, crossed through the pillars into the courtyard. He passed by the flagpole with the rock wall around it then the oval medium with the bronze statue. From the long driveways, he made his way to the bus stop and plopped down. That was the first time he ever ditched class. The occasional pep rally or spirit assembly, maybe, but never actual class.

Over by A-building, a couple security guards were talking. It was hard to tell if they saw him or if they were glancing his way, but he just ignored it. If he had to, he could always bolt across to the shopping center. He had a feeling, though, they would leave him alone. Not like he was smoking cigarettes or anything, like some of the other kids. Evan leaned forward with his elbows on his knees planting his face in both palms. What was he going to do? One day, maybe two days, he could keep this up, avoid her, avoid most of the group, but at some time he would have to face them—face *her*—and deal with everything repressed inside.

Watching the second hand glide around the face, Evan stared into the clock from his desk. He slouched, cheek leaning against a lazy fist. Next to him, Jared already gathered his things, waiting to escape. Evan felt a slight nudge then closed his composition book, put his mechanical pencil away, standing with the others as the bell sounded. In the crowd, the two followed along out into the hall then turned the corner down the walkway to admin. Both were silent, both awkward. Evan followed, almost going through the motions in his body where his mind wasn't present. As they passed through the stairwell down to the first floor where the vending machines were, Evan became nervous. His palms were sweaty, knees weak. His arms were heavy.

"Okay, lemme just go get my soda."

Evan watched as Jared walked to the machine. He panned around at all the kids passing by, happy and carefree. A part of him envied them. Another loathed them.

"So . . . What's going on, E? None of us have seen you since, like, last Friday." Jared twisted the cap, let out the hissy fizz. "Someone said you ditched class?"

He didn't respond right away.

"Let's, uh, go somewhere else first. Okay? We can't exactly talk here."

"A'ight. Sure, man."

They went out the back of admin towards the portables. Evan faced down at his feet as he walked. Next to him, Jared lifted the bottle and took a nice long chug, wiping his mouth.

"I . . . I don't even know what to say, Jar. It's too much to even think."

"Hmm."

On the outskirts of the fields, they sat down on the bleachers in the shade. Jared sat back with his bottle at his side. Evan leaned forward, rested folded arms on both his knees. Packs of students made their way across the baseball diamond, through the track and football field like herds of animals migrating.

Evan lifted his head, turned towards Jared, looked him in the eye. Jared nodded, stared back.

"It's Jude."

He was quiet, straightened up.

"I don't know what happened, but I think I . . . I think I like her."

"Oh . . . Shit . . ."

Jared crossed his arms, dazed off in the distance.

"Yeah. I mean, we always did get along and everything, in Chemistry."

"Chemistry!?" Jared's eyes widened.

Evan half-smirked. "Yeah."

"I didn't even know you were in Chem. Aw, crap. When did this happen?"

"I guess, well, I realized last Friday."

"The talent show . . ."

"Yeah. Like, I mean, not like I planned it. Obviously. It's just, she looked so . . . And I guess we'd been getting closer and closer."

Jared brought the soda to his mouth but just hovered, until he put it back down shaking his head.

"Can't believe I never noticed."

Evan turned, furled his brow.

"Back at the arcade, I think. You knew her. Right?" Jared turned as Evan nodded, blinked. "And then you guys danced. And then she kicked your ass, bad."

"Hey. She didn't kick my ass."

Evan smirked. Jared chuckled.

"Nah, but seriously. What you gonna do?"

"I . . . I don't know." Evan leaned forward again. "Guess that's the problem."

"Can you just forget about it?"

"It's hard, man. Like, just looking at her, just hearing her voice. And then if she's gonna have his arm around and be all kissing him and stuff. God, even thinking . . ."

He shook his head, let out a long and heavy sigh.

"That's gotta suck." Jared lifted one hand from crossed arms, rubbed at his chin. "Maybe try talking to them?"

"Nah. No way. What would I even say? I don't know about that." Evan clasped his palms together, interlaced his fingers.

"I guess so, huh."

"If I don't say anything, I suffer inside. If I say something or do something then I'm an asshole."

"Pretty much lose-lose for you."

"And, confirming she doesn't feel the same way, that'll be even worse, right? Maybe it's just best not to know." Evan straightened up, arched his head back with a sigh.

"Then again, I mean, you do kind of need to know. Or, hell, she prolly needs to know too."

"Ah, I'm not so sure . . . Just . . ."

There was silence as the clouds churned in the sky, a gradient of silver and gray. It became still as the wind died down. Evan faced ahead, saw translucent versions of himself and Judith running through the field holding hands, laughing, rolling in the grass.

"I do got this one idea."

Beneath the blankets, lying on his stomach in the prone position, Evan stared at the composition book on his pillow. In his fingers, he twirled the mechanical pencil, nibbled on the eraser end. There was a small flashlight on its side that illuminated the blank page and the faint blue lines. The bed jiggled from the top bunk as his little brother adjusted in his sleep. He wondered if he was doing the right thing, wondered how she was going to react, if at all. Then again, this was his chance. It was the one way to say what needed to be said, to do what needed to be done. Her face, her voice, these flashed through his mind in the darkness where his imagination drew swooshing circles and squiggly lines, swirling around different shades of color.

The problem wasn't having nothing to say, but rather, having too much. Evan wanted to tell Judith every little speckle of emotion she sparked in him—from her eyes to her hair to her fingernails, her dimples, how they mesmerized and beckoned him so—but didn't want to overwhelm her with this flood of flowery words. Evan wanted to list off every seemingly insignificant event that led to this discovery, but again, it would go on for pages and pages and he didn't want to ramble or rant. He just needed to tell her the truth: how he felt, the dilemma, and what he was going to do. It took a long time mulling and wondering, worrying, all weekend until late that night, and it was just time to pull the trigger. It was the best conclusion he could come up with. He held the pencil in his hand, pressed the tip to the paper.

Dear Jude,

7

Jan 19th
12:10pm

LEANING INTO THE open doorway, gazing in the empty classroom, Evan felt his heart drop. There was nothing. There was nobody. It was already the third classroom he checked. His skin was damp from sweat, his hair messy from running. Evan kicked at the frame of the door, touched his forehead against the wood paneling, letting out a subdued shout. He turned around, forced himself to continue. *Think, think* . . . With the back of his hand, he wiped at his forehead with the cuff of his sleeve. Now, he was in B-building where she had Economics. He already checked D-building where she would've had Calculus II, and he already checked lower H-building where she had Japanese. Evan wasn't sure what other classes she might be taking. Those were the few he could remember.

Time was already running out, not to mention Derek set a kind of time limit. With each attempt, Evan grew more and more desperate. He walked back out into the courtyard, glanced up at the roof of admin, where the first silhouetted dark figure stood with a rifle aimed. His mind almost entertained the tragic possibility of a worst-case outcome but he stopped himself, forced himself not to.

No. No, where else?

Come on. I've got to find her.

And then the thought popped in his head—maybe it wasn't a "regular" class in upper campus but a different type of class, like in the gym, or maybe one of the portables, somewhere in lower campus. Whenever he thought of her, he always associated her with higher level academic courses, but she took other courses just like everyone else.

Of all the different options, his intuition nudged him towards the gym. That's where she would be, somehow he just knew it. Deep in his psyche, deep in his soul, he could feel her presence that direction.

8

9th Grade

When he saw her face, Evan was overcome with a spectrum of various emotions: bittersweet, mixed smitten and anxiousness. In his back pocket, the letter remained hidden and folded. Each step towards her seemed to take longer than it should have. As he passed the podium, walked towards the third column, fourth row, Judith watched him almost unblinking. It was hard to determine what emotion she herself might have felt, perhaps mixed as well. Her brows were narrowed, yet her eyes remained soft. Her lips thinned, her face lifted and glowed with each slow step closer. She was back in her normal everyday wear but still appeared so beautiful. Evan cleared his throat, sat down in the chair.

Judith tapped him on the shoulder. "Where were you? I tried searching, tried calling . . ."

He turned back, faced her, gazed straight into her almond eyes that now were somber.

"I was worried . . ."

No longer could he avoid her. No longer could he continue to hide the truth.

"Uh, I know. I'm sorry." Evan licked his lips, leaned

closer in to speak in a whisper. "We'll talk after class, okay? I'll explain everything."

The teacher began speaking, instructed them to turn to the next chapter. With that, they both scooted their desks close. It was how it all began—his back turned, their heads tilted in, her pretty fingernail following each word in the sentence. He glanced up at her eyes as she read along. The way she was engrossed in it, almost in a trance, was still so fascinating to him. A light puff of her perfume wafted. He stared at her hair, at the curve in her cheek.

It was the shorter day in the middle of the week with all their classes, so it went by quick. With the sound of the bell, they each stood and walked through the door and into the hall together. Evan let her pass first, Judith adjusted her books in front of her. She stood over by one of the pillars, waited for him to follow. At first, neither spoke, just turned to the other in silence. He could see the smooth skin of her legs, from her ankles to her knees and thighs. He could see the softness of her neck as well as the delicate angles of her collar bone. Her lips were pouted, and her hair fell just around her face.

Evan shook his head. All the intrusive thoughts—he wanted to kiss her, wanted to hold her in his arms. It was hard enough standing there, let alone talk.

"What's wrong? Are you okay?"

She reached one hand forward, brushed the bangs out of his eyes. In that very brief moment, his entire body flooded with an electrical charge. No longer were they two far corners of a triangle but one straight line. It was like the clouds brightened, opened up. Like even the force of gravity lessened and let them fly. Just the two of them, while the rest of the school continued.

"Jude, I . . ." He swallowed as she drew her hand back.

The electricity died and he was left feeling hollow. The line was broken. It was back to cloudy and gray, back to standing on concrete with the crowd passing by.

He reached back and took the letter in his hand, held it out to her. She stared at it. It was torn from his composition book, sure, but it was also torn from the heart in his very chest. After some hesitation, she took it between her fingertips and started to unfold it as he left. He knew she wanted to ask, wanted to say more, but he just couldn't stay there. Like the stage behind the curtain in the auditorium the other night, with her music, her aura, her being, it was all too much. He needed to get out of there.

Evan could feel her eyes watching him from behind as he walked away. Judith stood there by the pillar, his open letter in her hand. A part of him wanted to turn back around, wanted to stay, but he also didn't want her to be late for her class.

Facing down into the stairwell, resting folded arms on both knees, Evan sat on the top step. It was cool out, with the clouds full and ready to pour. He was now in hiding, since he told her every last detail. In his tiny messy chicken-scratch, he confessed that something happened the night of the talent show. Something clicked. There was always a little spark between them, maybe, but it grew and became a raging fire he could no longer contain. In fact, he admitted, he liked her. Of course, there wasn't anything he could do about that. He was stuck. The best course of action, he decided, was to leave . . . Leave the group. Leave the school perhaps, leave her class at least. Leave, so that everyone could be happy and could be together, so that everything could go on like normal as it should.

Evan tilted his head, rested it sideways on his arms. He felt warm tears gather in the corners of his eyes, but fought them back. He felt a shuddering in his chest, at his shoulder blades, but struggled not to cry. Shutting his eyes, he just breathed in and out.

I shouldn't have come here.

It would have been best if I never met her.

None of this would have happened . . . None of this should *have happened, it's all a mistake.*

I wish I could go back in time.

All the thoughts bombarded his subconscious, one by one, like hot needles. The teardrops rolled from his eyelids down his cheeks past his lips that began to curl. There was a soft jerking in his torso as he gasped in short spurts of breath, sobbing.

He lifted his head up, wiped his face, then leaned against the wall. Staring into the cold hard bricks on the painted walls, the sanded strips along each step, Evan felt as if he was no longer part of the school, no longer part of this world.

Echoing off the walls, he could hear kids in the courtyard talking and laughing. Yet, here he was, all alone, in deep thought, lost, in a dark place. It was Roosevelt all over again but worse.

That was when he felt a light tap from behind, to which he turned. And there she was.

"I found you."

9

Jan 19th
12:13pm

Walking from pillar to pillar, down the walkway behind the cafeteria to the gymnasium, Evan checked his surroundings. Again, he could see there were round holes dug in the concrete as well as blackened streaks. It was quiet, just the occasional gunshot somewhere on the other side of campus. The gym grew in his sight and he broke into a jog towards the front doors. As he neared, he could tell something was wrong. The handles were chained together, with a big lock hanging down in the middle. He rattled these in his hands, yanked them, but it wouldn't budge. From the other side, he could hear a large group of students. They were all shouting and crying out.

Jude . . .

At first, he just stood there, not sure what to do. He stepped closer, pounded his palm on the door, shouting through to the inside. He leaned an ear against it to listen.

"Hey! Hello?"

Keeping his ear close to the panel of the door, he pounded again, this time harder, with a closed fist, shouting even louder.

"Hello!? Can anybody hear me?"

There was slamming against the door, like in a riotous frenzy. Kicking at the bottom, hard slaps all over the sides and middle, enough to cause him to flinch as the doors pressed outward toward him. He could hear voices inside: yelling, screaming, scattered cries and pleas.

The doors opened just enough to squeeze a tiny crack between the space, in which Evan could see eyes and mouths and fingers about to poke through. He stepped backward again, shaking his head with a sharp gasp. It was a strange sight, the kind from a half-forgotten nightmare.

10

9th Grade

SITTING DOWN NEXT to him on the top stair, her eyes locked onto his. Evan felt her arm rub against his as Judith scooted closer. The two turned, gazed into the stairwell, at each step and at the landing between. It was already midway through recess, most of the other kids either eating lunch or hanging out. Apart from the school, separated from the rest of the world, the two sat together side by side. He didn't say anything, just let out a sigh and hung his head low. She inclined her head, rested it on his shoulder. As he breathed, he could smell her perfume. Leaning back toward her, he smelled her hair, then faced forward again. Judith nuzzled her face, which felt warm, into his upper arm. Evan heard a soft sniffle as she lifted herself up and turned to him.

"I read it, Evan. Every word."

He swallowed. "I . . . I'm so sorry. I didn't know how else to tell you, I didn't know what else to do."

She turned away, wiped a hand on her face.

"It was the best I could do."

"You're really going to leave? School? Class? You're really going to leave . . . me?" Judith's eyes were red, moist.

Evan wrapped an arm around her, pulled her close.

Although he hadn't decided, he considered transferring over to Marine Biology like he was supposed to be or maybe getting a new geographic exception form or canceling the current.

"I have to, Jude. There's no other way."

His arm on her shoulders felt right, although he knew it was wrong. He felt a small flutter in his chest. They sat together like that for a few seconds, then Evan pulled his arm away and Judith raised her head back up.

"I . . . It's just too hard. I mean, I have to go away. At least for a little while, something. Get my head wrapped around things. Maybe the day will come when these feelings fade, and then I can come back?"

"You know nobody wants you to leave. I don't want you to leave." Her voice started to crack. "You don't have to do this. You shouldn't."

"Yeah. I don't want to leave, either, but it's the right thing to do."

There was silence again. And then it sounded like it was beginning to rain. Above, they heard the light pitter-patter grow in momentum from the raindrops falling. It sounded almost like a leaky faucet.

"Does anyone else know?"

"No. I read your letter in third and fourth period, and the minute the bell rang, I just came looking for you." Judith turned, looked him in the eye.

Evan half-smirked. "How'd you even find me?"

"I know you already." She smiled, sad sparkles in her almond eyes. "You told me once how you used to spend lunch at your old school."

He nodded, a *hmm* sound leaking through thinned lips.

"So I went to the library, figured you might be drawing or something, then just made my way from there. It took a while but, well, here we are."

The light tapping on the roof and walls grew to a heavy downpour, and it grew colder.

As she began to shiver and rub at her arms, he wrapped his arm around her again.

"Sorry you had to come looking. But thank you for finding me. It's all gonna be okay. Did you eat?"

"No, I'm not hungry."

She nestled her cheek on his shoulder.

"I don't want you to go . . ."

"I know. I'm sorry, Jude." He swallowed, squeezed her tight pulling her in close. "But I don't have a choice. There just isn't anything left for me here."

As he held her, she began to shudder beneath his arm. He could hear sniffling and it felt warm and wet through the fabric in his shirt where she nuzzled her face.

"Hey, hey . . ." Evan touched his chin to the top of her head. "Don't cry. It's okay, really."

The sniffle turned to a sob. He rubbed his hand over her arm, her shoulder, leaned the line of his jaw into her hair trying to console her.

Man. I'm such a jerk.

I didn't know she would be this upset.

Judith calmed down, forced steady breaths with the occasional sharp sniff. She lifted her head, faced him as he stared ahead into the stairwell.

"Evan . . . What if . . ."

He turned, watched her face that was still beautiful even though she was sad.

"What if I want to be with you too?"

11

Jan 19th
12:15pm

There were more gunshots in the distance, but Evan ignored them. He made his way around the gym towards the fields. On the wall outside the locker room, he found an axe in a metal box with a glass cover. Smashing it with his elbow, he reached in and pulled it out, feeling the weight of it, then began jogging back. To the side, there was a garbage can full of leaves and twigs next to a rake, a broom and a few other items. A golf cart was toppled over, the fender smashed. Evan squinted, inclined his head to one side, glanced around. By the far corner of the tennis courts nearby, there was a small shed that he walked towards.

It was one of those things he knew was always there but never noticed or thought of. The door left ajar, he pulled it open and peeped inside. A coiled length of hose hung from a hook on the side wall. There were boots in the corner, goggles on a shelf. In the back, he could see a rusty manual lawn mower.

Huh. This might work.

Evan lifted a piece of cloth, from which protruded a plastic handle. It was a long hedge trimmers. In one hand, he took it and held it at his side. With the axe and the hedge trimmers, one from each arm, he felt like he was entering some medieval battle.

Returning to the front doors of the gym, he weighed the two, threw the axe into the grass. Evan stepped forward with the hedge trimmers, opening each handle and fitting the shears around a link in the chain. He squeezed but it wouldn't move. It just made the tiniest indentation. Again, he squeezed, this time putting all his weight and might into it.

"Damn it!!! Come on!"

In frustration, he threw the hedge trimmers on the concrete. He stepped back towards the grass, picked up the axe and held it in both hands. He breathed, felt beads of sweat already forming on his skin.

Lifting the axe high, the image of the hammer in the jester's hand popped in his head. Evan felt fear take over, linger. *What if . . .* No. He shook the idea away, gripped the axe tight then swung down, swung again and again. The blade of the axe knocked the links of the chain into the panel of the door, making hard oval indentations. Other than a few light chinks, they remained intact.

"Jude! Jude!!!"

Finding himself in a rage, almost in a fugue state, he began to smash the axe against the chains.

"JUDE!!!"

He bent down, leaned closer. Against the metallic housing of the door handles, one of the links in the chain almost snapped open. That was the key: metal on metal.

Hang on, Jude.

I'm coming.

Again, he lifted the axe, panting already, the muscles in his arms shaking from fatigue in small tremors. Staring into the door handles, at the chains in place, at the one link almost broken open, he gripped the handle again and swung it down putting all of his force into it.

12

9th Grade

PEERING BACK AT her, mouth agape, eyes wide, Evan was in disbelief of what he just heard. All the wondering and worrying, thinking how to deal with the situation, he hadn't even thought about if she might feel the same way. He instead focused on how to respect his best friend, what the right thing to do was, keeping the group intact. Now, though, as she uttered those impossible words and faced him with soft and somber eyes, her lips pouted beckoning him like candy, Evan was put in another dilemma altogether. It wasn't that he had feelings for a girl he couldn't be with, but that they had feelings for each other.

"But . . ." Evan swallowed, cleared his throat.

Judith shook her head. "I know."

They could hear the rain coming down hard, felt it on the roof and on the walls. The eye of the tornado passed, and they were well into the height of its ferocity.

"If you wanna be with me, and I wanna be with you . . ."

His other arm moved, their hands finding one another and interlacing at the fingers. With his arm wrapped around her shoulders, holding hands now, sitting atop the top stair, the two corners of the triangle became one. They weren't two far corners, weren't two points separated by a straight line, but rather a single point—two small circles overlapped, like a Venn diagram.

"I've struggled with this too."

He wanted to lean in and kiss her right then, but held back. She lifted his hand, pecked it with her soft lips, gazing into the empty stairwell.

His eyes traced her face, from her brows to the bridge of her nose, her bangs, her chin.

"Oh, man . . ."

"What do we do now?"

Evan shook his head. "This is gonna be rough. It's going to kill him. I mean, it could break up our entire group."

"Like you, I just couldn't hold it in anymore. Not like I wanted this. It's how I feel."

"I know that." Evan licked his lips. "I mean, it's not like this kinda thing happens every day."

Judith leaned her head again, this time closer, against his cheek and his neck. "So, what should we do?"

"We need time to think. Let's, uh, meet after school." Evan turned his head in towards hers, felt her hair rustle against his collar bone. "Can you meet me?"

She nodded, squeezed his hand.

"Okay, how about by the goal post. Ocean side, out on the football field. Right after class, okay?"

He felt her breathe in and out, dazed at her eyes that were now closed.

"Meet me, all right? Come find me. And we'll figure out a way we can be together."

13

Jan 19th
12:19pm

THE FIRST HIT cut the chain, but didn't break it. Evan lifted the axe right back up and swung again. With each smash down, he hit the axe harder and harder into the wrapped chains. After a good couple of solid hits, the banging of metal on metal, one of the links snapped. He reached forward and began undoing the chains with one hand. The clinking of the metal rattled in his ear as he pulled. About to reach for the handles and yank them open, the doors burst open at him, and out came a flood of students and faculty. There were a couple of janitors as well, even a security guard—all just as confused and terrified as everyone else. It was as if he was thrust onto the median on the freeway with cars and trucks blazing past. All around him surged a relentless mob, like a mosh pit at a rock concert. The doors flung open and banged in place on their hinges.

Evan was bumped into and rammed, close to losing his balance and falling to the ground. It would be hell if he were knocked down and trampled. He pivoted on his feet, squeezed through the passing bodies, pushing forward, glancing at each face that rushed past.

"Jude!? Jude???"

Somebody knocked him sideways, then someone else knocked him backward. His foot rolled on his ankle and he almost tripped but managed to catch himself.

As the crowd began to thin, he entered the inside of the gymnasium where there was a basketball court between two sets of bleachers. It could either be a basketball court or a volleyball court. Depending on the layout and nets, it was interchangeable.

Evan walked to the free throw line, spun around, searching. He continued to move, with a side step, backwards, until he was at the top of the key.

On the back wall, behind the backboard written in red spray paint that dripped, he saw ominous words sprawled.

DOWN WITH SCHOOL

BURN IT DOWN

The words were sprawled over the image of the school's mascot on the back wall: the head of an eagle from a side view, with its determined bold eye and prominent beak.

He brought a loose fist over his mouth, stepped away with a sporadic blink. That was when he felt a light tap on the small of his back and turned, eyes still half on the words on the back wall.

"That was it. The one good pic." It was Michelle's voice, soft, almost a whisper. "I finally got what I'd been looking for."

"Oh, God. I thought you . . ."

When he saw his friend, her face was different than before. She was so dead set on capturing the event on film, desperately eager, almost excited. But now, she wore a look of exhaustion and trauma, seemed more like a journalist on the front lines of war than a photographer for the school paper.

"Are you okay?"

She shook her head, with a blank stare.

"I should've got off campus like you said. There was another shooter, and . . ."

Her voice trailed off, cracked.

"What happened, Michelle?"

"They shot at us, chased us in this direction. It was a bigger gun, like the kind the military uses. Evan, there was so many . . . that didn't . . ." Michelle shook her head again, stared ahead. "When we got inside, there was already this huge crowd. And then they locked us in."

"Yeah, I saw the chains."

It was just the two of them left in the gym. They stood between the center circle and the sideline.

"Did you f-find her?" She was afraid to ask.

"Not yet." Evan hung his head with a sigh, threw his arms out to the side, axe in hand still. "I can't think of where else she might be. I mean, unless—"

He stopped himself mid-sentence, as the thought entered his mind, then faced Michelle.

"Evan?"

"I've gotta go."

"Hey. Wait, wait . . ." She called out as he turned away, grabbed him at the arm. "You find her, okay, then just get out. Get off campus."

Both exchanged a look, as if it might be the last time they ever spoke. Each had sadness in their eyes, had a knowledge most people would never gain. He nodded then broke into a jog back towards the front doors that hung wide open.

14

9th Grade

Most kids walked through the fields from the baseball diamond side, so Evan went the opposite way to the field behind the gym. He could see Judith standing by the goal post, waiting for him. When he reached her, they hugged, and she leaned on him with her head on his chest. From there, they watched as the droves of students made their way through lower campus back home. Both their hands found one another and interlinked, lacing through each finger and dangling between their bodies. He wondered if anyone could see them and what the group might be doing right now, might be thinking. Tracing her face, her eyes and her lips, he again wanted to kiss her but resisted the urge.

"I was gonna say we could sit on the grass, but it looks like it's still wet."

Judith glanced up at him. "Bleachers?"

"Nah, too many people . . ."

He held her hand, led her further towards the side of the field where there was a small stream running from the canal. By a big tree, in front of the flowing water, there was a line of large rocks. Evan led her to a rounded flatter one, let her sit down first.

"Such a gentleman." Judith's dimples peeked through her wide smile as she sat down and scooted. "Here, come sit by me."

"I don't know. 'Gentleman' might be the wrong word. I mean, I like my best friend's girlfriend."

It was a terrible joke, but it was also the truth.

She sighed, leaned her head on his shoulder. "Yeah, I feel so awful. I'm, like, the worst."

"Hey, I feel bad too. It's not like either of us *wanted* this to happen. We're not just out to hurt people's feelings or anything. Again, I mean, should we be doing this? Maybe it's not too late to—"

"But it is. I know how you feel, Evan, and you know how I feel, and you know that I know that you know." She laughed at the absurdity of her wording. "How could we even pretend, if we both know that? We would just be lying to ourselves, lying to him too. Lying to everybody."

He arched his head back, faced up at the sky with its darkened clouds. "Damn, why's this so hard . . ."

"I don't want to hurt him."

"Of course not. Me neither."

"You know, maybe the point is, are we really choosing to be together? And, is it worth that much, all that we'll be willing to lose?"

Evan leaned his cheek against the top of her head, grazed it as he inhaled the scent of her hair.

"I think so. I like you . . . It sucks to admit, because it's going to come at such a cost, but I do. To the point it makes me sick. To the point I can't eat, I can't think."

He licked his lips, stared in the fields as she wrapped an arm around his waist.

"And, if you feel the same, it's kinda messed up, but we can't just walk away from that. I don't wanna live my life knowing I let someone go that was so special."

"Then we'll be together."

"Man, we still gotta tell him, though. Tell everybody. It's not gonna be fun or easy."

He could feel her chest fill and rise, as she took a deep breath in.

"I know. But we have to."

&

It had been almost an entire week since he talked to or hung out with the guys, except for Jared that one day. As Evan walked towards the flagpole, he could see them standing and talking amongst themselves. Max stood with arms crossed, facing down to the ground. Jared leaned his head back chugging his soda. Mark turned to Evan, smiled a big smile with squinty eyes. Each step closer seemed to grow heavier, perhaps from guilt. The flag waved with just the slightest hint of wind. It was bleak against the gray sky. They all clapped palms and bumped fists and did their bro hugs as he joined in. It felt good to be amongst them again, although he had terrible news he was very reluctant to share.

"Ev-an! Where you been?" Mark shoved him at the shoulder. "Tweak your wrist from jerking too hard?"

He smirked at Mark's line, as Jared chuckled and Max laughed a hyena laugh. It was a good one.

"'Sup." Max had his usual awkward smile.

"I don't see Derek or Judy . . ." Jared glanced at Evan with the corner of his eye.

Max chimed in. "I think they were by the tennis courts, talking or something."

Evan cleared his throat, shuffled on his two feet. "Yeah, about that, uh, I gotta tell you guys something . . ."

The tone between them was always upbeat or downright inappropriate, but then, in that moment, they all grew serious, almost as if they already knew.

"I talked to Jar a little bit about it, but I . . . I like Jude."

Mark's jaw dropped. "What!?"

"Oh, shit." Max nodded, brow furled.

"Yeah. I know." Evan faced downward, twisted the ball of his foot into the grass. "I tried to ignore it. I tried to just walk away. I wrote her a letter, told her I was gonna leave, but then she came and found me."

"Okay, and?" Mark's voice was curious, expectant, annoyed. "What happened!"

He took a deep breath, exhaled out through pursed lips trying to maintain his composure. "Well, it turns out she likes me too."

"Oh. My. God." Mark slapped a hand to his forehead, paced in a circle around himself. "What in the hell, man!?"

"You should've seen him Tuesday, he was a wreck. This is all crazy, yes, but it's not—" Jared tried to interject but got cut off.

"Still! Frick, man, you can't just go doing that!"

"Okay, hold on." Max stepped between the two of them with arms outstretched.

Evan bit down on his lower lip, turned to Max. "You said you saw them by the tennis courts?"

Max folded his arms tight, nodded.

"Then we better head there. I . . . I gotta make sure she's all right."

Shaking his head, Mark hyperventilated. "And what was this great advice you told him, huh?"

Jared stared straight ahead as they walked. "I just said he had to tell her the truth."

"The truth???" Mark almost hopped up off the ground. "Oh, no. No, no, no. Hell no. You shove that down. You forget all about it."

"Well, I tried." Evan swallowed. "Believe me, if there was any other way . . ."

He stopped, turned back, looked Mark in his eye.

"You know I wouldn't screw over my best friend if it wasn't something real. I'm throwing my entire life away here. My world, my reputation. I can't help it. Okay? I'm sorry."

Evan glanced first at Max, then faced Jared. "I'm sorry, all of you. Really."

Mark calmed a little, jaw still dropped. "This is gonna be bad."

The clouds above were dark, loomed heavy and full with moisture, ready to pour down. Evan led them through admin, then between the auditorium and the cafe. Mark shook his head in disbelief still. Max was quiet.

"So, that's why you disappeared . . ."

Jared turned to Mark, nodded, sipped.

In front, Evan saw Judith standing with Derek by the fence along the tennis court. He raised his arm up, stopped the group in place as they stood beneath the trees.

"What do we do?"

Evan glanced at Max. "Just wait, I guess. Let 'em say what they need to say."

From that angle, they watched the back of Derek's head and his arms moving as he spoke. Judith's eyes were narrowed, worried, sad, as she peeped down blinking.

"I don't know. Is this really such a good idea?" Mark rested his hands on the back of his hips.

Jared leaned on the nearest tree. "Like Evan said, maybe it's best we're here."

"Yeah, I wanna make sure she's okay. I've gotta be here just in case—"

He didn't finish his sentence. He could see she was crying now, and with that, all semblance of thought and rationale left his mind and his body. Evan walked towards them as if he was sleepwalking or hypnotized. Unbeknownst to him, both his fists were clenched at his sides. Jared and Max followed, then Mark.

"Ah, shit, here we go . . ."

"Evan, wait."

He stared at the two of them, Judith crying, Derek shooting out his arms, grabbing her at the shoulders. Then he shook her, the movement hard enough it messed up her bangs. She began to sob more, facing down and away. Her cheeks were wet with streams running down to her chin.

From behind, Evan shoved Derek to the side of the fence.

"Hey! Don't you *ever* touch her!!!"

Evan shoved him, shoved him again. With each push, the metal links rattled. He could hear it scrape against the concrete at jagged points on the bottom. Derek wouldn't look him in the eye, wouldn't speak, just wore on his face a glare.

"Whatever you wanna do, you take it out on me. Don't you hurt her. This wasn't her fault."

Derek slipped out from between the fence and Evan, passed through Mark and Jared. Max swallowed, turned to the three of them then to Derek, hesitating, going after him.

Evan shifted, stepped over to Judith, wrapping his arms around her as she cried into his collar bone. He rocked her from side to side.

"Ya know, that actually went better than I thought."

Jared watched Mark with an expression that was mixed pity and loathing. He crushed the empty can in his hand and tossed it on the ground.

❧

Sitting on the couch, Judith leaned against Evan, both with their hands together and fingers laced. Jared sat on the carpet by the coffee table. He placed both his hands in his lap, facing down. Mark stood in the hallway, arms crossed, sideways against the wall. Max grabbed a bag of chips, a jar of pistachios, some cans of juice. The feeling in the air between them all was of disturbed gloom. They each sat down or stood in place not saying a word, not exchanging a glance. Evan turned, kissed the top of Judith's head, peeped across at Jared who peeped back. He felt this deep sense of guilt. After all, this was his fault, everything, and now he dragged them into it.

"Really? This all you got?" Jared stared at the can of juice being offered.

"I mean, I got tea."

Jared shook his head, raised his eyebrows. "I'm good."

Max offered Evan and Judith each one then sat on the carpet near Jared. Mark walked over, sat on the armrest by Evan leaning on his shoulder.

"Great. Well, this sucks." Mark grinned a grin both genuine and forced.

There was a quiet round of laughter.

"Hey. Again, guys, I'm—"

"Don't worry. It's gonna be fine." Jared held a hand up, nodded.

"What did he say, Max?"

He shook his head, nibbled his lips together. "I mean, he pretty much didn't wanna talk."

Evan gazed down at his hand holding Judith's, squeezed it, which felt so right. How could something that felt so right be so wrong?

"I don't know. I guess keep trying."

"Or maybe let him cool off?"

"He might be like that for a while, just honestly." Mark shook his head. "Like, I get what happened, and that it had to happen, but sheesh . . ."

"It'll be okay." Jared leaned forward. "If he's really your friend, really our friend, then he would want you to be happy. Then he would try to understand."

Mark scratched his head, almost wincing at the words.

"I hope so." Judith spoke in a whisper.

It appeared like Max spaced out then. He stood, grabbed a plastic bowl from the kitchen, set it on its side on the floor at the end of the hall. He put a small paper target over the front of it, then went in the other room. An odd time to be doing such a thing, but no one seemed to notice.

"I just hope he knows it's not like either of us meant for this to happen. You know?" Evan adjusted on the couch. "He's still, like, our friend. Of course. We still care about him."

"Give it time."

Out in the hall, Max sat down and loaded plastic pellets into the magazine, slammed it in place, pulled the slide back, aimed.

Evan watched him with the corner of his eye. Judith kept her head down, played with their fingers clasped together. Mark dazed out the window from the armrest still leaning on Evan's shoulder. It was just behind Jared, so he turned back when he heard the trigger, but returned to face the others.

When Max stood to check the target, Evan noticed the handle of the knife in his pocket. There was a small crack at the bottom of the bowl.

"Ah, crap . . ."

He went back to his room, put everything away. After that, he put the bowl back in the cabinet. When he joined the others in the living room, Evan noticed the knife had been put away too.

"Hey, Max. Those guys ever bother you again?"

"Nope. Not since . . ." Max shook his head, jutted out his lower lip.

"Okay, good."

It had been a long time coming. All the pieces were set in motion. All of the seeds had been planted. Now, with the truth being said, certain actions being taken, Evan and Judith were together. There was talk for many weeks about the possibility of a teacher's strike, and as it turned out, that Friday was the last day they would have class for a while. So, many of the students rejoiced and shouted in celebration in the halls. Paper was thrown in the air from the walkways on the second floor like confetti at a festive parade. Pens and pencils were flung into garbage cans, snapped into pieces. Notebooks and planners were hurled on the grass and stepped on. Mark, Jared and Max said they were going to Game Works then Jam Comics for the joyous occasion. Evan told them he was going to spend some time with Judith, which they joked about and teased him for.

He watched as the three walked from the oval median down the long driveways off campus. From the rock wall by the flagpole, he waited for her with his hands in his pockets, kicked at the grass.

It felt weird without Derek there. Also, though, it felt kind of weird to him that it all felt oddly okay too. Like, the others just accepted it. So much so that he himself could almost accept it.

This what it's gonna be like now?

Sigh.

From behind, Judith wrapped her arms around him at the waist and squeezed. They wobbled on their feet at first, then when he turned and they hugged face to face, they became steady once again.

"Where are the others?"

"Oh, they went to the shopping center."

"You wanna meet them?"

"No way! Come on. It's our first date."

She smiled, her cheeks reddening with a blush. As she buried her head in his torso, he touched the back of her head with the palm of his hand.

"Also, I mean, we'll probably hang with 'em next week since there's nothing else to do. School is out now."

"You know, it's funny. I dreaded this strike so bad, but now, I'm actually a little relieved."

He squeezed her tight, turned them both in tandem as he smirked.

"I'm supposed to go to tutoring, but I mean, with the strike in place . . ."

"First date then?"

Hand in hand, they walked through the admin building, past the portables into the fields. The sky was overcast, with a light blanket of cloud. It had a slight glow but remained dim. They could almost see, feel, the sun behind it.

"Wait, Evan."

She let go, stepped about a foot away.

"Oh, right."

They were at the crosswalk now, so they had to be careful just in case her parents drove by.

When they crossed to the other end, he led them towards the mountain side, the opposite way they always went. Instead of down the running path alongside the canal, this was a more secluded area with trees on either side. As they continued, their hands grasped one another's once again and their fingers laced together.

"I wanna show you something."

By one of the trees, there was an opening between the bushes that led down a small slope. It was a wet bank right off of a stream from the canal. There was a tree trunk that had either fallen down or grown sideways into the dirt. It was like a little picnic bench waiting for them right by the water's edge.

Evan took her by the hand, led her to the sideways tree trunk, each of them sitting down. He wrapped an arm around her shoulder, leaned in and kissed Judith on the cheek.

"Is this, like, your secret spot?"

He smirked, lifted up a brow. "One of them."

She leaned her head on his shoulder, kissed him on the arm.

"I'll show it all to you, Jude. Show you the whole entire world."

There was a moment of peace then, as the water rose up the bank then retreaded. Light ripples on the surface of the water chased after the small waves.

"It's kind of crazy, but I almost wish I could push the pause button and just . . ." Evan shook his head, rubbed at her far shoulder. "I wish I could fly away or something, like, take you somewhere new and exciting and far."

Judith smiled, nestled her face against his arm.

"Derek never said things like that . . ."

Evan gazed down at her as she closed her eyes.

Hope you know I'm sorry, man.

Really. I didn't mean for any of this.

"You think he's okay? That things will be okay?"

"I mean, there's no going back now." She opened her eyes, faced up at him. "Sorry, I'll try not to mention him."

"Nah, it's fine. We gotta get it out sometime, address the issue. You know?"

From behind the slope, off the bank of the stream, they felt safe. Beneath the canopy from the branches and leaves, with scattered bushes up top, no one else could see them. It was quiet, peaceful.

"I feel bad, I do . . . But, at the same time, I wanted you. I can't pretend it doesn't feel right holding you right now, Jude."

"I know . . . I'm glad school is on strike, too, so we don't have to worry what other people might say or think."

He swallowed, breathed. "Plus, it does kinda just give everybody a little break, time to let it all sink in."

"And time together."

With a half-smirk forming at the corner of his lips, he leaned in and kissed the top of her head. Evan took her hand in his, kissed the back of her hand.

Just then, a single duck floated in the water near them. It weaved between some of the low branches. Behind it, a line of ducklings trickled in formation.

"Oh, wow . . ."

Covering her mouth with an open palm, tiny beads welled in the corners of her almond eyes. The dimples in her cheeks peeked through as her lips widened in a smile, excited. He held a single finger in front of his face, nodded, pointed to the water where more ducks appeared.

There was another duck, with a couple ducklings behind it from the other side. Then other ducks gathering in twos and threes all around.

Judith leaned in, whispered. "This is so cool."

"Yeah. I don't know why they come here. Maybe someone feeds them or something."

She reached in her bag, pulled out a small packet of cookies. "You think they'll eat these?"

"Probably." He laughed.

Evan crunched the cookies in the bag, opened the packet, handed it back to her. She threw a crumbled piece in the water, watched as the ducks swarmed around.

"Oh, my God!"

Both laughed. Judith squealed and chortled, Evan snickered. Each of them teetered on the sideways tree trunk.

"Shh, shh . . ."

Again, she tossed cookie crumbs, causing the ducks to swim closer. One of them stepped onto the dirt from the water, waddling on its feet in anticipation.

In her fingers, she reached forward offering the duck a small piece. The duck pecked at it with its beak then hurried back in the water and swam away.

Judith laughed again, turning to Evan who stared in her eyes that were turned up like little crescent moons. With her lips spread in a wide smile, he watched her tongue dance behind her teeth. Her bangs landed right off her brows, some of the strands of hair falling on her shoulder. It was the perfect moment.

Evan leaned in, pausing midway. Judith turned, her eyes first meeting his then peeping down towards his mouth. Their lips came together, touched, touched again. As she closed her eyes, her lips parted, allowing his lips then his tongue.

From her hand, the rest of the cookies slipped and fell. She rubbed at his chest, reached up around his neck. He ran his fingers through her hair, touched her along her inner thigh.

At first, their motions were awkward: hands fumbling, tongues like slugs or like swords slashing, breathing out of rhythm. Little by little, they found the pattern and fell in sync. Their hands grazed each other's bodies and their tongues slithered in place between their open mouths, each breath timed with precision.

With each kiss and each touch, the ducks floating on the water, the two far corners of the triangle warped in space and time becoming one . . . From opposite corners to points connected by a single straight line, small circles overlapped, then spherical orbs in alignment . . . An eclipse.

15

Jan 19th
12:24pm

CARRYING THE AXE in hand, jogging back the way he came, the thoughts churned and turned over in Evan's mind. It had been the right direction after all, except he went past it, went too far. He didn't even notice—the cafeteria. Now, as he passed each window behind hard metallic mesh, he could hear the students inside, trapped, like at the gym but not as loud. Making his way through the walkway, past each pillar, around to the front doors across from E-building, he heard a gunshot in the distance, a little closer than before. There was another shot then another, followed by a sharp scream cut short. *Jude!* He rattled the chain around the handles, lining it up so that it would hit again metal on metal. He raised the axe in the air with both hands, squeezed tight.

Whack. The link showed a small chink, a light dent forming in the housing around the handle.

Jude!!!

Whack, whack. A small cut began to form in one link, then in a couple of the others, each growing from the next consecutive hit. Whack.

"C'mon, goddammit!"

The small cut became a large cut, until the link snapped open and part of the chain dangled down. Evan threw the axe at the ground, reached forward, undid the rest of the chains. He winded it like a sailor on the pier tightening rope around a cleat, or a fisherman struggling to snag a majestic beast from the ocean.

As he pulled the doors open, he braced for the rushing flood of students and some of the lunch staff. Evan felt them brush past, one bumped into him at the shoulder while another stomped on his foot. His eyes remained fixed, however, facing forward to the inside of the cafe.

He took a step forward, then another, his arms at his sides. She stood to her feet from where she sat on the floor against the wall wrapped in a ball around herself. Each of them stared into one another's face from opposite ends of the open area, the crowd thinning. Almost as if all the others around them didn't exist, more and more the light appeared to hone in on just the two of them alone.

Evan swallowed, licked his lips, stepped a little bit quicker towards her. Judith wiped a hand to the side of her cheek where a single tear rolled down.

She ran over to him and jumped, as he hugged her tight, holding her up with her legs wrapped around him. Her palms touched the sides of his face, lips pressing together and opening, tongues slipping in. It was the first time they held each other like that, kissed, in what felt like a lifetime. Yet, it somehow also felt as if no time had passed at all. Evan knew just where her buttocks was, one hand sliding up the slender of her back beneath her shirt. Judith knew just where his shoulder blades were, as she stroked from his arms to his back, reaching up to the base of his neck.

They continued to kiss while she slithered down his body back to her feet. Rushed, desperate pawing and deep, passionate kissing turned to small quick pecks as they each regained their composure.

With a heavy panting, Evan scanned her up and down.

"Are you okay?" He licked his lips, held her at both shoulders. "Jude, are you hurt?"

"I'm okay. I just . . ."

She began to sob as he pulled her in close, cradled her in his arms against his chest.

"I-I thought I might . . . It was so . . ." Her shoulders shuddered as he held her, with heavy whimpers and short gasps between breaths. "I'm just happy you . . ."

Judith nuzzled her face against him, a wet sniffle mixed in with her slurred speech.

"Hey. It's okay. I'm here now. Everything's gonna be all right. I'll get us out."

Almost as if on cue, his eyes glanced through to the pantry in the middle of the cafe where he could see into the space in back.

What in the hell is that?

He took a step, about to head towards them.

"No, Evan, don't." She wiped at her cheeks that were moist from tears. "A few of the others already looked and . . ."

There were wires running along the front of two large propane tanks by the row of stoves. At the bottom were two round microwaves with scattered PVC pipes, similar to the ones from earlier he witnessed. He could see a small digital timer counting down.

16

9th Grade

The sky was again a lighter gray, with the sun blurred behind a thin layer of cloud. Rolling out of bed, Evan was eager to see Judith. He got dressed and ran out the door to the outside world. As he plopped down the stairs, passed from his two-story apartment building to the back streets, he thought of what to bring her. In part of the neighborhood ahead, he saw a small garden where he decided to snatch a flower. Bending down over the brightly colored plants, he searched until he heard angry foreign yelling from the nearby window. He plucked one—a purplish rounder flower—and took off down the road. Jaywalking across to the other side, he cut through a yard just as water sprinklers went off spraying him in his leg and side but kept going.

When he was a safe enough distance away, he slowed to a walk again. As he wiped at his pants that got soaked, Evan checked to the see if the flower was okay.

Damn lady . . .

Turning the flower in his hand, he could still feel her tongue inside his mouth. His lips were tired and sore. The taste of her lip gloss was embedded in his mind, and the scent of her perfume loomed in his nostrils and lungs. Heading toward the park where they agreed to meet, it was as if he was in a dream state. Cars passed by as he crossed and waited at intersections, but none of that registered. Evan instead still sat on the sideways tree trunk in his mind—with Judith, kissing, touching, holding one another, surrounded by ducklings floating on the water.

As he neared, he could see her waiting for him. She wore short shorts that showed her milky smooth legs and a spaghetti strap top that bared her shoulders and part of her chest. In her hands, teetering to one side, was a bicycle.

"What happened to you?" She laughed, smiled.

"Oh . . ." He shook his head. "It's a funny story."

When he held out the battered flower, her skin flushed pink. She couldn't hide the deep dimples in her cheeks.

"A bike?"

"Yeah, I told my parents I wanted to ride around so I could escape and come meet you."

They moved from the parking lot past a sandbox over to a small gazebo with a bench. She put her bicycle against the side of it, sat down next to him. He put his arm around her and they kissed.

"God. You're wet." Judith coiled away, teasing, then scooted close again.

Evan brushed at the wet patches of his shirt and pants from the sprinklers earlier, leaned in and pecked her on the lips once more. Their eyes locked then their lips opened, for a longer passionate kiss with their heads tilted in.

As they each sat back against the bench, he pulled her in close and she rested her head on his shoulder.

"You know, that's a pretty good excuse actually." He nodded, turned towards her as he teased. "Love the basket."

There was an umbrella in there as well as a bottle of water, and tangerine slices in a plastic bag. He could also see a sweater rolled in a ball.

"It's not easy when your parentals treat life like a prison sentence. Like, maybe we can just talk on the phone tomorrow. If that's okay."

"Yeah, sure."

"Hey. You know . . . what's your family like?"

Evan stared ahead, arching his neck in silence. He swallowed, sighed, then spoke.

"We're not really that close. I don't get along with my dad. Like, you know how Derek and Max have parents that are divorced? Everybody cries for kids with divorced parents, but I think maybe it's almost better. I mean, if your parents fight all the time, argue, yell, it's kind of worse."

"Oh, I'm sorry."

"It's okay. I'm used to it already . . ." Evan's eyes wandered through the sea of grass, as he let the words continue to spill out. "Like, I don't get how you could yell, hit someone you're supposed to love. If I had kids, I would never ever do that. It's just wrong."

She pressed into him as he tightened up.

He shook his head, clenched his teeth. "I don't know. It's hard growing up poor sometimes. Or hey, maybe it's my fault actually. Maybe, like . . ."

Evan swallowed, turned to Judith. He felt his eyes blink and flutter, forced a smirk.

"Ah, I'm sorry, I shouldn't have said anything."

"Don't be. We're together now. I want to know you, and that's part of who you are. Though you might be ashamed of it, even hate it, it's what makes you *you.*"

He took a deep breath, glanced down at their shoes next

to each other. His were crossed over while hers were neatly side by side.

"I don't know. My parents have money, they have 'good' jobs and 'work hard' and all that. They don't fight." Judith's eyes wandered now, to the pebbles in the sand and children playing with plastic shovels. "But it's almost like they don't really talk, they don't bond or click . . . Like they're just robots, and there's no emotion or warmth. Almost a business arrangement between the two of them. Sure, they don't yell or fight, but there is such enormous pressure sometimes."

She bit down on her bottom lip, stared up into the cloudy sky.

"Like, I don't think they get how hard it can be to try and be perfect all the time. I'm a person too . . . I want to live life like everybody else, and be happy. Sometimes, what I wouldn't give to just be . . ."

"Not insane."

Evan kissed her on the cheek, stood with her hand in his, motioning with a nod.

They walked from the gazebo to the swings nearby. She sat in one, rocked. He twisted in his, turning until the chains were wrapped then let go. As he spun in place, he could see her smiling at him between rotations.

"Do you think things happen for a reason?"

Judith held a hand on the chains on either side, pushing back with her feet.

"Yeah, I think so. I mean, I transferred here to Wash, met you, and now here we are. What's the chances of a school strike happening right after we decide to be together?" Evan nodded to himself. "I definitely say things happen for a reason. I was supposed to meet you, Jude, always. And you were meant to be part of me."

“Even with everything that’s happened? Even with everything on the line?” Her eyes were soft dazing into his.

Sigh.

You’re right, it’s not exactly how I would have wanted things to go, no . . .

Mixed feelings started to rise to the surface but as he faced her, they dissipated. Fading away, it was just the two of them, a beautiful moment with a beautiful girl.

He smirked, waddled on his feet, pushing back on the chains. “Maybe that’s what makes it so special. You know? Like, we’re not like everybody else or something.”

She smiled again, watched him swing back then forward. On the other side of him was a slide, monkey bars and jungle gym that a couple little kids crawled upon like insects.

“Yeah, maybe.” Judith pouted her lips, twisted them to the corner of her mouth continuing to ponder. “Do you think . . . there’s a God?”

He nodded, turned away.

“Do you think it’s possible, that it’s okay, to believe in both Buddhism and Christianity?”

Evan laughed. “These are pretty deep questions. I think there is a God, for sure. In order for any and all the wonders in the world to make sense, there has to be a God. We’re not just bags of meat walking around. Each of us has a purpose, has a personality . . . It’s all about heart. And, if God really is so knowing and powerful, I’m sure He can see past certain barriers and boundaries to determine whether or not someone’s good.”

“I hope so.”

“You’re a good person, Jude.”

She sighed, the movement in the swing slowing until she sat still. He noticed the bracelet on her wrist with the wooden beads, the characters etched in.

"Recently, I've been feeling this kind of guilt."

"Me too. But, I mean, what else were we supposed to do, right? You like me and I like you, and it's not our fault the timing and circumstances were all twisted." Evan licked his lips, faced down to the artificial rubber floor beneath his feet. "All we can do from here is try our best, I think. It'll be okay. It has to be okay."

&

The cord of the phone was stretched out and tangled with knots, as Evan cradled it between his neck and shoulder. They used to have a cordless phone at home but it broke so they switched back to the old one. He rolled in his bed from on his back over to his belly, listening to the other side where Judith asked him to please hold on. As he laid one arm out in the front of him on the pillow, he rested his head down, gazed out the open jalousies to the gray sky. Past the telephone poles and electrical lines where the silhouette of birds sat upon, he could almost see the orb of the sun hidden in the background. After a while, Judith's voice returned on the other end and Evan perked up.

"Hello? Sorry to make you wait."

"It's okay."

Her voice sounded distant, just a little muffled with a touch of static. He pressed the phone against his cheek, with the speaker close to his ear.

"I wish I could see you, but we should lay low for a couple days. Like, I had to wait 'til my mom went shopping to even call you, and my dad's still at work."

"As long as I get to hear your voice."

Evan couldn't see but imagined Judith smiled at that, subconsciously tucked her hair behind her left ear.

"Tomorrow, I have tutoring so maybe we can try to sneak out to see each other real quick." He could hear her breathe, like she was blowing into his ear. "You know, when did you realize you liked me?"

"Hmm . . ." Evan adjusted on his side, facing the bricks in the wall. "It was a lotta little things, I guess. From just sitting together in class and studying, to hanging out with the group, too, and talking, getting to know each other."

"The same. But I have to say probably the big moment was reading your letter. I guess you really don't know how much someone means until they're gone, or about to be."

Judith cleared her throat. He could hear some kind of noise like she was repositioning the phone.

"Actually, you know, there was one moment now that I think about it. The talent show."

"Oh, that night?"

He smirked to himself. "Yeah. It was when I saw you onstage, and I heard you playing piano. That's when it all became clear to me. Like it had been there all along, but I just never noticed . . ."

"You, uh, want me to play you something now?"

"I would love that."

"Okay, hold on."

Evan heard her place the phone on its side, heard her footsteps as she walked away. Then, the sounds started to flow through the phone in his ear like flower petals falling to the ground.

The notes jumped up and down, sweeping down and tipping back up in this light melody that bounced almost as if the sounds danced in the air. That movement cycled, then shifted to a crescendo that lowered and became soft until it repeated once more. Then, the music changed in tune to this darker off-key that was slow and deliberate. It built back up like a fountain spraying then returned back to those initial notes again, that jumped and swept and tipped.

It was something that struck him on almost a molecular level. The way she played was with such proficiency and precision, the music itself having a sort of hallucinogenic effect on him. Evan closed his eyes, laid his head back deep into the pillow, let the music flow through him—through his arms to his fingers, his legs to his toes, his chest and stomach—almost shuddering in ecstasy as if her tongue slithered in all the right places. Though they were in different parts of the city, separated, and just their voices reached each other in the electronics and hard wiring, with the music flowing—from her hands and her fingertips to his eardrums, to his very heart beating—they melted into one.

Sitting towards the back of the bus, close to the exit door, Evan put his arm around Judith. He watched all the buildings zing past through the window as the bus winded and turned. There were little droplets of water on the window, tiny prisms, from the morning drizzle. She leaned her chin on his shoulder as she also peeked out the window, at passersby in the streets. Some walked their dogs. Some were out for a run, carrying bags of groceries. It was strange not being in school on a weekday, but with the strike in place, they at least had time to see each other. Between them, on their laps, their hands squeezed together tight with their fingers interlaced. Evan moved his fingers, felt her smooth skin and the warmth where their flesh met.

“I never get tired of holding your hand.”

He put his other hand over the top of hers, cradling both and rubbing them.

She smiled, leaned in, kissed him on the lips.

"I'll never get tired of making out."

Her lips were soft. He could taste the lip gloss. He could smell her perfume, the faint scene of her hair. It was intoxicating.

"You know, me and Derek were never like this."

Evan swallowed, rubbed at her far shoulder. Judith laid her other arm out across his torso to his other hip.

"Like, he wanted to. We kissed. We tried making out, but it just never felt right and then he would get mad. But, like, with you, it's different."

"Heh. Lucky me then."

She pulled down the collar of his shirt, pecked him on the collar bone.

"I wanna bite you . . ."

When they got off the bus and crossed the street to the mall where they were meeting the others, it was okay to hold her hand again. Evan didn't mind playing it safe in case she ever did catch her parents out in the open. In fact, it was kind of funny to him.

When they exited to the opposite side of the mall, he and Judith passed by a couple fast food joints until they reached their destination: the music store. They swung their hands together playfully in a wide arc as they passed the sensor inside.

"Oh, there they are."

"Huh? Where?"

"By the posters."

Mark, Jared and Max stood in front of the tall display with revolving metal frames. They turned to the next, pointed, examined and commented, laughed. A small round of fist bumps and high fives as they each greeted one another, to which even Judith joined in.

"Whoa. How 'bout this one?" Max held the frame in place for the rest. "It's like in 3-D."

"I see it." Jared was quick to respond, with zero effort. "Yup. Nice."

Mark crossed his arms, tilted his head. "Ah, I don't see anything . . ."

Judith strained, adjusted side to side. "Do you see it? I don't see either."

"Relax your eyes. Like, look at the reflection in the glass and step back. You know?" Evan did so, leaned his face forward then pulled away, nodding as the image formed.

"Oh, I see it now." She held him by the arm, squeezed.

Throwing up his hands, Mark laughed. "Nope. I still don't see shit."

Further into the store, each went to their respective areas going through the shelves and flipping through checking out various artists and albums. Max walked to the heavy metal section, put on big headphones that hung down from the wall, headbanging to himself as he sampled new music. Mark and Jared went over first to alternative rock, then to rap.

Evan followed Judith close, indifferent to his surroundings. Most of the time, he loved to see the photography and different artwork on the album covers and on the back. Today, though, he was just happy to be with his girl as well as with the boys.

It occurred to him then, that although it was seemingly okay without Derek there, it shouldn't have been. He didn't deserve the acceptance of all his friends. He didn't deserve to be with such a wonderful girl.

"What do you like to listen to?" Judith watched Evan from down the aisle, turning a CD over in her hand.

"I mean, anything, really. I like this kinda music." Evan panned around. "I like pop, I like R&B. The boy band stuff that's out now's good."

"What else do you like?"

"Gotta say, I do have a soft spot for rock and rap. It just speaks to me. Probably my number one."

"Boys . . ." Judith shook her head with a smile.

"What?" He laughed. "It's good! I mean, there's no other music that speaks the truth like that. And that's the thing about music, right? It's all about emotion. Well, anger is an emotion too. Not all lovey-dovey all the time."

Judith nodded along, admiring his genuine respect.

"Real art should say something. You know? Like, it should make you feel something, think something. It's not just making money." Evan laughed to himself.

She giggled, turned away. "I guess so, huh."

They wandered to a different section. This one was of music from around the world. He followed her as she perused down the aisle, running her fingers over each cover.

She stared at one CD. It was a close-up of a girl's face, bangs just off her brow and cheek, with full lips. Funny, it reminded him a lot of Judith.

"I like this one. You ever heard of it?"

He shook his head, shifted over as she turned to the back, pointing with her pretty fingernail.

"Actually, I don't know any of these . . ." He glanced around at the shelf. "What is this kind of music?"

"It's called J-Pop. This one has a song that's popular right now, about falling in love for the first time. About the heartbreak that comes after, and how that person will always be part of you."

Evan watched as she spoke, smirked to himself. Judith appreciated the song she was talking about, which touched him, because that's just what he was hinting at before.

"She's pretty, yeah?"

He took her hand in his. "You're prettier."

Blushing, she faced down to the floor. He licked his lips, watched her eyelids blink and her eyelashes flutter. They each leaned in and kissed with a quick peck.

"Oh, there's some other good ones, too, although a little bit different."

Judith led him further down the aisle.

"What does that say?" Evan squinted his eyes. "Jude, you can read that?"

"Yeah. A little. My parents speak at home."

He smirked, leaned close. "That's cool."

She smiled as she touched him on the chest.

"And what's all this?"

"Now, this. This is called C-Pop."

"Interesting."

They moved from world music to the back of the store where there were stickers and patches. Mark and Jared made their way down the wall, perusing and pointing out certain cool or funny ones. As Evan and Judith passed through, the wall transitioned to collectible t-shirts and hats.

Wandering over to heavy metal to check in on Max who still headbanged with the big headphones on, Evan shoved him from the side.

"'Sup." His usual mumble was louder than normal due to the music blasting in his ears.

Evan gazed down at some of the CDs he sampled.

One was of a naked gothic figure, almost androgynous. It was hard to tell whether the person was male or female. A creepy image, with the pale white skin and gangly limbs and darkened eyes. He observed the cover then Max who was engrossed in it, eyes closed. Evan could hear the guitar riff, the drums and the raspy voice leaking out of the headset. He himself listened to metal and harder rock from time to time, but nowhere near as much as Max who seemed to gravitate towards it. Then, in that moment, Evan noticed something. Max, who was always quieter, always hung back in the conversation, to this music was like a different person. He had life in him. He banged his head, thrashed, moved from side to side, bouncing on his feet. There was this boiling energy in him that was bursting to come forth, like a gun, like a knife. That destructive force inside.

With a careful quiet touch, Evan turned the doorknob and closed the door behind him. Judith waited on the bed, watched him lock it then walk over and join her. He sat down, put his arm around her, leaned in and kissed her. The look in her eyes was part nervous, part smitten, part embarrassed, yet at the same time exuding this sort of innocence. As he reached one hand up, over the cup of her bra beneath her shirt, that innocence slipped away. Their mouths parted and their tongues intertwined. In between the writhing of lips, they breathed and moaned as the touching grew more and more, to the point they almost could no longer contain themselves. He reached a hand behind her back, sliding his palm and fingers along her skin up to the clasp of her bra, the other hand touching at her buttocks. She put both hands on the button and the zipper of his pants, feeling at them.

"Hold on. Wait, wait . . ." Judith pulled away, licked her lips as she caught her breath. "I don't know if we should do this on the bed actually . . ."

Evan let out a hushed laugh, nodded.

They kissed again, touched again, making their way from the edge of the bed to the floor. As they slid down, he pivoted her and they landed on the carpet. He grabbed the hem of her shirt, lifted it up exposing her midriff and bra that was a light beige-pink. Evan admired her breasts, bosoms pressing beneath the cups with smooth skin, rising up and down with each shallow breath. Again, the look in her eyes was nervous, smitten, just a tad awkward and shy, somehow innocent still. His lips pressed onto hers, parted them, then he slipped in his tongue making her moan and squirm.

Judith grabbed him, turned him and rolled him to one side, getting on top with her legs wrapped around. She reached both hands down, undid the button first then the zipper, reaching in and rubbing over the fabric of his briefs.

"Is this okay?" She bit her bottom lip, leaned in and kissed him on the side of his neck.

He nodded, licked his lips, adjusted on the carpet. Each of them lifted their shirts and took them off, feeling the skin of each other's torsos touching as they kissed. Her midriff, his chest. The small of her back, his shoulders and arms. That was as far as they would go, making out and fooling around. Enjoying the rush, exploring their bodies, taking it slow. Reaching over the band of her shorts in front of her hips, his fingers at the seam of her panties, he pulled them open a bit and peeked inside. It was a little triangle, upside down, that mesmerized him on the floor of Max's mom's bedroom.

With his arm around her waist, they walked in through the front gates. Evan stuffed the tickets in his pocket, glanced over at Judith who smiled until her dimples showed in her cheeks. There was a big wagon with slices of pizza, cotton candy, hot dogs and slushies. Next to that were food booths with caramel popcorn and candied apples. Behind that, they could see tents with games lined as well as some of the rides spinning and raising up in the air, bright lights flashing and blinking. A small roller coaster zoomed in the background on a windy track, first on a steep downhill then looping around in three consecutive spins. Whimsical melodies played from each of the different areas, pop songs blaring from the speakers. All combined together—the laughter and chatter, rides whooshing and whirring, games dinging and crashing—the sea of noise swept them up like a riptide. It was dark out but against all the colored lights and lit signs, it was almost as if it were still day.

"Holy crap. This is freaking crazy!"

She giggled as she leaned in, squeezing his arm.

"Yeah, seriously. Pretty cool. Wow . . ." He gazed around them as scattered crowds surged past. "Uh, you wanna get in line for some food first?"

They walked hand in hand, stood in the line by the food wagon, which wasn't too long.

Evan peeped at the sign and how much tickets cost. "Ah, damn. We'll probably need to get more."

"No need to go crazy. I'm just here to be with you, as long as we're together and have fun."

"You sure?"

She nodded, pecked him on the cheek.

"Okay. Well, we should at least play one game then. We might get lucky. Definitely need to ride a couple a rides." He faced up at the sign again. "As for food, though, what you want, Jude?"

"Hmm. I'm not that hungry actually. But maybe we can do cotton candy?"

"Which flavor?"

"Blue."

"Blue . . . You don't want pink?"

Judith laughed. "Did I say I want pink?"

Evan turned to her, smirked. "Maybe they can do, like, half and half or something."

Next, they went from the food booths to the tented area where there were different games in rows. A man swung a hammer down hard, while a couple little kids reached forward and tossed rings. She tore a wad of cotton candy and popped it in her mouth, tore another piece and held it in front of his face. He opened his mouth letting her feed him the sugary threads like fluffy clouds melting on his tongue.

"Hey, Evan. Look." She stuck her tongue out that had turned a slight tinge of blue. "Lemme see yours."

At first he shook his head, continued to walk away, but she tugged on his arm.

"C'mon. Pleease."

Finally, he stuck out his tongue, but just for a second.

She hopped up and down, laughing aloud. Evan stood back, smirking to himself as he watched those tiny beads form in the corners of her almond eyes.

Judith pulled him by the hand, the plucked cotton candy in her other hand. There was a grid of balloons hanging on a back wall, with stuffed animals lined on the shelves.

"Maybe we'll try this one?" Evan shifted over, shrugged.

"Are you good at darts?"

"No." He shook his head. "I've never even tried."

Evan stepped to the counter, took the three darts. He felt the weight of it, felt the grip between his thumb and fingertips, moved his wrist.

"You can do it, Evan."

He swallowed, licked his lips then flung it.

Pop.

She held her hands over her face fighting back excitement as he prepared the same way with the next two. This time, he peered at the wall squinting, trying to better aim its trajectory.

Pop. Pop.

Evan flinched to himself in disbelief, as the worker pointed to the top row.

"The giraffe."

He turned to her, raising his eyebrows. "Really? You could've picked the monkey, the tiger, the bear . . ."

She smiled, taking the huge stuffed animal.

"Okay, well, lemme hold that. You just finish the cotton candy." Evan struggled to find a good position to hold it in, as it was so large and poofy. "All right, I almost wish I didn't win now . . . This thing is frickin' ridiculous."

Judith laughed, led them further down the tents.

"What are your parents gonna say when you come home with this big thing, huh?"

"Well, officially, I'm here with 'Sally,' a girl from my tutoring."

Evan smirked, nodded. "I guess that's a pretty good cover."

She kept walking until she stood in front of a large table with plastic cups. In each of the cups was a small fish floating.

"How 'bout this one?"

"I don't know, Jude. Maybe we should quit while we're ahead? Not push our luck?"

"Come on, you're on a winning streak." She shook him at the shoulders.

He waited for her to throw the empty cotton candy cone away then hold the giraffe again. Evan took the light ping-pong ball, felt the weight of it like the darts before as he moved his wrist. It bounced off the rim of the cup onto the ground with a hollow tick.

"God damn it." He stepped back as she hid her face behind the stuff animal. "You wanna try it?"

"Yeah, sure. Why not."

He handed her the next ping-pong ball, let her step to the counter, adjusted the stuffed animal that slid under his arm. Without thinking or trying, she threw the ball up and over and it clinked right into the cup.

"I won!!!"

She jumped up on him, hugging him tight, as he struggled to support both her and the giraffe becoming wobbly and unsteady, almost tripping over a little kid who ran past them chasing after a red balloon.

The worker held the cup out for them while they regained their balance and composure. She took it in her hands with a big smile.

"Nicely done." Evan watched her.

"Oh, wait. What should we name him?"

He scrunched his lips together, furling his brow. "I'm not sure. . . . Filbert?"

"Filbert?"

"Yeah, it's a type of paintbrush. I learned it when I was doing set design for the talent show. Just thought it was kinda funny, haha."

"Filbert. Hmm, I like it."

"Okay, then. Filbert the Fish."

They left the games area and passed by the largest tent. He could see there was a stage inside with bleachers set up.

"Looks like there's stunts and performances and stuff in there. Some kind of animal show. You wanna go?"

She held the cup in one hand, his hand in the other, pulled them further into the carnival towards the section in back with all the rides. He adjusted his stance as he walked, trying to keep the giraffe wedged between his side and his arm.

First, there was a fun house. They could see curved mirrors on the second floor, striped poles spinning and cushioned cylinders swinging, even a slide to one side that ran from the third floor down. Then there was a merry-go-round turning with little horsies moving up and down, chimey music playing in the midst of it, and a tilt-a-whirl whooshing past with kids screaming at the top of their lungs both in ecstasy and in horror.

Next, there were chairs hanging from chained swings that rotated high in the air. Evan and Judith gazed up at the dozens of legs and feet that hung down, whizzing past, against all of the bright lights. Just then, bubbles floated in between the two of them, one of them popping on his nose. The bubbles floated into the wide space like confetti in a parade, like dandelions or feathers.

"See anything you wanna try?"

"Let's keep looking."

He put his arm around her shoulder, she put her arm around his waist, as they continued on. Ahead, they could see a long line leading up to a ride with rickety cages spinning on their hinges as the machine rose and rotated the track. It seemed to be the most popular one.

"Oh, God."

"I know. That thing looks like a death trap."

"Wanna try it?"

"Hell yeah, maybe later."

Both continued just a bit further, to where there was a roller coaster and then a giant wheel. When they each saw it, they knew right away. That was the one.

They stepped up the little stairs, lining up with the rest. It wasn't too crowded compared to the other ride with the rickety cages. Evan squeezed her hand, stared into Judith's eyes. He smirked, she smiled, then they each leaned in and kissed. To the side, the roller coaster crept at the top then sped down the steep incline grinding along the rails. In the distance, the chairs with the chained swings started back up, sending a new batch of legs and feet through the air. More bubbles floated in the space above them. When their lips parted, it was time to enter.

"Is Filbert gonna be okay?" She held the cup with two hands, eyes narrowing.

He smirked, touched the small of her back. "Should be. This ride isn't going fast."

Evan let Judith climb in the car first. She put the cup against the corner then blocked it with her bag. He sat next to her on the bench, put the stuffed animal on the other side of him. A boy, a girl. A fish, a giraffe.

The car rose a little then stopped, the next batch climbing in then the next. Evan leaned back, put his arm around her shoulder. Judith rested her head against him, getting comfortable. He touched a hand to her thigh then up her midriff to her breast as she rubbed over his chest then down to his crotch. Not far off the ground, and they were already all over each other, making out.

When they snapped their eyes open again, they were almost at the top. The air around them was still and the sounds just a bit muted. It appeared darker as they hovered above all the shining lights.

"I hope it's okay, that we're waiting." She squirmed on the seat, readjusting her clothing. "You're not like dying?"

He leaned back in, pecked her on the cheek. "Of course not. Whenever you're ready. Whenever *I'm* ready. I mean, I'm just having fun doing this right now. You know?"

Judith nodded, rested her head again.

Now they were at the very top, high in the sky in the darkness, touching the upper atmosphere and the vastness of space. They couldn't see the stars since it was overcast but there was an orb glowing through from the half-moon, opaque behind the clouds.

"God. It's so beautiful . . ."

He took her hand in his, laced their fingers as he squeezed.

"I'm glad it's not raining."

"I know. But it'll probably rain again soon."

She reached her other arm across, wrapping around his torso nestling her face against the side of his neck. He touched a hand to her chin, lifted it, then brought his lips to hers. It was a nice soft touch, just for a second.

"I can't tell you how happy you make me, Evan."

"I'm happy, too, Jude."

He took another glance around, at the crowds below that were like tiny ants, at the city lights in the distance.

"I don't think I ever been this happy . . ."

She lifted her head, turned to him. Evan stared into her almond eyes with a slow blink. Judith smiled until her dimples peeked through.

"Me neither."

As she rested her head back down, he watched her close her eyes and exhale.

"Think we could ever have a Filbert of our own?" Her voice was quiet.

Evan laughed a hushed laugh. "Of course. Why not."

"Get married, have a big house. Three kids."

He kissed the top of her head. He could feel her breathing in and out, as if she was about to fall asleep.

"Hey. We could have three kids and three dogs."

Judith nuzzled into him. He could smell her hair, caught a whiff of her perfume. Evan leaned his head back, smirking to himself.

"I can't help but wonder sometimes. I actually had a dream about us the other night, that we were living this whole other life." She nibbled on her bottom lip. "Do you think . . . we can make this work? Do you really think that this could last forever?"

17

Jan 19th
12:28pm

SQUEEZING HER HAND tight, pulling her, Evan led them through the front doors back into the open. He skidded on his feet as he slowed, darting his head left then right, scanning around. Judith almost tripped as she stared in front of them in shock, in disbelief, with her jaw dropped. There were bullet casings scattered around in the grass. She glanced up at E-building, at deep holes burrowed in the brick wall along with blackened streaks, then further down at admin where there were two rising plumes of smoke. Evan pulled her again, running around the side between the auditorium and the cafeteria. There were gunshots somewhere near. It was a string of loud bangs in rapid succession, faster than any of the previous gunshots. He ducked low as they crossed to the other side of the tennis courts, edging along the chain-link fence.

"Evan!!! Oh my God, no!"

She gasped as she winded her way around a body on the ground, not moving, dripping in red.

Though she felt sick, short of breath, faint, Judith continued to run as more rapid shots sounded through upper campus.

He turned back with a finger to his lips, eyes wide, beads of sweat forming on his skin.

Now they were passing by a set of bleachers, about to run through the baseball diamond and cut through the track.

"Come on, Jude! This way!"

As they moved further into the fields, the outlines of two ambiguous figures appeared, running towards the goal post, becoming more pronounced as they drew closer. Evan could see one of them waving their arms, the other hopping up and down shouting something. By the far end of the field at the back fence, police cars and ambulances gathered on the street in a long blockade.

"Hurry up!"

"Over here, over here!"

It was Mark and Jared, Evan realized, and he had never been so happy to see them.

Evan and Judith struggled to reach them, hobbling on their feet, hugging them, then knelt down to catch their breath. Their little reunion was greeted with an unintelligible voice blaring over a megaphone from the end of the field.

"Looks like they finally got here, huh . . ." Mark bent down on one knee, put a hand on Evan's shoulder.

Jared stood by the three of them on the grass with his arms crossed, bent down, hanging his head. His usual neutral and carefree face now seemed empty and heavy.

"You guys okay?"

Wiping tears from her cheeks, Judith nodded back.

"H-how did you—"

Reaching around, Mark wiped dirt off the back of his jeans. He must have slipped and fallen at some point.

"Me and Jared were out in M-building, hiding with others underneath our desks. Our classes are close. There was a loud explosion, like a bomb or something, so we were forced to run. Most the others took off to the shopping center but we got separated, headed this way . . ."

Judith chimed in. "I was trapped in the cafeteria, worst cafe duty of my life. Evan came and found me."

"I searched everywhere else. And I don't know how, but the thought popped in my head."

Jared looked Evan in the eye, motioned with his chin, glancing down to the end of the field.

"Wait. Where's Der?" Lifting his head up, Evan furled his brow. "Is he all right?"

"Derek?"

Oh, shit. Did he not make it?

"We tried stopping to help a kid who hurt his leg. Looked like he jumped from the second floor. Then there were shots by admin, so we took off. I might've saw Derek in back of the crowd but not sure."

Evan bit his lip, pounded a fist to the ground.

"Shit . . ."

He staggered up, helped Judith to her feet.

"Guys. I gotta go back."

"What?"

"I was going to, anyway. 'Cause I still gotta find Max. But now I can't leave Der behind either."

"Evan, you can't—"

He cut Mark off, raised his voice.

"I *have* to, okay!? I owe him that much!"

There was silence now, amongst the group that stood together like a lopsided polygon. The silence was cut short by the sound of the megaphone again from one side of the field, and then gunshots echoing from the other.

Judith squeezed Evan's hand, watched him with tears in her eyes, lip quivering. "You can't, Evan. No."

He faced down at the ground, shaking his head.

"Please. Please don't do this . . ."

"I'm sorry, Jude."

"Guys. I think we gotta go." Jared peeked down at the end of the field where he could see authorities aiming their weapons.

"Mark, keep an eye on her, okay? Keep her safe. And Jar, you keep an eye on Mark. S-stick together." Evan could feel goosebumps on his skin as he stammered. "You guys are like brothers to me, no matter—"

Jared closed his eyes. "Evan, don't."

"Let me say this. You're my best friends, we been through hell and back, and I care about you. I'm asking y-you to go. I need you to do this, to watch out for Jude. For me."

"Are you sure you want to do this?" Mark swallowed, tilted his head.

Evan nodded, then turned to Judith.

"And I'm sorry. I am. I want you to know that . . ." He felt his eyes water but fought to contain them. "I need you to know that . . . I love you. I've always loved you, Jude. You're everything to me."

She glanced up in his eyes, mouth hanging open. Her cheeks streamed wet with tears. Pulling him close, she hugged him tight, swaying on both feet as she sniffled through short gasps that turned to sharp sobs and whimpering.

"Okay, really, we better go."

He reached up and wiped the tears from her cheeks with the cuff of his sleeve, leaning in, kissing her forehead. "I love you. It's all gonna be okay. You'll see. I'll be fine. Don't you worry."

Mark took a couple steps, waited to lead them down the field. Jared hesitated to follow. Judith stayed just a second longer, her hand not wanting to let go.

"It's time, Jude."

"Evan, I . . ." She licked her lips, moved her fingers in his hand as tears streamed down once more. "I . . ."

He reached up again, dabbed a sleeve to her face.

"I love you too."

With that, his eyes filled with water and a single tear rolled down the side of his face. He smiled a big smile, as he kissed her on the hand and let go. She walked backward on the grass, turned, jogged with the others.

At first, he stood and watched as they made their way. He could see a couple officers waving them down, heard the megaphone blare again, maybe directed at himself who lingered in place not moving. Evan turned around, back to the school. There were rapid gunshots that echoed in the distance. He could feel the goosebumps, the tiny hairs standing on end, a cold sweat, and then fear. But he wasn't finished yet. He had one last mission before he could rest, before he was free: to find Max, to find Derek.

18

9th Grade

THE REST OF the teacher's strike went by quick, and before they knew, they were all back in school again. On that first day back, the rains had come at last, and it was pouring out. Evan ran from G-building to F-building down the walkway on the second floor, getting drenched along the way. Judith smiled, shook her head as he joined her under the covering by the wall. It wasn't her usual smile, though, and he noticed right away. Still, he leaned in and kissed her, smirked as he did so. In the short time between classes, with students passing by—some taking out umbrellas, others running with backpacks over their heads—he bent down and unzipped his bag. Evan rifled through, pulled it out, then stood up.

Before he handed it, he looked her in the eye again. "Are you sure you're okay, Jude? You seem . . ."

She faced down to her feet. "Yeah, sorry. It's just weird being back, I guess. That's all."

"Hmm. Well, anyway, you remember the art contest?" Evan raised an eyebrow. "I finally drew this."

Judith took the drawing in her hands. It was of two birds sitting side by side on a tree branch. The birds nuzzled their heads and touched their beaks like lovers. She traced the details in the bark, in every feather, in each leaf, in the clouds in the background.

"One of the first times we laid in the park. Remember? Those two gray doves. Close enough we could touch them if we wanted. Pecking at the ground, bouncing closer, then flying in the tree. You said their little eyes were like a doll."

"It's . . . Wow. So beautiful, Evan. Perfect." She darted her eyes up from the paper, smiling. "And this couldn't wait? You had to show me, now, risk us being late?"

"Well, I couldn't hold it in anymore." He laughed, turned away from her with a slight blush. "And it's really just for you. I didn't want the others to see. I know you have tutoring after school so . . ."

She opened her umbrella, stepped close, held it out over the two of them. "Okay, we better hurry."

Evan put his arm around her shoulder and Judith put her arm around his waist as they went down the walkway together. About midway through, he stopped, turned, and kissed her, to which she gave in and kissed him right back. Their lips parted and their tongues slithered as a slight gust of wind sent tiny particles in beneath the cover of the umbrella, spraying them in a soft spritz like waves splashing against the side of a ship.

With the heavy downpour and the wind blowing, it became an icy cold kiss. Like they were in the middle of a tornado that tore through and swept them both up. None of the other students walked by, all already in the classrooms, but the two of them remained there just a moment longer, on the walkway kissing in the rain. She adjusted the umbrella in her hand, reached around to his shoulders as he held at her hips and the small of her back, dipping her down and backwards. From watching ducks by the stream to lying in the grass at the park, to movies, to the carnival, to the floor of Max's mom's bedroom, and now right there . . . It had all been so perfect and wonderful and amazing, until it wasn't.

❧

It didn't happen until the weekend. At the end of the week, Evan saw Judith in Chem in the morning then at lunch and after school, just like that, she was nowhere to be found. He tried calling but no one would answer or her parents would say she wasn't home or she was asleep. All weekend, he was wracked in agony wondering where she was or what was going on. Was she mad at him? His mind ran rampant with all the different potential scenarios. If anything, he knew he would at least see her again in class, but he just couldn't wait that long. Lying in bed, staring out the window, he obsessed over it. Each second passed by so slow that he couldn't escape the thoughts.

From the edge of the bed, he felt a light tug on his shirt. It was his little brother, with innocent eyes, not one word. Evan sat up, gave him a hug, forced a smirk.

"H-hey, you wanna draw? You must be bored, huh." He patted him on the head then on the shoulder. "I just been sleepin' here all day."

On the floor, they scattered papers and color pencils and crayons, began to sketch and doodle. For a moment, Evan glanced over and watched, as his little brother concentrated with his tongue sticking out.

I'm not around enough, I know.

But it's hard. High school is hard, and now with friend drama and girl trouble . . .

From the other room, there was yelling and arguing that escalated with the shattering of glass. Evan reached back and turned on the TV, loud enough to drown out the noise either his brother didn't notice or was already used to.

He pondered how much of an escape his group of friends had become, and now also this girl he had met.

Jude. I hope everything's okay.

The following week, on the first day back, Evan searched all over campus. He went to the library, the computer lab, checked through buildings A through D, then in the upper east wing of admin before recess, he came across her.

Judith swayed on her feet, arms half-crossed in front of her, avoiding his eyes.

"Talk to me. Is everything okay? Did something happen?"

Evan took her hand in his. He led them to a stairwell where they sat down on the top step, like when they first shared their feelings for one another.

"I'm sorry. For everything."

He shook his head, let out a deep sigh. "I was going insane, Jude. What the hell."

"I just didn't know what to do. It was all too much to take, and I needed some time . . ."

She placed both her arms over her knees then rested her head on them. He put his arm around her shoulder, rubbed her arm and leaned in close.

"You can tell me. It's okay, Jude. I'm not mad, I was just worried." Evan started feeling like himself again. "You didn't come to lunch. You don't come out after school. And then you're not answering the phone."

In that moment, it began to rain. A soft, slow rain with heavy droplets that tapped on the walls and roof.

"Okay."

She lifted her head back up, let out a slow exhale through pursed lips, staring straight ahead.

"It's a lot of things, Evan."

He nodded as he listened, starting to feel nervous. His palms dampened as his ankles bounced on the concrete. In his throat, he swallowed a hard and dry lump.

"First of all, my parents know. They found out a while ago but finally confronted me."

"Ah, crap . . ."

"They said I can't see you, that I can't be with you."

Evan arched his head back. "What? Come on, Jude, we can't just let them—"

Judith turned and faced him, eyes reddening and welling up with tears. "It's true, though. They do have a point. My studies have been lacking, from even before. I've been so unfocused and distracted, and I really can't afford to blow it. You know? I've been late to classes, almost missed practice and tutoring. I even bombed a presentation in one of my classes . . . I can't let them down. I can't let myself down. I can't."

He was quiet, just stared ahead, pulled his arm back and laced his hands together in front of him.

"Maybe we shouldn't be together."

His brows furled as he grinded his teeth. He rubbed his palms together trying to stay calm.

"Not only that, but . . ."

"But what?"

"I don't know, I can see other people staring and whispering whenever I pass by. They're talking about us and what we did. I can't take it."

"Screw 'em. Your parents, all these other kids, what does their opinion matter? It's about *us.*" Evan motioned with his hand between the two of them. "It's about us, and how we feel. We like each other. Right?"

She closed her eyes, opened them again, but glanced down at each step and at the landing.

"Yeah, but they're saying I'm a slut and that you're an asshole. That we're both selfish, and . . ."

Judith could no longer contain herself, shuddered at the shoulders, breaking down. Now, Evan understood. It was all too much for her: disapproval from her parents, the pressure of school and studying, then judgment and guilt.

"All right. Fine."

Evan put his arm around her again, pulled her close.

"I'm sorry your parents got mad. I'm sorry that all this has been affecting your grades, and your concentration. And I'm sorry there's gossip now and that you feel, like, overwhelmed." He rubbed her arm again, inched in close enough to catch a whiff of her perfume. "But tell me. Do you still like me?"

"Of course. Evan, that didn't change."

A tear rolled down her cheek as she smiled.

He took her hand in his, lifted it and kissed it. "I still like you, too. I care about you. And, well, whatever it is you decide, I'll follow."

"I think . . ." Judith licked her lips, let out a slow breath. "We have to break up, at least for a little while. Go back to being friends. Like, it's just too much right now."

There was a long pause then the rain grew more intense, matching her tears.

"I'm so sorry, Evan."

"Me too." He swallowed as he squeezed her hand, sighing to himself. "Me too . . ."

Coming over him then wasn't a feeling of sad or mad, but rather a lack of feeling, hollow and empty. A part of him was severed and withered apart right there on the stairs.

"You think one day we'll be together again?"

"I hope so."

Their eyes locked, with her soft smile and his half-smirk, both holding hands in the stairwell while the rains poured down over the school washing away their short little love affair.

Next morning, in Chem, as they each scooted their desks close with the textbook turned sideways, he watched her pretty fingernail follow along the words. He gazed up in her almond eyes that were engrossed in it, feeling a dull beat from inside his chest, then peeped back down. Other than small moments in class, maybe the occasional study session, it was all over between them. They were friends now, just friends.

Before the others, Evan was first to get to the flagpole and wait. He sat down on the rock wall staring at the other kids who laughed and smiled as if things were normal, just happy to be out of school. Now, school was the one place he got to see her—on Tuesdays, Wednesdays and Fridays, in the mornings—so school was almost a haven to him. A haven in that he could at least see her still. But, at the same time, it was also a small personal hell—in that he was forced to see her. The flag above waved in place. A group of girls passed by, and they kind of glanced at him whispering amongst themselves with cupped hands, just as Judith described. He could feel a small rage building inside, but faced down and away, letting it go. It was the least of his concerns. All he needed was for the boys to come so he could vent to them, as soon as he could, as long as he could. It was like a rite of passage.

Evan panned once more around the courtyard, up at the walkways between buildings then at the second and third floor of admin. He closed his eyes, clenching his teeth and his fists, while his feet jittered in place.

A slight shove from his side, and his eyes snapped back open. It was Mark and Jared standing there.

"Hey. How ya holdin' up, man."

"You okay?"

All he could muster in return was a shake of his head from side to side, scrunching his lips together.

Mark sat down to the right, then Jared, left. The three friends watched the rest of the world together, as it continued in front of them and all around.

"I just feel like . . ."

Mark turned towards him. Jared listened, but faced straight ahead with arms crossed.

"It just feels like I totally screwed up."

This was Evan's confessional booth now.

"Ah, don't beat yourself up. Like, you did what you had to, what felt right."

"I mean, plus, think of all that you got to enjoy. You're the only one of us who's touched a boob." Mark's attempt at humor landed flat.

Evan did smirk a little, but returned to his somber state.

"I don't know. It almost feels like was it worth it? You know? For just a few weeks, look at us. Look at all this. What happened to our group? Where's Der? Where's Max?"

Jared cleared his throat, chiming in. "Uh, something happened. I think Max might be in detention . . . Not sure. He was caught tagging a wall or something. That's what I heard, anyway."

"Are you serious? See?" Evan planted his face in both palms. "Tagging . . . Graffiti . . . What's happening? What is going on?"

"That idiot." Mark shook his head.

Evan lifted himself up, sat straight, arching his neck back.

"And, well, the worst part, of course, is just missing her. I miss her so bad it frickin' hurts, you guys."

Both were quiet, sat there with him in his pain. The crowds thinned, and the courtyard became more calm.

"One day. Just wait. Maybe you'll get to be together again."

"We're trying to be friends."

"Can you really do that?" Mark kicked his feet out in front of him, scooted on the rock wall.

Evan sighed, ignored it. "Guys. Any of you heard anything from Der?"

"Not since Max tried reaching out last. He's like the only one that's actually talked to him." Jared slumped now, laying his hands in his lap. "I tried calling a few times, but he just says he doesn't wanna talk and hangs up."

"God . . . I really made a mess of things."

"Hey, man. We'll get through this. And, you know, Derek really wasn't so great." Mark forced a laugh. "Forget him. Cut the cord. Better off without him."

He felt Mark put his arm around his shoulder, felt Jared tap him on the back.

"I just wish things weren't so screwed up. I wish I could talk to him, somehow. You know? He'd know just what to say, ironically." Evan laughed to himself.

"Eh, one day. Maybe not today, but one day." Jared shifted over, nodded.

"Yeah. I guess so." Evan licked his lips, breathed in a slow breath, his eyes staring into the patches of grass.

The memories came, as he sat there with his friends trying to console him. He thought of Derek and his goofy smile. He thought of how they grew up together, how they played with toys and went to the beach to watch fireworks. Then, of course, he remembered Judith, her dimples and her almond eyes, and all their passion: holding hands, kissing, making out, touching one another. In the midst of the flood of images, Derek flashed once more through his mind, and the last thing that happened between them, the fight by the edge of the tennis courts, over Judith.

Evan sighed, swallowed, with his brow furled. “And how long, you think, until we ever talk again?”

19

12th Grade

IN THE BATHROOM mirror, Evan peered at his own reflection peering back. His fingers brushed his hair that was a little longer and parted in the middle, then he straightened and adjusted his collar shirt. Around his neck was a set of cheap headphones like a backwards necklace, the crooked wire running down his front. He grabbed the discman from the sink, held it in his hand, pressed play. As he walked back out onto campus, he let the sounds blast in his ears. One of the vocalists screamed at first in one octave then again in another, while the other rapped in rhythm to it. In the background, turntables scratched along to guitars and drums. Now, as Evan walked through the halls, he got nods and waves, clapping palms together as he passed through. Being in one place long enough will do that to a person. You become another familiar face, one of the fixtures on the wall. You become institutionalized.

Some of the girls were more curvy, dressed more provocative, and Evan let his eyes wander and linger. He smiled at those he knew, admired those he didn't. A few guys had grown in proportion, too, with spurts of facial hair and muscles. It was a different world than when he first strolled on campus. And, well, he was a different person too.

He had Spanish in the morning, then after that, he had Health. When there was enough time left at the end of class, he worked on a new masterpiece. First he would etch in pencil, get the main outline and all the essential shapes, then switch to black marker—a Micron 0.8mm—and sometimes straight ink along with a calligraphy brush to help fill in. After the inking process, he streaked lines through using a small squeeze bottle of whiteout which helped highlight. Instead of a composition book, he now used a real sketchbook.

His latest work was of a bow turned sideways, a wooden arrow in place, aimed, about to shoot a tranquil deer that chewed grass in the trees and shrubbery.

With those two classes out of the way, it was time for lunch and he was on his way to the cafe where he, Mark and Jared sat in back, further past the old spot.

"Evan!"

Turning around, he saw Michelle. Her camera hung from a lanyard around her neck, and she nudged the glasses to the crook of her nose. They were in Newswriting together, which was his third and final class for the day. She was one of the photographers while he was a cartoonist. Wiping the sweat from her brow, she caught up to him then caught her breath.

"Hey. Think you could get us a quote?"

"Are you serious . . ."

"Yeah. We're behind on this one article, you know which one, and everybody's real slammed."

At the end of the month, they all scrambled to get their articles and photographs and illustrations together, fitting them, and sending them off to the printers.

"I knew it." He shook his head, sighed. "I mean, I guess. I got a friend there so, if he's around, fine."

"Awesome. See ya in class."

"But hey, like, if he's not, then what?"

She shrugged, turned back and rushed off. Michelle was kind of an outsider, strange to most, but the two of them always got along. Every now and again, he, Michelle and some of the other staff (they called them that if they were part of the school paper or yearbook) would joke around in the darkroom while the photos developed. They all grew close since the end-of-the-month scrambles often ran late into the afternoon, sometimes even until night. And then they had to deliver the damn things, which wasn't too bad because it did get them out of class.

Heading from G-building across the courtyard, between admin and D-building towards the portables, Evan let the music blast some more. With his backpack over one shoulder, sketchbook and discman in one hand by his side, there were more waves and nods along the way.

Now, in front of him was P1, the largest of the new renovations in the portable buildings. Some renovations were made to the library on both floors as well. Buildings A through H now all had air conditioning in the classrooms, and the campus got a fresh coat of paint along with brand new benches. They put a mural in back of the admin building and a big design of the school mascot up in the gym. The computer lab was improved, with better computers and better internet. The auditorium got new lights, a new sound system and new curtains and seats. An exchange student program was implemented. There were a lot of little changes like that from freshman to senior year, before all that would occur.

He stepped towards the open doors, could hear faint

grinding from the woodshop in the next portable over in P2. Some kids in uniform glanced up, but Evan ignored them as he saw who he was searching for—sitting with his back turned, at one of the tables flipping through a pamphlet.

Evan tapped him on the back, waited.

Turning around, Max stood with him. "'Sup."

"Looking good in that uniform, man." Evan smirked, punching him. "I still can't believe it sometimes."

They didn't hang as often as they used to, but they were still close. Max had some trouble in his classes, not paying attention and falling behind, so he had to retake them during summer, which put a little space between him and the rest of the group. His acne cleared, his braces were off, and he seemed to be doing good overall.

"So, we're kinda taking a poll thing for a story based on the towers, and I'd like to get a quote from you, if that's cool. Represent the ROTC and all that."

"Yeah, sure."

Evan noticed the pamphlet, reached down and touched it, rotated it so that he could see it straight.

"Are you . . . joining?"

"I actually swore in last week."

"No shit. Really?"

He took it in his hand, leafed through to the inside which showed men in salute, tanks and planes, a ropes course being tackled, facing back up at Max.

"Interesting. You know, we've all talked about what we wanted to do when we graduated, but I never knew yours."

"I mean, me either." Max laughed, with arms folded. "Kind of just happened."

Evan was happy to hear his friend found a direction in

life, had made this big decision. Still, though, it was kind of strange to him.

"Hmm. If you don't mind . . . Like, what made you choose this?"

"There's a lotta benefits. They pay for college, pay for housing and travel. Also . . ." Max balled a hand in front of his mouth, cleared his throat, rubbed his nose that was turning red. "Sorry, allergies."

"Also what?"

His reply was so blank and so matter of fact, it was disturbing.

"I want to kill people."

20

Jan 19th
12:34pm

THERE WAS SOMETHING different this time, heading back from the fields. Evan heard the megaphone blaring from behind him, as well as rapid gunfire echoing the opposite way. Police had begun clearing the school, starting from the ends of upper and lower campus toward the interior, building by building. He ducked down as he passed the bleachers in front of the baseball diamond, then strafed between the portables towards the walkway on the side of D-building. He headed to the west wing of admin, about to enter inside. Evan slowed, stepped, as he saw blood splattered, blood pooling and spilling, along with bloody footprints and a handprint smeared.

Oh, no . . .

Evan thought of the one shooter in E-building on the second floor, darted his head back then forward again keeping an eye out for the other shooter. It was eerily quiet now entering the admin building.

The vending machine was shattered in front, its pane of glass cracked like a spiderweb. The water fountain was filled in the bowl, the spout half-stuck in the on position, dripping over the side. Pieces of paper blew across the floor as if they were dry leaves or tumbleweeds.

Bang, bang, bang.

Rapid gunshots sounded, close, from behind in the west wing. Evan raced forward without thinking.

Bang, bang, bang, bang.

It was even louder, and there was a shout that panned from left to right reverberating off the walls around him. Glancing back over one shoulder, Evan saw someone run past the opening outside the building.

As he turned back around, he tripped and fell down, hard, right on his knees, rolling to his side.

Keeping his gaze down the west wing, Evan continued to inch backwards on the floor starting to hyperventilate. The lights above him dimmed, flickered, cut out.

Bang. Bang.

The long pleading shout was cut short with the abrupt gunshots.

Shit!

He turned over on all fours, about to stagger up, then he heard it.

"E-Evan?"

It was almost inaudible, like a stammered murmur in the dimly lit hallway wheezing through a crushed throat. There was a deep gasp followed by sharp coughing.

"Evan, h-help."

As his eyes adjusted in the darkness, he could see the outline of someone on their back on the floor just a few feet away, hands over the front of their torso with their head sideways on the tile.

He crawled a little closer, until he could see the features in the face.

God. Please.

Please don't let it . . .

Now, as he hovered over, Evan could make out the whites of his eyes, the beads of sweat, the tears gathering, a slight shiver in his fingertips that grasped at his abdomen. He could hear the gasps and wheezes, almost like a gurgling noise as he struggled to stay alive.

"Max?"

Through gritted teeth, he attempted a nod in return.

"Oh, God."

Evan sat up on his knees, holding a hand out over the top of Max, whose front was stained in dark crimson. He was in civilian clothes instead of in uniform, just a plain shirt and denim shorts.

"I . . . I can't move . . ." The gasp muttered through pursed lips, another slight gurgle with a sharp hiss. "I can't f-feel my l-legs . . ."

"God. No, no."

Evan attempted to swallow, dry heaving instead, turning to the side to fight it back.

Throughout this time, he had been so preoccupied with Judith, with finding her, with saving her. She was the priority, above any one of his friends—above himself. Feelings of helplessness and guilt and melancholy permeated deep down inside him.

"You're gonna be okay."

Evan nodded, unsteady in his movement, telling it to himself as well. His lips thinned and began to quiver, but he shook his head and faced the other way.

"I'll get us out of here."

"D-d-don't leave me, Evan . . ." Max pleaded from the floor, his eyes bulged.

Evan began to unbutton his collar shirt, removed it so all he wore was a white undershirt. He balled the collar shirt, stared down at Max's torso, not sure where to place it.

"I'm not, I won't."

He placed it over Max's front, closer to his stomach. Max adjusted his hands and fingers over it. Already, the fabric stained and started to soak through.

"I promise."

Max gasped again, a wheezing hiss as he settled in his next breath. He tried to speak but mere gurgling emerged, followed by nodding.

"But I can't move you like this. Okay?" He raised his brows, tilted his head as he spoke. "I gotta go get something to help move you."

Shaking his head, Max closed his eyes, leaned against the tile floor.

"It'll only be a minute, maybe two."

Evan scanned around. There wasn't a maintenance shed this time or any carts near, but maybe he could find one.

"What i-if . . ."

He looked Max straight in the eye, nodded. "I'll be right back, I swear."

Strands of spittle dangled as Max opened his mouth to speak but instead just breathed.

Evan stood, faced down at him.

"You hold on, okay?"

He turned, walked away, first with a side step then with a slow jog. From behind, he could still hear Max moaning like a wounded puppy.

"Waait . . ."

Evan went to the bottom of the nearest stairwell but it was locked. Each stairs had a gate at the bottom and top that were always open, held in place by a simple hook, but this one was closed and chained together like at the gym and the cafe.

Ah, come on.

He remembered the herd of bodies clogged in the stairwell when the shooting began, and how he walked backwards in shock against one of the pillars.

That's why they were stuck like that.

It clicked in his head then. The second floor, where this all started. By the library. There had to be a cart inside, a shelving cart.

Just hang on, Max.

I'll get ya outta here.

He ran down the east wing of admin over to the inner stairwell of F-building, sprinted up the steps to the second floor. Evan was already out of breath, already beginning to feel a sharp pain in his side.

Making his way back across, a silhouetted figure turned the corner from the direction he was headed. A bigger military style rifle was held up in both hands, aimed straight at him.

Evan skidded on the soles of his feet, froze in place with his hands out.

Bang, bang. Bang.

In back of him, doors at the opening of the walkway bursted with splinters and wood chips. To the side, pieces of the wall crumbled, and tiny concrete pebbles spiraled onto the floor.

Ducking down, Evan zigzagged toward the automatic doors that whooshed open in front of him.

Bang. Bang.

He entered the library, could see others hiding behind counters and under tables, between the different rows of shelves.

The automatic doors whooshed open again, and Evan rushed forward, unsteady and haphazard.

Bang, bang, bang, bang.

A rapid succession of gunfire echoed through the quiet space, blasting apart metal housing in each shelf, glass displays of computer monitors, even a copy machine in the corner that sparked then smoked.

Pieces of paper wafted down all around like leaflets or like snow, as if from a small blizzard, pages torn from books that had been shot through and ripped apart.

Evan glanced over by the stairs, wondered if he should try to run up, peeked back toward the automatic doors and the turnstile and sensor.

More shots fired, forcing him to pull away, leaning against the shelf lined. The wooden rail of the stairs cracked open, the glass pane beneath it shattering, and the shards fell on the carpet. Sheets of paper wafted again with some of the pieces landing near him.

There was a loud high-pitched cackling that pierced through the air, causing some of the students hiding to shudder in place and cover their ears and their mouths.

Oh, no . . .

"Now LISTEN UP, boys and girls."

It was the jester, from back at the auditorium.

"The TIME has AL-MOST COME."

No, no, no, no, no.

Evan inched around the side of the shelf, saw the jester stepping, almost prancing. She held the bulky handgun in one hand.

"I'm giving you ALL this ONE chance. You're FREE to GO."

Nobody moved, not sure if it was some sort of trick.

"I see you HIDING over there. C'mon, get up."

He saw the jester jerk somebody up from under one of the tables, knocking over a potted plant. He peeped around again, saw whoever it was walk with their hands up towards the automatic doors.

"You too, behind the counter. Let's go."

Evan glanced down to the next shelf, where a cheerleader stooped on one knee and another hugged themselves in a ball on the floor. There was confusion and hesitation on their faces, as they each turned to one another mouthing what they should do.

Just then, the jester stepped into his line of sight. She stared first at Evan then at the other two.

"What did I say, huh? GET OUTTA HERE."

They both stood and walked away with their hands above their heads. Evan staggered from the floor, faced the jester. He could see her teeth showing through beneath the mask that covered the top half. For a moment, her malicious grin appeared like pointy teeth or like fangs.

"Hey there, pretty boy."

Evan gazed down at the floor, spreading his hands out in front of him as he walked. The jester continued to the next few shelves herding students out one by one or in pairs of two or three.

About to pass through the turnstile, a gun pointed at him from the other side. It was the bigger military style rifle from earlier out in the hallway.

He lifted his hands higher, stepped backward. All else seemed blurred except a long black trench coat and the barrel of the gun aimed right at his chest. His eyes shifted focus until Evan noticed that the mask they wore was different. Unlike the masquerade ball type of mask or the kabuki mask, this one was a gas mask, which could only mean . . .

Images of the puppet tilting his head in place, staring from behind the swirled black, white and red conjured in his subconscious. Evan turned back, watched the jester who started walking up the stairs to the second floor of the library. Her mask gleamed in the light, with its feathers and rhinestones. In front of him, the gas mask had two round circles for eyes, a grated metallic piece for the mouth, and a round cylinder sticking out to the side.

There was a third shooter.

Evan had come in contact with all three, and here he was now, held at gunpoint while the other students left one by one in a single file line. He watched them pass, some glancing back with worried eyes. There was a teacher among them, even a librarian and an aide.

"Okay, that should be all of them."

"Should be or it is?"

"It is."

"It better be."

Unlike the puppet, gas mask spoke. Watching their interaction, it was clear which one of them was in charge. The jester stood to one side, awaiting further instructions.

"Now go and follow them." The gas mask didn't break gaze, kept the gun steady. "Kill every last one."

Evan found himself blinking, his brow furled, listening as the voice was muffled behind the mask.

"You got it."

The jester was about to exit, turned back once more.

"Uh, the timers are about to . . ."

As the gun edged closer, lifting higher up, Evan raised his hands and faced the floor.

"La-di-freaking-dah."

Evan's eyes shot open wide and his head darted up, staring

across at the gas mask. The jester went through the automatic doors that slid open then closed.

Bang. Bang.

He could hear the cackling from outside.

Evan's lower jaw hung down, and he stepped forward, lowering both hands. He peered deep in the circles of the eyes, into the blackness there. Goosebumps formed on his skin. His breaths became quick, shallow.

It was just the two of them left in the quiet library, with paper scattered all over the floor. A part of him wanted to scream at the top of his lungs. Another part wanted to break right down and cry, as the inescapable conclusion became clear. His eyes narrowed as he fought back hot tears, shaking his head as the thoughts overwhelmed him like a raging flood.

". . . Derek?"

PART FOUR
BLEEDING HEARTS

1

12th Grade

As he headed from the portables to the cafeteria, Evan still thought of what Max said. There were more nods and waves, clapping palms, more smiles, but Evan couldn't help lingering on those words. How could someone say, even *think,* such a thing? He pulled the headphones from on his head and his ears to around his neck again, as he entered the front doors. It was always nice seeing Max since he wasn't around as often, but Max was also strange at times. The divide may have started with falling behind and being forced to take summer school classes, but there was also something more.

He walked by the old spot, thought of days long gone—Judith smiling, laughing, her hair swaying, Max nodding, spilling food in his lap, and of course, Derek—then he continued on past the line and the register to the new spot in back. Jared nodded at him, Mark waved.

"Hey. What up, guys."

Mark had a black beanie with a fox on it and a jacket, which was too hot for this weather. (The things you did to look cool, right?) He no longer had glasses and wore contacts instead. Jared had a long sleeve collar shirt on, kind of similar to Evan. Evan always wore plaid or stripes, maybe a light blue denim color. Jared liked to stick to solid colors: gray, beige, darker blue.

"Ev-an."

"Yo, E."

He sat down next to Mark, across from Jared. They slid some of their food over, a carton of milk as well.

"Thanks, man. I had to stop and talk to Max real quick."

"Oh yeah? How is that ol' ass-hat?" Mark grinned a wide grin, bit into a fry with the corner of his mouth. "Still a weirdo?"

"He said he's joining the military."

"Really?" Jared jutted out his lip, tilted his head with arms crossed. "I can't imagine."

There was a small round of laughter.

"Hey. We hangin' out tonight?"

"Ah, I gotta do Newswriting. It's the late night where we gotta get all our articles in and stuff. I also got a meeting for Eagles Club before that, too, so a little busy."

It was a social club where students did volunteer work, community service and charity events, things like that. So far, he'd helped with a beach cleanup, visiting terminally ill children, and some fundraising.

"Man . . ." Jared shook his head. "I don't know why you signed up for that."

"I told you." Evan laughed. "It just happened."

Leaning an elbow on the table, Mark grinned again. "Well, we'll be at the mall checking out chicks so."

That was Mark's new favorite hobby. It was all of their favorite hobby of course, but Mark was always the biggest advocate. Jared had the best eye for it, since he had twenty-ten vision and was super subtle—like a ninja or a spy. Mark just blatantly stared with no shame and no attempt at even trying to appear inconspicuous. Evan was pretty good, an opportunist catching a girl bending over or maybe going up the escalator, or by happy accident the wind blowing their skirt.

From time to time, they still played games at the arcade and went to the comic book shop, but now they hung out at the mall or just chilled at some fast food joint, maybe shot pool. Mark played for the tennis team and did judo so sometimes he had practice and was busy as well. Jared was the anti-social one who didn't join any clubs, never went to PE classes and had to take Home Economics instead. Evan was in the one club, but drew for the school paper, and also helped with some of the theater productions still.

With graduation looming, just a few months away, it was a mix of "senioritis" setting in and prepping for the so-called real world. It seemed like the main options were either to work, join the military, or to go to college—either at community college or university in state, or some bigger school out of state.

High school is just high school. A place filled with people, a campus filled with students. Chalkboards and analog clocks and shelves with textbooks and rows of desks. Acne and hormones and angst. A delicate little ecosystem, with balance and norms. You become so used to it, to the point you're almost institutionalized. It all makes sense and everything works out just fine. Soon, it would be time to migrate to a new ecosystem, and adjust to all new rules. For now, though, at least they still had this: hanging out, talking, joking, checking out girls. Down the road in the coming months, they would have prom and cut day and signing yearbooks, so on and so forth until actual graduation day.

Walking up the stairs, Evan let the music play through the headphones in his ears to his body and limbs. The rest of the world passed by as he remained in a different plane of existence, smirking to himself. In one hand was his sketchbook and the discman that played with the anti-skip on, draining extra battery. Over one shoulder he held the strap of his backpack, the exact same one from freshman year except written over and designed with Sharpie and whiteout, which was the cool thing to do. From the top of the stairwell, he turned and headed down the walkway. He always looked forward to club meetings, although he would never admit it. Stepping toward the side of the library where the meeting room was, Evan glanced down to the courtyard and cul-de-sac, at the flagpole. Further up the hallway, on a small ladder that one of her friends held in place, Judith put together a bulletin board. The way the sun beamed, she was like a celestial being. With her hair in a fiery sheen, nibbling at her lower lip, her almond eyes focused and concentrated on the task at hand.

Evan leaned on a nearby pillar, removing his headphones, crossing his arms and watching, as Judith arranged thumbtacks and construction paper and cardboard. He could see the slender of her legs and arms from that angle, inclined his head to one side as he admired her beauty. When she turned and bent to grab the glue stick, he could see in its entirety what she was putting together.

WASHINGTON
HIGH SCHOOL

There were notices and flyers hanging from it, and a picture of the school mascot from the side with its pointy beak and big bold eye.

"You know, you've gotten a lot better at that."

Judith shifted back, saw him standing there, began to step down.

Amongst themselves, the two girls spoke in a whisper.

"He's cute. You should date him."

"Actually . . ." Judith smiled, her deep dimples peeking through her cheeks. "You know, maybe."

"Here." Taking the other board, folding the small ladder, her friend started to walk away, giving her a look. "I'll take care of this one."

Stepping closer together, they faced one another for a moment, not moving, not speaking. She tucked her hair behind her left ear. He adjusted the headphones around his neck. Her light denim jumper had a flap over the shorts that made it appear almost like a skirt at the bottom. Beneath the jumper, she wore a tight sweater-shirt that accentuated her breasts. He could see the raised design along the lining of her bra. All this time gone by, and there was still an electricity there, this tension, in the space between them, whenever their eyes met or their skin would graze.

"I've been listening to some of that J-Pop you gave me, pretty good."

"Oh yeah? I have another new song I wanted you to listen to, too. You'll love it."

He led them to the ledge of the second floor where they leaned on the wall and gazed out over the upper campus. It was a beautiful day, with the sun up and light clouds scattered and spread thin.

"So. How's it going, Jude?"

"Things are good. Busy as usual, with tutoring, with practice. Not to mention I'm still submitting applications and letters of recommendation, statements, transcripts . . ."

"Ah, you got this. It'll all be okay. Oh, hey, know what I found out? So weird. Max said he's joining the military."

"Really? Wow."

Evan squinted as he panned down the long driveways running parallel, then at the shopping center. "Crazy, right?"

She nodded, smiled as she watched him lost in thought, his eyes peering out in the distance.

"With you applying out-of-state, Mark already accepted to the university on scholarship, Jar planning on community college, and now Max going into the service, it's like we covered it all, huh? Hmm."

"And what are you planning?"

He was quiet, faced downward. "I don't know. Like, my SAT scores are good enough to get into university, but I don't know how I'd pay for it. I talked to a recruiter and even went to base, got suckered into doing some physical and combat training."

She covered her mouth, tried not to laugh. "What?"

"Yeah, haha. I was only supposed to get like a tour, and next thing I know I'm running around, doing sit-ups, then getting grappled by some buff dude. I took the computer test and aced it, so they said I can pick any MOS I want, from computers to special intelligence. But I just don't know if that's the right thing . . ."

"You're kind of a free spirit."

Evan turned towards her, smirked.

She licked her lips, leaned in.

"And how 'bout art, Evan?"

Letting his shoulders slump, he leaned forward. "I've talked to my art teacher about that. If I take drawing and painting seriously, I mean, I would probably have to move somewhere like Cali or New York, and I just don't know. I was thinking maybe I could just take a year off. What you think?"

"Maybe talk to the counselor?"

"You know, I did that. I went in there and said all this stuff, about the recruiter and my SAT scores and art, and they didn't really take me seriously. It's like, if you're not struggling at the bottom or some darling at the top, they don't give a crap . . ."

"I'm sorry."

"Eh, it's okay."

He pulled from the wall, motioned with a nod. "Hey, uh, we better get going."

They walked together side by side. No one else was around, just the two of them.

It wasn't a far walk, since the meeting room was just on the other side of the library. After a few pillars, Evan stopped and turned to Judith.

"Wait. Before we go in . . ."

He traced her up and down, breathed in and out as he twisted on the ball of his foot. She peeped up at him with reddened checks, blinking, holding one arm over her midriff.

"Do you wanna go to prom with me?"

Her almond eyes lit up, and her deep dimples poked through as she smiled a wide smile.

"I thought you'd never ask. I'd love to."

"Great. Then it's a date."

2

Jan 19th
12:47pm

THE TWO OLD friends stared at one another, one from behind a mask, with a gun in both hands. Evan's jaw hanging open and his narrowed eyes became a disapproving glare. His teeth clenched and grinded. His fists tightened. Derek stepped to the side, placed the gun on the counter, taking the gas mask off. He stood like that for a moment, with his back turned, as he basked in satisfaction and relief. The quiet of the library emphasized every single step that dragged across the carpet, every tap and glide of the gunmetal against the marble. Evan's body trembled without his knowledge, as the undeniable truth turned the initial disbelief into disgust, then into seething repulsion. He could see Derek put on a backwards cap before turning around. Whatever bond there used to be was no longer there, and this mutual malice lingered in the air from both ends. A violent confrontation was brewing beneath the surface in the deafening silence that seeped through the open space. Evan furled his brow. Derek smiled.

"You like that, huh?" Derek motioned with his head. "That's an AR-15. Well, generic version."

They each stepped in tandem to the space between the tables and the checkout area. Behind Evan were rows of shelves, and the stairs leading to the second floor. Derek stood with the counter to one side and the turnstile and sensor on the other.

Earlier, he didn't have the trench coat or the mask, but he did have on all black. He almost always dressed like that in recent years so Evan must not have noticed. Now, Derek in his black shirt and jeans, donning the trench coat, showed his true self. And Evan, in his white undershirt and beige khakis, stripped away of the light blue denim collar shirt, felt naked and vulnerable. He glanced up at the red backwards cap, which was like the red on his hands.

"What did you do, Derek?"

His eyelids fluttered as he grinned, lips thin, on the brink of an outburst of laughter.

"The hell, Evan. You know the answer to that . . ."

"You're working with these freaks?"

As they stepped in unison, they rotated clockwise. "It was my idea."

Evan forced a swallow, faced down to the carpet then back up, shook his head and scrunched his lips.

What happened to you, Der . . .

"For years, I've been waiting for this moment. I studied and practiced, planned, like from out of a cookbook, like a blueprint."

Derek shot out one of his arms as he emphasized the words, flapping the trench coat behind him.

"You could've cornered me earlier. Why didn't you?"

"I wasn't ready yet. No. There was still work to do. Plus, I just knew you'd be stupid enough to stay on campus."

He let him speak, listened, glared, mirroring his movement in turn.

"Remember how we used to play Killer?"

With a blank stare back, Evan stood with his arms to his side.

"Some people get dealt all the good cards in life. They got the upper hand. The aces and the kings and queens, face cards, while all I got are *fucking* single digits."

Evan snapped then, shouted out. "Oh, don't give me that bullshit, Derek! Life's not fair. So what. You deal with it."

He nodded along, lowered his voice. "Deal with it . . ."

"Yeah. Get over yourself. This little sob story is crap, and it's pathetic. Look out there. People are dead! The school is burning, shot up!"

All the anger had been brewing, then spilled out. Evan felt nervous, almost regretted the words.

Derek ignored whatever it is he said, continuing his own train of thought.

"And, in our little game, what was that one rule? Do you remember? 'Loser deals,' right?"

They each took another clockwise step.

"Well, not today."

"Oh yeah?" Evan nodded with conviction, spread his arms out in a taunting manner. "And what you gonna do? Huh? You wanna fuckin' fight me, is that it?"

"That's part of it, yeah." Derek smiled.

Evan lurched forward with a fist winded back, throwing a right hook that Derek dodged. He followed with a kick that Derek blocked. Derek then pivoted, countered, and knocked Evan away.

"I told you. I've waited a long time for this."

Derek shifted on his feet, jabbed Evan in the face, punched him hard in the torso then kneed him. He took swings to his jaw, cheek, then his ear, turning him around and toppling him forward. With a good swift kick to the back, Derek sent Evan stumbling onto the floor. Evan turned over on the carpet, knocking Derek down with a sweep of the leg.

"Ah, there we go."

Dusting himself off, Derek stood from the floor, shaking out the trench coat.

"Let me get my monies' worth."

Evan wiped at his nose that bled around one nostril, staggering up with a slight hunch in his posture. His breathing grew heavier.

"You did this to yourself, Evan. All because you let some bitch get between us."

"She's *NOT!* A bitch!!!"

Evan yelled through clenched teeth, straightened up ready to fight again.

"Okay, Der. This what you want!?"

He stepped forward, uppercutted Derek right in the jaw, followed with two jabs to the left side of his cheek. Then he pivoted, lashed out his leg in a quick kick to the ribs, spun the other way on the ball of his foot, swinging around and hitting him with his heel.

"I haven't seen you do that since we were kids!"

Derek held his arm close to his side, smiling and gritting his teeth at the same time. He was about to say more but Evan didn't let him, cut him off as he tackled him backward into a table, breaking one of the legs. They then grappled on the floor turning over sideways in a hard roll. Evan lifted a fist, about to punch down. Derek let out a sharp maniacal laugh, headbutted Evan knocking him off wincing in pain.

"Now see, Evan." He stood, leaned over and spat on the carpet. "I learned some new tricks."

"S-screw you . . ." Evan spoke through open fingers, covering his face, staggering to his feet again. "Shut the hell up and let's go."

Derek laughed again.

They circled each other, this time counterclockwise. Evan held one fist up, one fist down. Derek held his hands in front of him, keeping them open. Both their bodies were slanted in attack positions.

As Derek stepped forward, Evan stepped back. They both were slower and had slight limps.

Rushing at him, Derek swung left then right, jumping with a kick to Evan's chest that sent him back. He struggled not to fall, stumbling on his feet, regaining balance then faced Derek again. Evan jabbed but Derek blocked it. Evan kicked him right in the ribs, kicked again. He lunged, grabbing the collar of his shirt, shoving Derek back into a shelf just shy of toppling it over. Some of the books slipped off and thudded on the carpet.

Derek shot both arms between Evan's hands, pressed his elbows out, shoved him off. He then rammed into him and knocked him down.

"You mother—"

The two wrestled on the floor, seeing who would get the upper hand. Papers rustled and crinkled beneath them as they writhed and squirmed.

Evan punched him in the side, in the stomach, getting on top.

"You! Son of a—!"

He winded back and swung across, hard, knocking Derek in the face.

"This is what you wanted, right!?"

Evan punched him again, again, again, until there was a swollen bruise around the eye. He reached back to his pocket, pulled out the knife—swish, swish, flick, click.

Derek laughed, a slur in his voice, with a crackle of mixed spittle and blood.

"Yeah. Do it." He smiled up at him through a bloody grin, the one good eye white and wide, staring, unblinking. "Come on, bestie. Go ahead. Finish what you started."

The knife rattled in Evan's hand as he squeezed tight, glaring down with clenched teeth, his breathing more rapid.

Stop, no.

What am I doing?

Judith came to mind, and her dimples and her almond eyes. Mark and Jared and Max, standing by the flagpole, laughing and joking. He even thought of his little brother drawing with crayons and color pencils.

He then shook his head, tossed the knife aside.

"No, Derek."

Evan staggered up, turned the other way.

"Do you even realize . . ."

He closed his eyes, holding in the tears as his voice became stifled. There was so much he wanted to say, so much he wanted to ask. How could he have done all this?

"I-I don't wanna fight you, Derek."

At that moment, a sharp pain penetrated through his right shoulder blade, searing out to the base of his neck and to the small of his back, forcing him to stagger down to one knee.

Evan gasped in pain, reaching back, arching in place with his mouth wide open.

"There. Now you know."

Behind him, Derek paced sideways.

"Now you know what it feels like, to have your best friend stab you in the back."

"D-Der . . ."

Evan fell forward on his palm, gritted his teeth, hissing as he struggled to remain upright.

He watched Derek walk around in front of him, towards the counter. Evan shuddered, plopping down sideways and knocking over a nearby chair.

"D-D-Derek . . ."

Moving the opposite hand to his far shoulder, he reached behind and yanked the knife out, shouted, felt a warm splash of liquid. Pulling his hand back, he turned his palm over. It was covered in red, dripped and spilled.

He inched back, leaned against one of the tables, peering up at Derek. His body trembled as he gasped on the floor.

"Y-you did this, 'cause of what happened?"

Evan shut his eyes then opened them, tensing in place on the floor. Derek watched him suffer.

"Well. That's not entirely true, no. But it's definitely a big ol' cherry on top."

"Go ahead, then. . . . Kill me."

Derek leaned back bawling in a howl of laughter, bent forward slapping a hand to his knee.

"Kill you? You think I planned all this just to kill you?"

He stepped closer, knelt down in front of him, raising both eyebrows.

"No, no, no, Evan. You must live."

Derek grinned, put a hand on his shoulder causing Evan to hiss and squirm. He straightened up, sent a quick flap through the trench coat.

"No, bestie, you get to live. And you get to know that these people are dead or hurt or scarred for life, all because of you. Because of you, and your fucking dick."

Derek tilted his head as he spoke.

"I-it wasn't like that, Der. I *loved* her. I fell in love. I wouldn't throw everything away if it wasn't—"

"I don't wanna hear it."

Derek stepped right next to the counter, reached and grabbed the gun.

"Wait, wait. Der, no. It's still not too late—"

"It is too late." Derek swallowed. "You prolly thought one day we'd all be friends again, but no, it's far too late. It was too late ever since that day by the tennis courts."

He turned the gun backwards then held it upside down, pointing it towards himself.

"Please, Derek, don't do this."

Evan reached a hand out, shifted his weight, forced his legs to move, trying to stand.

"Derek!!!"

He put the barrel between his lips, touched the muzzle to the roof of his mouth, middle of the gun firm in one hand, his thumb over the trigger in the other.

"Derr, no!"

Bang.

The final gunshot was loud, hard, yet somehow also hollow and muted.

"DEREK!!!!!"

The body fell in front of him, collapsing on the carpet with a few dull thuds like a toy chest that had been knocked over.

Evan wobbled on his feet, rushed down to the carpet near his friend. He wanted to lift his head up, wanted to cradle it in his lap, but just stroked it instead. He ran his fingers through the wave of poofy hair, stared down at the face, now with a swollen bruise around the eye, and near it, a wet tattered fleshy portion.

"Why . . ."

He whimpered and sobbed, like a child. The tears rolled down his cheeks and dripped off his chin.

The exit wound was on the side of his head, behind the temple and above the ear. An angle through the tissue precise enough to leave a last few sparks of electrical current. He could feel Derek's breathing slowing, and he could see Derek's eyes glazing over.

"Why did you do this?"

"I . . ."

One last shallow breath, and Derek turned his eye, parted his trembling lips.

"I'm not like you, Evan . . ."

The library became emptier, quieter, as he felt complete stillness take over and linger.

Evan broke down in a stifled cry, leaning down and hugging his friend. His white shirt stained red, mixed with both their blood. Peeking down to his face, the eyes and the lips seemed sad, seemed scared, dazing off as if asking an unanswered question or receiving an unwanted answer.

God, Der. Why.

A single memory floated to the surface. He remembered the two of them obsessing with their toys, their little model airplanes. They each held one firm in their hands, running and playing, imitating the noises of jet thrusters and missiles firing. Doing barrel rolls and somersaults in a vicious dogfight, in a sonic boom. Two little kids high up in the air, free, flying through the clouds.

Although he wanted to stay there like that, remain with his friend, holding him, reality ripped him back. There was a far explosion that shook through the library, sending small shockwaves in the floor and on the shelves.

Evan stood, gazed down once more.

The backwards cap hovered diagonally to one side, some space between, with spatters of blood. The gun ran parallel alongside his body, a light trail of smoke wafting from the chamber. From that angle, he appeared almost like a scarecrow that had fallen, with a tear in the side of the head and a patch of mud across the eye.

"I'm sorry."

There was another explosion, this one a little further away, then another, setting off distant ringing.

Evan limped towards the turnstile and sensor, hobbled out the automatic doors that whooshed open. He fought through the pain across the walkway, down each stair, all the way back into admin. Now the ringing was louder and sharp. He started to feel dizzy, numb, like he might pass out, but kept going.

In the darkened hallway, he could see Max still laying on the floor. He was no longer wheezing or gasping.

Please, please. No.

Not you too.

Without thinking, Evan knelt down and scooped him up in his arms. Although he tried standing and lifting him, Max wouldn't budge from the floor. He bit down on his lip, took in a deep breath, stumbled to his feet with a long hard grunt.

Heading towards the front doors, Evan carried Max in his arms, wobbling on his feet, feeling a constant throb. He kicked open the door with a slight sway, stepped down the wide set of stairs. At the end of the long driveways, a mob of police and fire officials gathered. Several ambulances lined the road between campus and the shopping center, their lights timed intermittently, sporadic flashing at conflicting angles. Passing the oval median and bronze statue, a group of police raced over just as Evan fell to one knee.

"Help him . . ."

Two of them took Max, another prepared supplies. One came around and tried assisting Evan but he waved them away, flailed his arms, shook his head, pointing over to Max.

"He's been shot. H-he can't move his legs . . ."

Evan leaned backward, plopped on the ground, the lids of his eyes closing.

"H-h-help 'im . . ."

3

Motionless, in the hospital room, Evan stared ahead with a blank expression. He leaned forward, rested his chin in his palm, adjusted the other arm that was in a sling. Max lay on the bed with his eyes closed, not moving except for his chest that rose. His breaths were shallow, weak, as the machine bleeped. There was a pulse oximeter on his finger, an IV line in his forearm near his wrist, and a nasal cannula wrapped around the back of his ears to the front of his face. According to the doctors, they both had been lucky. Evan was struck between the bones, not hitting any major arteries or nerves, and didn't puncture the lung. It was risky moving Max, they told him, but since he had lost so much blood by that time, it was good Evan got to them when he did, because he was right on the edge, in critical condition. That said, the bullet hit Max right in the spinal cord, a vital section that meant he might be paralyzed from the waist down, and never walk again.

There was so much on his mind, the thoughts and feelings overwhelmed him. He was happy to be alive. He was also afraid for his friend who might be paraplegic. Over and over again, he replayed the last two hours in his mind: the auditorium, back and forth from the fields, the cafeteria, then the library.

His specific ordeal and the way that it turned out, compared to how many countless others. Max's mom was there awhile, but stepped out to go through paperwork. Evan's parents came as well. His mom hugged him, which was rare, and his dad patted him on the arm. The circumstances were so extreme it lit a spark of hope for his fractured home. He insisted he was fine and that all he wanted to do was stay with Max. It was his worst fear throughout the shooting, and it had come true.

In one word, Evan was experiencing shock. How could this have happened? What was supposed to be a beautiful day turned out so tragically and horrifically. Evan remembered the sun up and the clear blue skies, and a distinct feeling when he gazed at it all, with his hands in his pockets. There was just a slight hint of clouds, and the way the sun hit the whirling puffs of steam was like from out of a timeless painting. It was such a good feeling, and everything seemed so right and well with the world. Classes were going smooth, and he couldn't help thinking about Judith. A small smirk crept across his face as he strutted through the hallway, escaping to the bathroom just to get a break from the monotony. That was when . . .

Bang.

Bang, bang, bang.

How could Derek do this? Evan shook his head to himself, closing his eyes and leaning back, his brow furled. It always bothered him that they never did hash it out, although he did try. The attempts at an apology and reconciliation over time turned into this sort of awkward tension whenever they saw each other or passed by. Whenever one of them saw the other, it was always the same. Evan would peep over, right in his face, with curious eyes that observed. A part of him wanted to say something, to do something, but knew better. Derek stared straight in front, almost right through him, as if he wasn't even there. It was hard to pinpoint what that certain stare might have meant. He wondered if perhaps it was loathing or hatred, or maybe it could have been indifference. Now he would never know.

Just as he would never know why Derek began to wear all black, began to wear a backwards cap, or began to run with the wrong crowd. Why it was he slacked off in school, why he ditched classes, why he got suspended.

Evan opened his eyes and glanced up at the TV, which played the same thing on all channels. Every news station devoured the story of the attack, almost like it was a flattened cell on a clear slide in a microscope, one they could study and dissect. There was footage of the school from an aerial view, with plumes of smoke, and police cars and firetrucks lined. It cut to officials directing staff and students on the scene, then to a testimonial. One witness spoke through tears in a stammer as multiple microphones pointed at their face. None of the words seemed to resonate, however. It was mere sounds, all just movement. When it transitioned back to the main news anchor, the woman peered down at her stack of notes then into the camera with a somber face.

The nation mourns today as one city high school is in shambles. For those of you just tuning in, a vicious shooting occurred at approximately 11:00am, lasting for nearly two hours in what is being called the Washington Massacre. Students fled from the campus, some hiding in classrooms beneath their desks, as President George Washington High School was under brutal attack. Three shooters carried a combination of knives, hammers, semi-automatic weapons, and homemade explosives. An alarming number of guns have been retrieved from the scene so far including a Glock 19 and Glock 20, a Walther P22, a TEC-9, two sawed-off shotguns, one pump-action and one double-barreled, as well as two carbine rifles, including an AR-15 type model. It appears the suspected shooters amassed various ammunitions ranging from 9mm to 10mm, to 12-gauge, to .22- and .223-caliber from nearby superstores. Some of the weapons had been modified using illegal bump stocks, meaning rounds could be fired at accelerated rates mimicking fully automatic weapons. In addition to this arsenal, shooters carried Molotov cocktails and PVC pipe bombs, and placed pressure cooker bombs near propane tanks in the school's cafeteria. At approximately 12:45pm, bombs went off first in H-building, then in A-building and F-building. The pressure cooker bombs set in the cafeteria, fortunately, failed to trigger. Students who were trapped in the cafeteria and the gymnasium were able to escape prior to the timers set.

Law enforcement and fire departments were slow to respond to the shooting, due to an apparent car bomb and ensuing fire by a freeway overpass not far from the school, which many are assuming was likely a type of diversion. It was discovered the phone lines had also been cut, leaving staff and students unable to contact 9-1-1 from campus or nearby. A total of twenty-three students lost their lives today, but that number may still rise as officials continue to thoroughly search the campus. So far, the number of students and staff injured tallies up to a staggering seventy-one. Hospitals in the vicinity are all overflowing, filled to capacity in efforts to assist those hurt. Triage was established right off campus for those in serious condition needing immediate care. Our deepest condolences to each of the victims and their families, and to those still suffering from this traumatic event.

Each suspected shooter was found with self-inflicted gunshot wounds to the head, appearing to have taken their own lives as authorities arrived. Two of the suspects have been identified as Adrian Lorenza and Cheng-Fai Ho. Lorenza, who was diagnosed with depression and mild Asperger's, was taking several prescribed medications including anti-depressants, and was noted to have been suffering from severe anorexia. The level of anorexia exhibited could have been a contributing factor as cognitive impairment and brain damage may result from the malnutrition, particularly in females. Ho was noted to have anxiety and selective mutism. A quiet student, who was reportedly ostracized by his peers. In months prior to the shooting, he was subject to disciplinary actions for many disturbing behaviors including stalking and harassment. The third suspected shooter, now believed to be the main perpetrator and instrumental in planning the attack, was Derek Harrison. In journal entries as well as a two-thousand-word manifesto discovered in his mother's home, it is believed Harrison showed notable anti-social and aggressive tendencies, possible narcissistic personality disorder, as well as a superiority complex. At our HNN offices this afternoon, a mysterious package arrived containing a video diatribe of the suspect's final thoughts. Viewer discretion is advised as the following may be considered disturbing or graphic.

For those of you that don't know me, of course you don't know me. You walk right on by, past that pathetic loser. I'm just the guy in back of the class, not paying attention, not included in any conversation or any jokes. I'm just the guy waiting to smoke cigarettes at recess with my dejected friends who are equally despised. All the rich kids doing well in life, going out and partying, liquored up, showing their titties. All the cool kids who pat each other on the back, laughing and joking and spreading gossip. And all the teachers and even the fat principal who allow this nonsense to occur daily. Well, this is for you. You shat all over me my entire life. You pushed me so far back against the wall, I had no other choice. You left me out, left me by the wayside. I was subjected to the daily torture of an unjust world. I was forced to march to my death, by the cruel and corrupt, and by the ignorant who do nothing. I hate you all. I hate what you represent. I'm offended by the system, by the status quo. Our entire society has descended into utter chaos and savagery. Crime is run rampant, homelessness on the rise. Poverty. War. The rich get richer, and the government floods the public with more and more lies. How do we fix this? Where does it all even begin? And the answer, it's school. In silly classrooms behind silly chalkboards, with teachers saying their big fancy words and making you repeat after them like god damn fascist dictators. Let this act awaken the people who have been locked away in their slumber, pretending like things were ever good enough. Let it spread like a virus amongst them for which there is no cure, as you've done to me this whole time. I will set your precious school on fire and use the student body to fan its beautiful flames. As for me, I don't plan on making it out of this alive. No, I will be the flint to the spark, of what will grow into a raging moat of heat and a blaze of glorious anarchy. Just know, however, the way things are, in this world as you all designed it, I was already dead.

It returned to an aerial view of the school, voiced over by the helicopter pilot in static. Evan leaned back with his eyes still darted up at the TV, shaking his head, his mouth hanging open. He didn't recognize the person saying those words, who had allegedly planned and carried out this atrocious crime. The face was that of his former best friend, but the words being spoken and their delivery was like a different person altogether. It was as if they were the words of a deranged madman, hell-bent on destruction. Again, he panned over to Max on the bed, who gasped, shuddered in place, causing the machine to alarm. With a few quick wheezes, a slight raspy cough, his face winced. He then returned to his normal state, the machine again with a steady bleep. A dread came over the room as Evan buried his face in both palms, sniffling.

"God. I still can't believe it . . ."

"Poor Max."

Evan lifted his head, saw Mark and Jared there. Mark put a hand on his good shoulder, lowered to sit on the armrest of the chair. Jared stood with his arms crossed.

Wiping the back of his forearm across his face, Evan turned away with another sniffle.

"How could he have done this?" Jared shook his head.

Mark remained stoic as he watched the news on the screen.

"That guy is a frickin' psychopath. I wish I never met the piece of shit."

"Like, the Derek we know would never . . ."

"I don't know what happened over the years, but it doesn't matter. A normal decent human being with a conscience could never do what he did. This is sick, and I'm not gonna pretend it isn't."

Jared stared down to the tile floor.

Evan remained silent through the little exchange, focusing on quieting his sniffles. He blinked and took a deep breath in and out.

There was a short pause between them.

"Hey, what did they say? Is Max gonna be all right?"

"W-we don't know anything yet . . ." Evan adjusted on the chair, straightening up, regaining his composure. "Like, they told his mom they'll know more when he wakes up."

"And, is it true? That he might never walk again?"

Evan hesitated, then nodded.

"Damn it."

"See, this is all his fault. That mother . . ."

There wasn't enough profanity in the English language to express all the disgust Mark felt. He resigned to sitting there with a quiet scowl.

Evan swallowed a lump of dry air. "You know, it probably would've been more, if the bombs in the cafeteria had gone off."

"And why those other buildings?"

"Pssh. He probably thought it was funny. That sick bastard."

It was clear Jared was the one in denial, and Mark was the one that was angry. Which meant Evan must have been either depression or bargaining, perhaps a little of both. Of course, collectively, it was all the same: grief, and its many stages.

"Uh, we going tonight?"

"I mean, we kinda have to. For Max. For everybody."

4

The flames of the candles matched the stars in the sky, lights twinkling and flickering in place. Both the road between the campus and the shopping center, and the street behind the school alongside the canal were flooded. Mark and Jared walked in front, both holding a lit candle close to their chest. Evan walked just behind them, one arm in a sling, holding a candle in the other. Judith glanced over at Evan with tears in her eyes, an arm wrapped around his waist. Along the back fence were letters and cards, small posters with pictures of the victims in memoriam. Up and down the fence, scattered all along and tied with bows, were varied flowers. There were bouquets, wreaths, single roses. Some were attached with little letters in little envelopes, the names of the addressees written in eloquent cursive. It was an incredible moment, touching and tender, although bittersweet, born out of loss and mourning. Attendees joined hands and swayed in song, even those that didn't know one another hugged and cried together. Warmth from the bright candles emanated through the cool air, blending the unity, love and support from the large crowd gathered.

"I'm glad you made it, Jude."

"Of course. No way my parents could stop me."

Sometimes it takes the darkest of tragedies to bring people together, to bring out the best in people. Sometimes there's a glimmer of light amongst the heartbreak and emptiness, in this case hundreds. Evan held the candle, leaned in and pecked Judith on the side of her head, scanning around at the crowd, at each stranger, taking in that moment.

Mark remained stoic, displaying a simple thousand yard stare. Jared gazed down at his feet on the ground, sad yet blank, shaking his head from time to time. There was not a word, there was not a joke. Judith kept her eyes closed, her lip quivering, while her cheeks remained wet and warm. Evan let the streams roll down from the corners of his eyes, blinking to himself. He felt a sensation like fainting, but fought it back. There was an aching in his bones, in his chest, in his very soul.

5

Unlike the vigil, the funeral was a bleak affair. There weren't many attendees. There wasn't much flowers or letters or cards, and there wasn't any kind of uplift or catharsis. Evan and Jared walked side by side up the small hill through the cemetery grounds to the mortuary, both wearing all black. Mark decided right away that, hell no, he wasn't coming—that Derek was dead to him, both literally and metaphorically. It was too much for Judith to process, to comprehend. She couldn't decide either way, and almost had not gone just by default. As for Max, well, he was still in recovery, and couldn't go even if he wanted to. Evan adjusted his arm in a sling, stared down at his feet as he walked. He glanced around at the headstones, at the final words, at the years of life and epithets.

"Can't believe it, still . . ."

"I know." Evan nodded.

There was no way Derek could've pinpointed how his plan would unfold, what exact movements and what exact reactions there might have been. And, it maybe didn't matter whether or not he got his final moment or if it all lined up and timed right. It was, in the end, a suicide mission.

Out front was a table with a few pamphlets. There was a

small bouquet of flowers in a glass vase. A picture of Derek was framed, hung above the table. He had that goofy smile and wave of poofy hair, like when they were kids.

"Man. I can't help but keep thinking, the Derek we know would never, could never, do such a thing . . . I know how everyone else feels, but there's just no way."

"I get it. I do. Probably more than most." Evan turned to Jared, picked up one of the pamphlets. "But the thing is, he did do it. He did it all and then some. Like you said, that was *not* the Derek we know. No. That Derek was lost, gone, changed somehow, sadly."

As he opened the pamphlet, he could see Derek's mom standing inside the small chapel. There were just a handful of people in the pews. When Evan saw Max's mom at the hospital, she was blank, at a loss for words, expressionless. Here, now, Derek's mom was a total wreck. She bawled, cheeks sopping wet as she shuddered throughout her upper body, gasping with each breath.

"You ready?" Jared faced up from the table.

Evan licked his lips, breathed. "No."

6

Entering into the lobby of the hotel, each with a boutonniere on their lapel, Evan walked behind Jared arm in arm with his date. Mark led the way, holding one hand behind his date's hip who had a long flowy dress and heels. Jared's date dressed a little more plain, carrying a small tote in one hand. They pointed to a sign with information printed and an arrow indicating which way to go, then walked up a few steps to an area with elevators. The attendant nodded, waving a metal detector over and between them, and pushed the button. Evan watched Mark who had a big wide grin. He then glanced at Jared who tried to hide an embarrassed smile. Two of his closest friends, from when they were little kids, now appeared like young men, accompanied by two beautiful young women. When the elevator dinged and the doors opened, they all stepped out to a space with balloons and streamers and a big banner hanging across. He slowed behind the others, lingering just a bit.

"Evan, you coming?"

"Uh. I think I'll wait." He stepped to the side of the doorway, leaning on the frame, holding the small hand bouquet. "Jude should be here soon."

"All right, man. We'll be at the table."

He panned from the doors to where there were round tables lined in clusters. There was a long table to the side with plates stacked and trays of food, with bowls of punch and dispensers full of juice. In front was a stage where a DJ was setting up, and a dance floor with a shiny ball spinning from the ceiling. Colored lights pointed at different angles from aluminum beams set up on either side.

On one of the nearby tables, Evan noticed somebody staring at him. At first, he almost didn't recognize the person. It was one of the kids from the auditorium, the one with the bandana who laid on the cart. He got a haircut, cleaned up, had two crutches near him that leaned against the side of the chair. They exchanged a nod as his date returned with two cups, sitting back down. At another table on the other side, closer to the buffet, Evan saw the short girl with glasses smiling and talking to somebody. She paused, gazed back at Evan from the corner of her eye, also nodded, then returned to conversation.

At least there was some good, huh.

From behind, the elevator dinged again. When Evan turned back around, Judith stepped towards him. He was stunned, taken aback at how extraordinary she appeared. It reminded him of the night of the talent show, and how he fell in love with her in an instant. Her dress was astonishing and tasteful. Her hair was done up perfect, her makeup was immaculate.

"You look beautiful, Jude."

"And, wow, you're so handsome. Like a true gentleman."

He handed her the bouquet, took her hand in his, led them between the round tables, each one with napkins folded and multiple sets of forks and knives. On the middle of each table was a centerpiece arrangement.

Judith glanced around at the decor, smiled to herself. She

brought the bouquet close to her face and breathed in the scent of each flower.

They each sat down. Evan could see Mark and Jared with their dates standing in line by the long table, about to get food and drink.

"Sorry we couldn't arrive together . . ."

Judith faced down to her bouquet, rubbed one of the petals, twirled one of the ribbons.

He smirked. "It's okay. I mean, we both know how your parents can be."

"They've actually mellowed a lot recently. I mean, they know you're my boyfriend. Just, they still wanted to make sure to drop me themselves, and pick me up themselves."

"Oh, how long can you stay?"

"I'm supposed to be done by midnight, but I'll just stay a little later. I mean, it's prom." She shook her head with a smile.

He peered into her eyes peering into his, leaned in, and they kissed.

"We'll dance later?"

Judith nodded, placed the bouquet on the table. She held both his hands, squeezed them, then rested her head on his shoulder.

"You should've wore the sling."

She raised her head, pecked him on the cheek.

He laughed, catching a slight whiff of her perfume.

"We talked about this. I'm not a wearing a sling to our prom. I'll be fine."

Evan felt the electricity flow between their bodies, and warmth from her neck and shoulder. He breathed out a long and deep sigh of contentment.

"Picture?"

It was Michelle, and she already aimed the camera at the

two of them, adjusting the dial around the lens. When she pressed the round button, it sent out a bright flash.

"Sweet. Yeah, I'll print these and give them to you later. I plan to take pics through the night."

"Cool, sounds good."

Michelle turned, snapped a couple shots of the next table.

Judith hugged Mark's date, who was the one friend by the ladder before. Jared pulled the chair out and waited while his date sat down. As the others placed their plates and their glasses down, Evan and Judith stood to leave.

"So, what you think, Jude?"

He held her hand as they got in the short line.

"You know, it is beautiful, and I'm sure we'll all have fun. Of course. But there is still this kind of sadness."

"Well, I have a feeling that'll remain. Probably past graduation even. Like, it's just gonna take time. And a lot of time for some people."

"Right."

He took the ladle, swirled it in the bowl, scooped the punch and a few ice cubes. She held the glass for him to pour it into, then another.

"Like, what other prom's got metal detectors?"

"True. I guess we should just be lucky they didn't make us all take off our shoes."

She stepped, scanning around the room.

"Even these security guards around us, some of them look like cops."

"Yeah, I know. So weird."

As they made their way back to the table with their glasses and plates, the DJ started playing. Before they could touch their food or even take a sip, a slideshow flashed on the screen. The crowd oohed, applauded, and laughed accordingly. In the middle of the presentation, the slides turned from lighthearted to more of a morose and melancholic tone, as it then showed some of the faces of those that had passed on.

After it ended, a voice over the speaker asked for all guests to remain quiet in a short moment of silence. Mark put his arm around his date. Jared clasped his fingers together, rested his chin on them. Evan and Judith held hands under the table. The screen went blank and the lights dimmed.

"Well, that was depressing."

Jared let out a quiet chuckle. Mark's date hit him.

Evan took a piece of fish in his fork, smirked as he shook his head. Judith sipped her juice, rolling her eyes to her friend that hit Mark once more for good measure.

The music at first was sad, then transitioned to slower yet neutral pieces. When a love song came on, couples started to make their way to the dance floor.

"You ready?"

"Sure, let's go."

As they walked from the table, hand in hand, they entered the small dance floor already filling. The colored lights shined down from the metal beams, and the spinning ball lit up and emanated sparkling circles.

Evan placed his hands on her hips. Judith wrapped her arms around his shoulders. They each stared into each other's eyes as different colors and patterns shined over their skin and their clothes. It was kind of like when they played the dance game together at the arcade.

"Hey, I listened to that song."

"Oh. Did you like it?"

"Yeah, it was really good. Of course, I didn't understand what they were saying . . ."

She laughed, her deep dimples peeking through.

"What's it about?"

"Basically, it says that love is like a tornado. It sweeps you up. You're helpless, and it's out of your control."

"Hmm, wow. That's actually kind of true."

As they swayed, they turned in unison.

"Well, this is it. Our prom. The last days before we all get out there in the so-called 'real' world."

"Crazy, huh?"

"I'm just glad we're here together, dancing, you in that dress, and me in this tux."

She smiled. "I don't think there was any other way."

"You feel ready for it all? I mean, you get to go away to your dream school. Get to become a doctor like you wanted."

"I feel . . ." Judith panned down, then over his shoulder, searching for the right words. "I feel like everything that happened was horrible, of course, but it also kind of woke me up in a way, if that makes sense."

Evan didn't say anything, just listened. Her gaze again met his, and he smirked back.

"Like, I always wanted to be a doctor. But why? Just 'cause my parents made me? Now, well, I kinda have an answer, at least for myself. I wanna be able to help people. If someone's been hit by a car, or if they had a heart attack, or if they've been shot even . . ."

Judith nodded, nibbling her bottom lip.

"I don't know. But I think that's what makes sense to me right now. Like, I want to be able to help people who have been hurt, and try to save them."

Evan's smirk grew into a wide smile.

"I think that's terrific."

They both continued to sway. She interlaced her fingers

tight behind his neck. He held her close, his hands along the slender curve of her lower back.

"How 'bout you, Evan? You fully process it yet? Does everything make sense?"

"Getting there."

Licking his lips, he faced down to the floor then back up in her eyes.

"It's been hard. You know? To think, someone you used to know and love could go down such a dark hole. You could make the argument that maybe he was born with a defect, or maybe he suffered certain things in life. The media is trying to spin it so that it was violence in pop culture . . ."

Judith watched as Evan spoke, like a button had been clicked or a lever had been pulled. Doors that had been shut and locked were wedged open and left ajar.

"But, I mean, we all played the same video games, all listened to the same music, and we all watched the same movies and TV. It's not that. No. I think I've come to understand, deep down, inside, we all make a choice of who we want to be and what we want to do."

Evan peered up at the ceiling then out at the back wall, his eyes staring into a void that he alone could see. The words continued to pour out of him into the air.

"Just like how you wanted to be a doctor, and now it's coming true. Same thing. If a smoker wants to quit smoking or an overweight person wants to lose weight, there's no stopping someone that's truly set their mind to something. And, well, he must have decided a while back that he was going to do something terrible."

She leaned in close, rested her head on his chest.

"Yeah, I think you're right. For a while, I wondered if this was our fault even. But, after seeing the footage, hearing his true thoughts and intentions, it was clear he wasn't in the right state of mind. He was angry at the world, blamed everyone else for his problems, and now he'll burn in hell for it."

He nodded along, blinking.

"You think there'll be more, that this is going to happen again, like a copycat?"

Evan shook his head, shifted downward.

"I think, if someone looks at everything that happened here, hears our story, the true story, and comes out wanting to commit acts of terror and violence, then they really didn't get it."

Judith took a deep breath in and out, closed her eyes, held him tight.

"Too bad Max couldn't be here . . ."

"I know."

Between dancing and talking, food and drink, taking picture after picture, the night went on. Mark danced goofily on the floor, with awkward poses and pelvic thrusts, much to his date's dismay. Jared just bobbed his head, bopped his shoulders up and down, hands out in front of him. Evan held Judith's hands, pulling her in, pushing her back, spinning them around in a faux swing move, dipping her down.

As the night drew to a close, Mark and Jared waited with their dates out front while Evan and Judith decided to take a walk along the beach. Judith hugged her one friend. Evan, Mark and Jared clapped their palms together.

"You sure you can stay?"

"My mom's actually the one picking me up, and she gave me a look before she left. She knows it's a special occasion. I'm not supposed to, but I mean come on."

Evan laughed, glanced over at Judith who smiled. He felt happy, and also proud.

"Wow, Jude."

It was a beautiful night, and the moon and stars were clear in the sky. They could see the small dunes of sand and the water creeping up then back in little waves. His bowtie was loosened and his vest unbuttoned. She held her sandals and purse in her other hand as they meandered up the quiet and empty beach.

There was a darker spot at the base of one of the nearby buildings, and they sat down together. As the waves splashed on the sand, with nobody else around, under the starry night sky, it was so peaceful.

"Evan?"

He put one arm around her shoulder, kissed her on the side of her head.

"Yeah?"

"I love you."

He smiled, and they each leaned their face in.

As their lips and tongues writhed, their hands came together and interlocked.

"I love you too."

She took a deep breath, bit her bottom lip. He swallowed, gazed into her almond eyes. They kissed again, this time more intense, lowering down on the sand. She fumbled with the jewel buttons of his shirt, pulled the tie off and tossed it aside. He undid the straps from her shoulders, lifted up the silky hem of her dress, parted her legs. She felt for the buckle of his belt, reached in her purse taking out a small square wrapper.

Just as the ocean and the shore became one in the tide and the waves, so did their bodies. The horizon where the heavens and the earth came together was a long straight line, but in that moment, that line seemed to have blurred, spilling like a cascading waterfall over a wide lake. Above, the moon and stars were obscured by the gliding clouds. Her eyes were shut tight, mouth agape, as her fingers dug into the sand. He slid his hand up her torso to the line of her jaw, cradling her head as he kissed her neck. Sand clung to their skin, caught in between strands of hair. Their bodies moved in rhythm like the palm trees in the breeze. The sparkles on the water were a near perfect reflection of the starlight. The world in rotation synced with their hearts beating and their lungs breathing. Neither of them knew what the future might bring, but then and there, they were together, they were in love.

7

WITH HIS SKETCHBOOK under one arm, discman in hand, Evan walked around the courtyard. He took the mechanical pencil from behind his ear, stuck it in his backpack that hung from one shoulder. It was still strange being back after everything that happened. Mostly, they were able to feel normal, to actually be normal, but some of the traumas crept to the surface. For a while, they shared classrooms and facilities with Roosevelt, which was ironic because Evan thought he had escaped that school. After a few weeks of thorough cleaning and restoration, as well as implementing new security protocols, they returned to their home campus, which now became infamous. Here, seeing all the kids talk and joke and run around, Evan breathed in a light sigh. Some of them tossed pieces of paper from the second floor like confetti, reminding him for a moment of his ordeal in the library. Others chased each other spraying shaving cream and silly string, which sent flashbacks of running through the fields. A good number just sat down and traded yearbooks, taking out different colored felt-tip and Gelly Roll pens, writing heartfelt goodbyes and sincere thanks and well wishes.

High school really is just high school, except that it's

not. It is more than just a place filled with people, not just a campus, not just chalkboards and analog clocks and shelves with textbooks and rows of desks. In actuality, it's kind of everything in a lot of ways. This precious moment in time, filled with many emotions, is a significant journey towards coming to understand the world in one's own unique sense. Some people view the world with love, with hope and with courage. They know exactly what they want. They know who it is that they are, that they want to be. And some people view the world with fear. They still have a lot of growing up to do, and a lot of learning the hard way.

"Ev-an!"

"Yo, E."

When he passed from the walkway through the pillars towards the flagpole, they all were waiting. Judith held both hands on either strap of her backpack, her dimples growing. Mark adjusted the beanie on his head. Jared took a slow sip from his soda. Max sat in the wheelchair, one palm on the rim of the wheel, an awkward smile across his face. The group together formed a lopsided polygon as Evan joined in, each of them hugging, and clapping palms and bumping fists.

8

THE LAST DAYS felt like some of the longest days, other than the day of the actual shooting. Regular classes were just formality by then: turning in last projects, filing away assigned text-books, scraping gum off the bottom of desks. It was the actual graduation ceremony itself after that. Since its status as a now infamous school, it was decided that the Ocarina Amphitheatre would be used as the site of commencement. For one, it would be receiving a lot of media coverage so that allowed for more video and broadcast equipment. But two, it was also easier for police to secure. Like at prom, there were metal detectors, checking interiors of bags, then regular patrolling and sur-veying by officers on the premises and around the perimeter. Evan stood in line with each of his peers, his dark green cap and gown feeling awkward, the light silver tassel hanging to the appropriate side. He could hear the corny music playing from onstage, and one by one, all the names being announced.

They were lined alphabetically, and separated into male and female. Evan would be the first of his friends, then Mark and Max, then Jared, and close to last was Judith.

From the side of the structure, the line trickled along the grounds behind the building. Evan now could see the stage itself, its abstract shape reminding him of one of his favorite video games. There were rows of seats filled with friends and families sitting with balloons, posters and banners, holding up makeshift necklaces, even inflatable animals. The females were on one side, males on the other, and they each walked down to meet, linking arm in arm in the middle of the rows to the stage. As they stepped up and across the platform, their names were called. His partner was someone he'd never met until they started practice runs in weeks prior. They called her name first, then his.

"Evan Kleinbeck."

He grabbed the diploma, winded around to the chairs on the raised platform taking his seat. Then he saw the entirety of the audience and it was a huge crowd gathered, even bigger than the candlelight vigil.

General applause continued, name after name, until loud whistling and cheers grew to a standing ovation. It was Mark pushing Max down the middle of the rows to a ramp on the side of the stage. Evan stood and clapped as well, smirking to himself as his friends made their way.

Amongst those towards the middle-back, Jared and the rest went almost ignored, due to fatigue setting in. But he didn't seem to mind it.

"Judith Zhang."

She was one of the last few remaining in the procession, but she walked proud still. Her wide smile showed her deep dimples, and her cheeks reddened. Evan shouted through cupped hands, as did Mark, Max and Jared. Judith glanced over at Evan as she took her diploma, tucking her hair behind her left ear. He watched her the whole way to her seat, with a big smile on his face.

When all students were seated, there was a keynote address

from a guest speaker. The governor herself had attended, and talked of bravery in the face of adversity, and of coming together as one. As she broke the ice, mentioning the tragedy that occurred, the mood seemed to darken, along with the clouds above. There was a light drizzle, and it fell in a diagonal motion. At last, a round of applause as the governor stepped down and the valedictorian was introduced.

The original valedictorian, sad to say, had been killed during the attack. It was then decided that the honor of speaking would go to the student with the next highest GPA, which turned out to be Judith.

She stepped to the podium, adjusting her cap and gown, clearing her throat. Friends and families in the audience on the lawn began to cover up, taking out umbrellas as the drizzling continued. It was fortunate each graduate was under the covering of the roof to keep them dry.

"It is with a heavy heart, I speak on behalf of the former valedictorian to this graduating class, to all the staff and faculty, to law enforcement, and to the governor. Friends and families, thank you all for joining us this afternoon at our special commencement ceremony. We are very lucky to be here, to be together. We're lucky to be alive, to be okay. Many of our fellow classmates didn't make it, and for every one of them, we mourn . . ."

Evan thought about the kid in the JROTC uniform, who was one of those lost. He aspired to join the military as an officer, imagined he might die from a bullet, perhaps in war, or in a training gone wrong maybe, but never like this. An article was printed about him in one of the big national magazines, and he was hailed as a young hero—which he was.

Evan thought about the guy on the cart he saw at prom. He was headed down a bad path, the opposite of the kid in uniform.

He had been in fights, always in and out of detention, close to being expelled even, but now was trying to get his act together.

"Today is about graduating, about growing up. But I think a lot of us feel we may have already done so, that dreadful day just a few months ago. It's easy to feel sadness, to feel rage, and also to feel afraid. How do we carry on, and what do we do from here? We have to keep moving forward. Yet we can never forget what happened. The best way to remember our fallen classmates is to honor them, by making a difference, by changing the world and the future. It is up to each and every one of us. We can help one another, build each other up. Improve current laws. Improve safety in schools, and in public areas. Improve our sense of community."

Evan thought about the girl with piercings, who ended up dropping out of school and getting her GED. After everything that happened, it was all too much for her to take. She didn't care for school to begin with, but now could no longer stand it. She just didn't believe in it anymore.

"Over the course of the past four years, a lot of us have changed in many ways. Some of us made incredible friends. Some of us fell in love. Some found a dream, and are working towards it. Now, even in the wake of tragedy, those bonds are made stronger. Those stories can be even greater. All our dreams are that much more important . . ."

As her words echoed through the speaker system, the drizzling ceased, and the sun began to pierce back through the veil. In the tiny prisms of each raindrop, the light refracted in a beautiful flash of iridescence. Some in the audience started lowering their umbrellas, peeking up at the sky streaked with bright red blending into orange, vibrant yellow blending into green, then back to pure blue, to purple. It was a full and round rainbow stretching across the sky in a long arch.

Oh, wow. Look at that.

Just maybe, everything's gonna be okay.

"We will forever be Washington Eagles, the symbol of our nation, a symbol of courage and of strength. We will fly together, and we will fly high."

It was a slow clap at first that built like a wave to a roar of applause, along with more whistling and cheers. The principal thanked their valedictorian, asked the graduating class to stand to their feet. Each of them waited, placing a hand on the light silver tassel as instructed, then moved them in unison over to the other side. Once the principal congratulated them, they all jumped up and down, screaming, shouting, hugging one another. Some threw their caps in the air even though they were specifically told not to.

After the chaotic frenzy, they made their way from the stage to meet family and friends, to take pictures, setting off poppers and streamers, and releasing balloons. There was a celebration to follow for those that signed up, which was most of the students. It would run all night to the next morning, from place to place to place.

Evan changed out of his cap and gown into baggy cargo pants, his school t-shirt and sneakers, giving the dress clothes and dress shoes in a plastic bag to his family who was getting ready to leave. Again, his mom hugged him and his dad patted him on the arm. Evan knelt down, rubbed the top of his little brother's head, messing up his hair. Then he followed the crowd that gathered outside in the parking lot near trolleys that were waiting, and he could see Mark and Jared huddled next to Max.

Before heading towards them, Evan glanced around, caught Judith amongst the sea of people, walking his direction. It was getting darker out, almost night as the sun faded.

"So, was it okay?"

"You did fantastic! It couldn't have been better."

Judith smiled, hugged Evan tight. As they embraced, he pecked her on the side of her head with a quick kiss.

"Okay, hey, not too much. My parents are here."

"Right. That's probably why they're not letting you come along tonight, huh?"

"Exactly."

They both laughed, holding each other's hands.

"Well. You be careful, okay? Have fun."

"I will. And I'll see you tomorrow?"

She nodded with a smile. He lifted her hand and kissed the top of it, stared deep in her eyes.

"They're getting ready . . ."

Evan turned back as Judith waved over to the others, starting to step away.

He wanted to pull her toward him again, hug her once more but decided not to. His eyes followed her all the way as she rejoined her parents.

Mark waited for Evan while the others lined up. Jared was in line already, towards the front, so he could save them all seats. Max was off to the side since staff would assist him with boarding.

"Finally. What the hell?" Mark teased as he and Evan clapped their palms and snapped their fingers.

Evan reached over, bumped fists with Max. "'Sup."

The staff was about to come over when a couple of jocks grabbed Max and lifted him up. His eyes stretched wide open, worried and anxious, but softened with a chuckle as the jocks helped him onto the trolley themselves in a spontaneous gesture of kindness.

"Yeah!!!"

Mark shouted along with the rest who cheered and chanted, loud. Everybody wearing their gray shirts with eagle symbols was like a lynch mob hyped up on sugary caffeinated drinks.

Evan smirked to himself, nodding, as the line inched forward.

"Hey, you know what's going on tonight? I mean, they've been keeping it secret."

"No clue. I heard it might be a cruise, then like a hotel or something."

"Ah, I see. Hmm."

Mark squinted his eyes, grinned, then nudged him with his elbow.

"I saw you with Judy earlier. Looks like things are going pretty good, huh?"

"Yeah, man. Totally. We're both really happy."

"Awesome. What you guys planning to do after summer?"

They each took a step forward as the line moved.

"Well, we talked about ways we could make it work. Like, if we both call regularly, and try to visit. I could even move out there . . ."

Mark nodded along, climbed in the trolley.

Evan followed him and they made their way towards the back where Max and Jared were already sitting.

"There you guys are."

Jared had his arms crossed as he slumped. Max spread one arm out across the top of the bench.

"Looks like we're about to get going."

Again, the hyper lynch mob shouted and yelled, cheering and chanting, now also stomping the floor of the trolley as it pulled into the city streets.

Evan dazed out the side of the trolley into the open air

as buildings glided by in a blur. The city lights were brilliant with each wind through, turning from a five-way intersection towards the uptown area. The driver honked the horn and rang the bell as they passed pedestrians in the street—couples, families, college kids, tourists—who all waved back and cheered along, some of them blowing kisses.

Most of the others stood, joining in celebration and jumping up and down, screaming like they were on some roller coaster ride.

Jared hung from one of the handles as he observed the madness occur around him. Max shouted out from the seat, waving his arms up and down. Mark went wild, let loose completely, swinging from the bars across the ceiling like a chimpanzee. Evan held onto one of the poles, leaned out the opening, felt the cool air rush over his skin.

As the friends celebrated with their fellow graduates into the night, riding along to some unknown destination, they temporarily forgot all they had been through. It didn't matter who was an athlete or a top scholar, or a gangster or a goth. It didn't matter if anybody was off to boot camp or some vocational school, working in retail, or going to help with the family business. All that mattered was they were alive. They were young, they were free, and they had their whole lives ahead of them. With each loud shout and each sharp scream, of joy, of happiness, they let the past slip away. Each wide smile and each excited jump in the air, they lightened up and opened, ready to embrace the future to come. Each hug, each laugh, each playful shove brought them all closer together and bonded them forever.

ACKNOWLEDGEMENTS

First of all, I would like to thank my wife, Donna, for all her ongoing encouragement and support. We got married while I was writing the first draft and I sent out my last query letters to agents in the hospital while she was giving birth to our son, Andrew Nolan Gebhardt. She bought me my printer, she was the very first to read this work, and she even chipped in a chunk of our savings to make this dream a reality. Thank you, babe. We did it.

Second, I want to thank my little brother, Daniel, who has shaped my taste in all things art. He and I are huge movie buffs, are nerds and gamers, but are also creators. He was the first person in my life to ever read my writing, has read the most of all my works, has consistently given me great advice, and even served as final proofreader for this book. Also, my brother is fantastic at video editing and was essential in teaching me to launch my channel.

I want to thank my writing partner, Jeremiah, who writes under JM Payer. We have been working together for years ever since we met at NaNoWriMo where I tried and failed to write this novel. He helped me to build my foundation as a writer, and kept me coming back when I had fallen hard off the wagon. He took me to the shooting range multiple times so I could learn what it felt like to hold and shoot a gun. This is the second work of mine he's critiqued, and he tore apart the thousands of adverbs and all the inconsistences.

I want to thank my beta reader, Stephanie Takenaka. This is the second work of mine that she's critiqued. Her genuine excitement over the romance and geek humor gave me the green light to go all out. She answered my many questions over text and set fire to my grammar and punctuation.

My professional editor, Erin Young, with her background as an agent and her experience with some big names really leveled me up from aspiring writer to published author. She helped to punch up the pacing and emphasis and effect of the story, while pushing me to also remain sensible. Our many e-mails and phone calls forced me to focus and develop while preparing for the true author journey to come.

I would also like to thank Tate Tsukamoto. From the beginning, he was one of the only few that even knew I wrote, and helped to nourish that. He regularly checked in, watched my work grow and change, and I am so happy to have earned his respect and confidence. He graciously served as the first proofreader.

The professional team under Damon Freeman with their experience producing thousands of books turned this project into something tangible and of value. Robynne was a joy to work with, coordinated everything and handled my many detailed requests. The cover design absolutely blew me away, and was created by Giovanni. Benjamin handled all of the interior formatting and the superb final touches.

SPECIAL THANKS

This book would not be possible without the generous contributions from the following extraordinary supporters. Their efforts helped to spread awareness of this project and discussion of the subject matter.

Brianna Thomas
Christine Shimada
Cindy Chang
Dan Rebb Leano
Elizabeth Fitzpatrick
Janie Brown
Jarrett Tang
Kelvin Jhovanni Malvar
Kerridan Lopez
Lauren Dudas
Lianne Kaneshiro
Marc Miura
Matthew Lau
Michael Lee
Rachel Wacker
Sandy Ly
Sara Herrick
Stephanie Clements
William Pacana

A portion of all profit from this book is donated to various charities that help prevent these kind of tragedies, and assist and console all of the unfortunate affected. Visit my website for a full list of organizations.

www.tjgiii.com

If you enjoyed this work, please leave a review on Amazon and on Goodreads. Every little bit counts and will help the novel get ranked in the algorithm for others to discover.

To stay up to date with all of the latest posts, follow me on social media. Every like, comment and follow is much appreciated.

www.facebook.com/tjg3words
www.instagram.com/tjg3words
www.twitter.com/tjg3words

ABOUT THE AUTHOR

Thomas J. Gebhardt III has been seriously writing for seven years after long days in healthcare, doing occupational therapy with the elderly. He lives with his wife and newborn son in his hometown of Honolulu, Hawaii. This is his debut novel, which first began as an idea from when he himself was in high school, was attempted when he lived in Japan and in Seattle, as well as during National Novel Writing Month, and finally completed in March 2020. His work is heavily influenced by pop culture including movies, music, shows, video games, comic books, anime and manga.

www.ingramcontent.com/pod-product-compliance
Lightning Source LLC
Chambersburg PA
CBHW030130310726
48970CB00005B/1371
* 9 7 9 8 9 8 5 7 1 6 0 1 6 *